Black Satin

BLACK SATIN

Joan Elizabeth Lloyd

Carroll & Graf Publishers, Inc.
New York

Carroll & Graf Publishers, Inc.
260 Fifth Avenue
New York, NY 10001

ISBN: 0-7867-0236-2

Text design by Terry McCabe

Manufactured in the United States of America

This book is dedicated to all the men and women who have discovered that sexual experimentation is one of the most wonderful pleasures ever created.

And, as always, to Ed.

Black Satin

Chapter 1

"You sent for me, Miss Gilbert?" the man said. Although he looked about forty, paunchy, with a neatly trimmed moustache, he was dressed in a traditional boy's school uniform: short navy pants, white formal shirt, a green-and-navy plaid blazer, and white, knee-length socks. Incongruously, he also wore Gucci loafers with small tassels on the vamp.

"I certainly did, Bobby," Miss Gilbert said. She sat behind an antique desk that she had previously moved to the center of the large, beautifully furnished living room. As arranged, she was dressed in a high-collared, long-sleeved white blouse fastened with a classic cameo at the neck. Her straight black skirt was pulled primly over her knees, covering most of her sheer hose. Her grey hair was swept up and pinned into a bun on the top of her head and her rimless glasses were perched on the end of her nose. She stared at Bobby over the top of her spectacles. "I'm afraid you're in serious trouble."

As Bobby looked at the floor he could see her heavy, black sensible shoes with their thick heels. Although the sound was muffled by the plush carpet, he could see her toe tapping rhythmically. "Yes, ma'am."

"I've seen the results of your exams and they're totally unsatisfactory." Miss Gilbert picked up a ruler from the desk and smacked it into the palm of her hand.

"Yes, ma'am," Bobby said, his knees shaking and a bulge forming in the front of his shorts.

"Do you know what that means?" Again the ruler smacked her hand, her long slender fingers wrapping around the wooden slat.

"Yes, ma'am." Bobby's palms began to sweat and his breathing accelerated.

"Tell me, exactly." She smiled. Smack, smack.

"It means that either you'll tell my parents or. . . ."

"Or what, Bobby?" Smack, smack.

"Twenty?"

"There were three failures," Miss Gilbert said. Her index finger stroked the edge of the ruler slowly.

Bobby's eyes followed the bright red nail back and forth. "Th, th, thirty," he stammered.

"Yes, I'm afraid so." Her finger kept sliding from one end of the ruler to the other. "Thirty." Smack. "It's your choice."

"You can't call my parents," Bobby said. "My father would kill me." Inside he smiled. His father had been dead for almost five years but that didn't matter. This dialogue had been honed over many encounters. Sweat tickled his underarms.

"Then we know what it will be, don't we?"

Silently, Bobby pulled off his jacket and shirt revealing a slightly overweight body and hairless chest. Nervously, he ran his hand through his thick, dark brown hair and wiped a light film of sweat from his face. He dropped his hands to his sides and waited for the instructions he knew would come.

Her voice conversational, Miss Gilbert said, "That's good. Now drop them."

His fingers were barely able to unzip his fly as Bobby opened the uniform pants and let them drop to the floor around his sock-covered ankles.

"What are you waiting for?" Miss Gilbert said.

Trembling, he slipped his fingers into the elastic waistband of his white cotton drawers and started to pull them down. As usual, the task was made more difficult by the size of his erection. He pulled the shorts out over his hard cock and down so they fell and joined his navy blue uniform pants on the floor.

"Well," Miss Gilbert said, rising from her seat behind the large maple desk and staring at his cock. "I can see that dickie is anxious for what is next." She rounded the desk and tapped the end of the ruler against Bobby's hard cock. She reached across the desk and picked up an Ace bandage. She wrapped the wide elastic around Bobby's hard cock, attaching the first turn with a metal clip. Then she wound the stretchy fabric around his hips, then over his now-bulging erection. Around and around, she encased the area from Bobby's waist to his crotch in the stretchy fabric.

Bobby could barely contain his excitement. The first few times they had played out this scenario, he had come inside the elastic before they could get to the best part. By now he had developed some self-control. He bent his arms on the bright green blotter-covered surface and placed his forehead against his crossed wrists, his gold Tourneau watch showing the exact time and date.

"Now, Bobby," Miss Gilbert said, "you know that you must count for me and thank me for not calling your parents." She tapped the ruler against his shins, still covered by the white socks. He moved his legs back and spread them apart.

Swoosh. The first slap of the ruler fell across the elastic over his ass. It didn't really hurt but rather made his cheeks vibrate. "One, Miss Gilbert and thank you."

Nine more swats fell across his buttocks. Now the entire area covered by the Ace bandage tingled. "Ten, Miss Gilbert, and thank you." He knew what came next, but it didn't make it any easier.

With little warning, the eleventh swat fell across the back of his bare right thigh. Miss Gilbert made sure that it stung and left a slight red mark.

"Eleven," Bobby said, "and thank you Miss Gilbert." By the twentieth swat, the backs of both well-muscled thighs were bright red and sore.

"I think we'll wait for the last ten for a short while," Miss Gilbert said. She tapped the back of Bobby's neck and he raised his head. She put the ruler on the desk where he couldn't help but stare at it. "Are you very sore?" she asked innocently.

"It's not too bad," Bobby said. His legs were on fire but it wouldn't do to admit it.

"I'll make it better for you," Miss Gilbert said. Carefully, she unwrapped the elastic bandage from around his body and touched the deep indentations it had left. "Poor baby," she said, running a long fingernail over one particularly deep groove on one cheek. Holding the end of the pink stretch material still encasing his cock, she ran the tip of her tongue over the groove in his skin. As she yanked at the end of the material, Bobby's cock pulled toward her. She released the material and it snapped back. Alternately pulling and releasing the bandage, she continued to lick the marks on his ass.

As she straightened and looked toward his cock, she could see drops of sticky fluid oozing from the tip. "Is it hard not to come?" she asked sweetly.

"Oh, yes, Miss Gilbert," Bobby said.

"Well, we can't have you disgracing yourself, can we?"

"No, Miss Gilbert."

Still playing with the end of the elastic, she pulled at his cock and smiled. "You know the penalty for premature ejaculation, don't you?"

"Yes, Miss Gilbert." It happened occasionally. The last time they had been together, he had come like a fountain, spurting semen all over the desk. He had been forced to clean up the mess and had gotten ten extra swats from the ruler. He had come again then, but had been disappointed with his performance, his lack of fortitude. This time, however, he was sure he had enough self-control to finish.

Miss Gilbert unwound the elastic from Bobby's cock, put the roll down, and picked up the ruler. "You've been very good today," she said. "Should we reduce the punishment to twenty-five?"

As much as he might like to decrease his suffering, he wanted to continue to test his endurance. "No, ma'am," he said. "I need to be thoroughly punished."

Swat number twenty-one was a stinger, just hard enough to burn his now-bare ass. "Thank you Miss Gilbert. That was number twenty-one."

By number twenty-eight, Bobby's ass was as red as the backs of his thighs, but he stayed bent over the desk and took it.

Miss Gilbert knew what was expected now. For swat number twenty-nine she raised her arm as it would go and brought the wooden ruler down as hard as she could.

It hurt terribly, but Bobby didn't move. "Twenty-nine and thank you Miss Gilbert."

She heard Bobby's deep breathing and knew he was trying not to cry out. She raised her arm one last time and administered the final swat as hard as she could.

"Thirty and thank you Miss Gilbert." Bobby stood up, his hands at his sides, his erection enormous.

"Are you sure you've learned your lesson?"

"Oh yes, Miss Gilbert, and thank you. I'm ready for the rest of my punishment now."

Miss Gilbert went into the bathroom and returned with a large bath towel which she spread over the desk. She tapped the ruler across Bobby's inflamed buttocks and he moved so the fronts of his thighs pressed against the desk. "I'm going to watch you now. That's the rest of your punishment, you know. Show me what a bad boy you are," she said, her voice smooth and soft as cream. "Show me how you rub your dickie when no one's looking. Show me."

Bobby watched Miss Gilbert round the desk and sit down in her chair. He saw her ice-blue eyes riveted on his cock, still striped by the small folds that had been in the elastic. He hesitated. This was still the worst and best part.

"Bobby," Miss Gilbert said, "I want you to play with yourself so I can see. I want to watch everything. Now, wrap your hand around your dickie and rub." When he still hesitated, she picked up the ruler and snapped, "Now!"

His hands shaking, Bobby took his cock in his hands and began to rub.

"Wait," Miss Gilbert said. "I have an idea." She opened the

desk drawer and pulled out a tube of lubricating gel. "Hold out your hands."

Slippery stuff. This was new, Bobby thought, a deviation from the ritual. But it was wonderful. She had guessed what he wanted without his having to tell her anything. That was what made her so special. He held his hands out, palm up, in front of him, and Miss Gilbert squeezed a huge glob of slippery goo into one hand. "Now rub," she said.

It feels so cold, he thought as his hands surrounded his hot cock. The moment he touched himself, he was lost. He closed his eyes and slid his fingers up and down his cock.

"Open your eyes you naughty boy," Miss Gilbert snapped. "I want you to see me watching your hands play with your cock." When he didn't obey immediately, she snapped again, "Now! Do it!"

He opened his eyes and looked into her face. Her eyes were riveted on his hands stroking his cock. It was sensational. It only took a moment until spurts of come erupted, falling on the white surface of the towel. His knees almost buckled, but he held on, enjoying the afterglow of one of the best orgasms of his life.

Miss Gilbert sat, unmoving, until Bobby swept up the towel and disappeared into the bathroom. Fifteen minutes later, she was sitting behind the desk reading when Bobby emerged from the bathroom, dressed in a grey pinstriped suit, light blue shirt, and paisley tie. He wore black socks and the Gucci loafers.

Without another word, he checked the time on his gold watch, put a handful of bills on the green blotter, and left the room.

The slam of metal against metal, the impact of her chest against her car's shoulder belt, and Carla's "Oh shit," came almost simultaneously. She shifted the car into park and stared out through the windshield. "Where the hell did he come from? There wasn't anything there a second ago," she said aloud, slumping against the seat. The front bumper of her six-year-old Ford had put a significant dent in the passenger-side rear quarter panel of a classy, gleaming dark blue Cadillac. "Oh God," she moaned. "Oh God, why me?"

Several pedestrians and a bicyclist had stopped to gawk at the tableau. Carla's car was blocking the sidewalk, halfway out of a Kinney underground garage between First and Second Avenues on East 53rd Street, an upscale Manhattan neighborhood. The Cadillac, which had been heading west across 53rd, sat in the road, the front of Carla's car resting against its side.

With a deep sigh, Carla climbed out of her car and watched the driver of the Cadillac emerge. As the woman stood up, Carla stared. The driver was a tall, slender statuesque woman with dark blond hair twisted into a perfect French knot. As the classically beautiful woman stared at her through dark, tortoiseshell sunglasses, Carla self-consciously ran her palms down the thighs of her comfortable, well-washed jeans.

The more Carla studied the woman, the more stunning she looked. The woman removed her designer sunglasses and shaded her eyes from the afternoon sun. She had perfectly arched brows over deep blue eyes, a long slender nose, and coral lips. Carla thought that she looked like Grace Kelly at her best.

Carla ran her fingers through her shoulder-length, brown hair, and tucked an errant strand behind one ear. "I'm terribly sorry," she called as the woman closed the Cadillac's door. "I can't imagine how this happened." Now that's an inane statement she thought.

Carla had been so happy when her doctor's visit had confirmed that all her worries had been needless. The lump in her breast had turned out to be nothing but a fluid-filled cyst. She had been so relieved after a week of suspense that she had almost run to the garage, bailed her car out, and started for home. Why was she going home? She wasn't really sure. The kids were still at school and her mom and dad were both out for the day. And anyway, she hadn't told her parents or her three boys about the lump. No need to worry anyone, she had reasoned. Unfortunately, that meant that she now had no one with whom to celebrate.

As Carla watched, the blond walked around the joined vehicles, calmly assessed the situation, and shook her head. God, Carla thought, I had to hit someone like her. The woman wore a classic dark red Donna Karan suit, a matching red-and-white patterned blouse, and perfectly coordinated Robert Clergerie pumps. She adjusted a gold, red, and white Hermes scarf over her shoulder with long, slender, perfectly manicured fingers. "Oh dear," the woman said, her voice soft and well modulated. "I'm so sorry."

"You're sorry?" Carla said.

"Of course," the woman said. "I was going a bit too fast and I wasn't watching where I was going." The woman hesitated, staring. "Wait. It couldn't be." She continued to stare. "Carla?"

"Excuse me?"

"Carla. You're Carla MacKensie."

"Carla Barrett," she answered. "But I was Carla MacKensie before I married. Do we know each other?"

"It's Veronica. Ronnie Browning, now Talmidge."

"Ronnie? It can't be." Carla and Ronnie had been roommates at Michigan State and had graduated together fifteen years before. During their three years together they had shared everything: field hockey, the debate team, the drama club and even, unintentionally, a few boyfriends.

Ronnie's laugh was a full rich sound. "I'd know you anywhere. You haven't changed a bit." She looked down. "I guess I've changed a little since then."

Carla remembered the moderately attractive brunette with wire-rimmed glasses and little makeup whom she had loved like a sister. "Have you ever! You look sensational." She smiled ruefully. "And you're right, I haven't changed. Unfortunately I look pretty much like I did fifteen years ago: Medium brown and average, average, average." Carla looked Ronnie over carefully. "What in the world have you been doing for the last fifteen years?"

"More than you can possibly imagine." Ronnie looked at the two cars and waved her hand. "You know, this seems relatively minor. Listen. Where were you off to?"

"Minor?" There had to be thousands of dollars worth of damage. You couldn't have an accident that didn't cost thousands these days. "I was going home to Bronxville—where I live now."

"That's silly. Now that we've found each other let's not lose track again. Why don't we park here and have lunch? We can catch up on all those years. And anyway I'm starved."

"Weren't you going somewhere?"

"I have an appointment at two," Ronnie said, glancing at her gold Cartier watch, "but that gives us over an hour, and there's a great little Italian place down the block."

When Carla hesitated, Ronnie's voice dropped. "Please. I'd love the company and we have so much to catch up on."

The parking lot attendant ran up waving his hands, trying to clear the entrance way. "You'll have to move these cars," the uniformed man yelled.

Ronnie's voice was soft, yet authoritative. "If you'll wait just a moment, Tom, we'll be out of the way." She turned to Carla and said, "I'm in this neighborhood a lot. I used to park here all the time but I've found a less expensive place around the corner."

As Ronnie returned to her car, Carla climbed into her Ford and backed up. The cars separated and Carla noticed that the damage to the Cadillac was less than she'd expected. Just a nasty dent and some chipped paint. She'd have to examine her car, but since the bumper had been the point of contact she thought it should be okay.

"Over here," Tom said. "Back it right over here." He waved Carla into one parking space and Ronnie drove into the one next to it.

As she climbed out, Ronnie said, "We'll be a few hours, Tom." She leaned into the passenger seat to grab a fashionable bag that Carla knew had to be either a Fendi or a great knockoff and slung the chain strap over her shoulder. Carla reached through the open passenger window of the Ford and grabbed her ersatz leather purse and camel-colored wool jacket. She slipped her arms in the sleeves and buttoned the blazer over her denim-blue-and-white striped shirt.

"Oh, Carla, this is so wonderful," Ronnie said. She looked at the front end of Carla's car. "Not bad," Ronnie said. "Looks like you got out of this little accident with almost no damage at all."

Carla nodded and wrapped her arm around Ronnie's waist. "I'm so glad I ran into you." She laughed. "Literally."

"Me too. This way." Ronnie led Carla under a small awning that proclaimed the restaurant to be The Villa Luigi. As they entered, Carla inhaled the enticing odor of garlic, oregano, and olive oil. They were shown to a quiet table in the back. "Give us a bottle of your Ruffino and some garlic bread," Ronnie told the waitress who seated them. As she left, Ronnie laughed. "Remember the night we got a gallon of jug-red and drank it with an entire package of Oreos with Double Stuff?"

"All I remember is how sick we were the next morning. I had to hold onto the floor to keep from falling off."

"And I puked my guts up for over an hour." The two women laughed. "Tell me what's new with you now," Ronnie said.

Carla took a deep breath. "Well, I was married for almost nine years but Bill was killed in a car accident almost five years ago."

"I'm so sorry."

"Well. . . . Bill wasn't exactly Prince Charming. He drank too much and was not a nice drunk. I had been thinking about a divorce for a year before his death."

"Kids?"

"BJ—that's Bill Junior—is thirteen, Tommy's eleven, and Mike's ten. Three boys. Where did I go wrong?"

"I remember that you wanted ten kids, all girls. And you never wanted to work."

"Never work? God, imagine thinking that being a mommy wasn't work."

"So you're a mommy full time?"

"Fortunately Bill left me pretty well provided for. That, and I sell a little real estate. I got my license about two years ago and I put what I make away for college for the boys. Sometimes I think I should work more, what with the boys in school all day and my folks right next door, but I can't think of what I could do, college degree or no college degree." Carla put her napkin in her lap. "English literature. A useful degree if ever there was one. Anyway, what about you? Married? Where do you live?"

Carla waggled her left hand under Carla's nose. The wide gold band on her third finger flashed. She also wore a thin band of diamonds on her index finger and a heavy free-form gold ring on the middle finger of her other hand. "Jack's an independent geologist who does consulting for a number of oil companies. It's a combination of lots of travel and a house full of computers. He's only home about one week a month." She heaved a sigh. "Unfortunately, no kids. I found out early on that I couldn't have any and neither of us wanted to adopt. We live in Hopewell Junction, in Dutchess County, almost two hours north of here. What were you doing in town, by the way?"

"Doctor's appointment."

Ronnie jumped in. "Nothing serious, I hope."

"Nothing. A lump in my breast that turned out to be a benign cyst."

"I'm glad." She squeezed her friend's hand.

Carla was touched. Ronnie was someone with whom she had always shared everything. It felt good sharing now. "So, Ronnie, I couldn't help noticing the quality of your wardrobe. And the new Cadillac. Jack's obviously doing well."

"Well enough. But the Caddie's mine."

"You work?"

Ronnie smiled in a way that puzzled Carla. "Yes, I work." She paused, then continued. "And I take occasional courses in creative writing at NYU. I've even had a few articles published."

"That's great." The waitress brought their wine and a basket of bread dripping with butter, garlic, and herbs. When she had poured them each a glass and left, the two women picked up their glasses and tapped them together.

"To work in all its forms," Ronnie said mysteriously, then laughed.

Puzzled, Carla drank.

For the next hour, Carla and Ronnie caught up on everything that had happened since they lost touch after graduation when Ronnie traveled in Europe for a year. As the two women finished espressos and the last of the bottle of wine, Ronnie looked at her watch. "I hate to say this, but I have to run. Someone's meeting me at two. But let's get together next week. Noon. Why don't we meet out front and eat somewhere else? And, don't worry about the damage to my car. I'll let my collision coverage take care of it." Carla took the check, added a generous tip, and split the amount. After settling up, the two women stood and Ronnie reached out and hugged Carla. "God, I've missed you."

For each of the next three Mondays the two women lunched in the same neighborhood: at a Chinese restaurant specializing in Peking Duck, an Indian hole-in-the-wall that made the best mulligatawny Carla had ever tasted, and today at a sushi bar where Carla sampled raw fish for the first time. Over ginger ice cream and green tea, Ronnie suggested their next meeting place. "I'd like you to see my place," she said. "Let's have lunch chez moi next week."

"In Hopewell Junction? I guess I could. You'll have to give me directions."

"Not Hopewell Junction. Around the corner." With an enigmatic smile, Ronnie gave Carla an address on East 54th.

"I don't get it, Ronnie. You have an apartment right here?" She saw Ronnie nod, then pause. "No wonder you know all the good spots to eat. Have you got a secret life? Tell me everything."

"Next week I promise you'll know all." As Ronnie left for her usual two o'clock meeting, she added, "I'll arrange to have the whole afternoon free. We'll talk."

The address that Ronnie had given Carla led her to a small, three-story brownstone on East 54th. Carla climbed the four steps to the entrance and rang the bell. Ronnie opened the door dressed in a soft grey wool long-sleeved jumpsuit, her dark blond hair loose around her shoulders. A pair of large, free-form silver earrings and a silver herringbone choker were her only jewelry. Carla was glad that she had chosen to forgo her usual jeans and had worn a dark green wool suit with a beige raw silk blouse.

The two women bussed cheeks, and Carla followed Ronnie through a small vestibule and into a beautifully furnished living room.

"Some fantastic place," Carla said as she looked around. Everything was done in black, white, and shades of grey. The sofa was overstuffed, covered in black leather banded with leather straps secured with heavy metal buckles. It was accented with throw pillows in black-and-white stripes and plaids. The two comfortable-looking soft chairs were white jacquard fabric with identical black-and-white pillows. A fluffy white rug covered the center of the floor; Carla could see the original highly polished inlaid wood where the rug ended. The walls were covered with a soft silver-grey silk and the windows were draped in a slightly darker grey damask. End tables of black lacquer held white-based, modern lamps that filled the room with light.

Vases and pots of flowers placed on tables and pedestals around the room provided the only color. Roses, chrysanthemums, and geraniums added their hues to blooming cactuses and unusual blossoms that Carla didn't recognize. Several hanging baskets of living blooms hung from hooks in both the walls and ceiling. One wall was all windows with a decorative but highly functional iron grill outside. The opposite wall contained a long, white, glass-fronted wall unit filled with books of every kind, from popular novels to poetry to volumes on natural sciences and history. The other walls held black-and-white Ansel Adams prints and other, smaller black-and-white photographs by artists Carla didn't know. At one end of the room sat an antique maple desk.

Carla whistled. "Holy cow." Through her real estate wanderings, she had learned enough to appreciate the class and expense of the decorating.

"Just a little hideaway," Ronnie said, laughing.

"Little? Either you inherited a small fortune, your writing is doing extremely well, or Jack indulges you and your 'little hideaway.' ''

"Or 'D' none of the above." Ronnie handed Carla a champagne flute and filled it from an already opened bottle of Dom Pérignon. She clinked her glass against her friend's and, with an enigmatic smile, said, "To 'none of the above.' ''

They drank. "Okay," Carla said, "give."

"I think we know each other well enough for me to show you my photographs. Sit down." She motioned toward the sofa and Carla picked up a photo album covered in black satin and sat down next to her friend. When she opened the album Carla saw a picture unlike anything she had expected. A statuesque brunette posed, wearing a black leather and chain bathing suit-like outfit. The links draped over her naked breasts, the supple leather caressed her hips and belly. On her hands she wore soft, elbow-length, black leather gloves and her legs were covered with thigh-high patent leather boots with five-inch heels.

The woman's wavy, auburn hair hung softly across her chest with one curl surrounding an erect dark brown nipple. In one hand she had a short, black leather riding crop. Her makeup was heavy, with bright red lipstick and exaggerated eyeshadow and liner. "I don't get it," said Carla.

"Turn the page."

The picture on the following page was of a woman with pale white-blond braids that hung down in front of her dress. She was turned slightly sideways, looking shy and vulnerable and dressed in a puffed-sleeve pink dress, an adult version of the dress a five-year-old girl might wear, with a fluffy full skirt over several petticoats and a wide sash tied into a large bow which peeked out from behind. Her white ankle socks were neatly cuffed and her black patent leather maryjanes gleamed. Her face, artfully made up with soft rouge and pale pink lipstick, looked youthful and familiar. As Carla examined the face more carefully, she gasped. "That's you." She flipped the page backward. "So's this."

"Turn the page."

The pictures that followed were all of Ronnie in various costumes: a harem girl with a transparent veil covering the lower half of her face, a prim grey-haired woman in a white high-necked blouse and sensible shoes, a voluptuous female pirate wearing short shorts that showed the half-moons of her ass peeking beneath and a blouse unbuttoned to the waist, and a woman in a black satin teddy standing over a man whose arms and legs were secured to the frame of a brass bed with lengths of heavy-link chain and padlocks.

"Phew. Ronnie, I'm amazed here. Okay, fill me in."

"I call the album Black Satin and it's really a menu. Selected people get to pick their . . . shall we say entrée and I supply the dessert."

"You're trying to tell me that you're a hooker."

"I'm a very selective, high-priced prostitute."

Carla was flabbergasted. She had expected something unusual. After all Ronnie had never been mainstream. But this? What could she say?

Ronnie spoke, her voice a bit tentative. "No condemnation? No 'how could you?' "

"I'm too much in shock to say much of anything. But, of course, your life is your own."

Ronnie smiled. "And it's wonderful. I enjoy every bit of my secret existence."

"What about Jack?"

Ronnie smiled. "I think he knows what's going on. He travels and I know that he entertains himself while he's away, and so do I."

"What about AIDS?"

"I thought about that a lot when all this began. Many of my friends—that's what I call them, my friends—don't want actual intercourse. They want oral sex, toys, and/or mutual masturbation. And those who do want to have intercourse must wear condoms."

"What about oral sex? Isn't that risky?"

"Not as risky as unprotected intercourse, but yes, it is. I thought about it a lot at the beginning, and I decided it was a risk I was willing to take.''

"How in the world did you get involved in this?''

Ronnie leaned back and put her feet on the coffee table. "How, indeed."

Chapter 2

"I guess it all started just over three years ago," Ronnie explained. "You have to understand that Jack and I have always had an open relationship. I guess you'd say we were swingers. We both enjoy sex a lot and find that outside activities actually enhance what we have."

"You mean . . . with other people?"

Ronnie chuckled. "Yes, both of us were. And it didn't bother me at all. I loved the idea that someone else was making Jack happy, particularly since he was—and still is—away so much. And back then he'd come home with new ideas, toys, sexy lingerie." When she saw Carla's expression, Ronnie added, "Put your eyebrows down, Carla. You remember I was always the experimenter."

"I remember some of your experiments. Like Oreos and peanut butter. Go on."

"Well, the only strict requirement that Jack and I had, and still have, is that no one has intercourse without a condom. Period."

"Weren't you jealous?"

"I can say truthfully that I'm not jealous. I can't speak for what goes on in Jack's mind, but for me, not a bit. Anyway, because of his traveling, Jack and I spend at least three weeks out of every month apart. We are always very careful with each other's feelings. We talk often, and I'm sure that Jack has no objections to what I'm doing, although he doesn't know all the details. I have

23

no problem with his flirtations. And they're just that, flirtations.
Nothing serious, just lust and good sex. For me too.''

"If you can really handle it. . . ." Carla paused. "I'm not sure
I could.''

"I don't actually know of many who can, but Jack and I seem
to do okay.''

"You were telling me how this thing," Carla waved her hand
around the luxurious room, "got started.''

"Jack and I were having dinner with a business associate of
his, TJ Sorenson of American Oil and Gas Products." Ronnie
closed her eyes. "It was Christmastime about three years ago. I
remember that there were tiny trees and red candles on the tables.''

"What a meal," Jack said, settling back with a cup of espresso.
"I've never been here before but you can be sure I'll come here
again.''

"I discovered Chez Martin several months ago," TJ said, "and
I keep hoping that no one else will. I read the restaurant columns
and am relieved every time I find other places discussed. So far
no reviewer had found Chez Martin. I'm particularly glad I could
share it with you. You're two of my favorite people." TJ Sorenson
was about fifty, with a head full of white hair and a bushy white
moustache, which he stroked with one index finger when he was
thinking. An old-time wildcatter, TJ's eyes were the color of corn-
flowers with deep lines at the corners from squinting in the bright
sun for dozens of years. He was a handsome man, with the outdoor
look of someone who spent a great deal of time in the sun, wind,
and weather. He didn't look old enough to have a grown son, a
married daughter, and three grandchildren.

"Thanks so much, TJ," Ronnie said. "I'm so full I could
burst." She took a sip of her white crème de menthe on the rocks
and gazed at the two men, both looking mildly uncomfortable in
double-breasted suits, white shirts, and ties. Although he looks
great in his usual jeans and sweatshirt, I love how Jack looks in
a suit, Ronnie thought. And the slight grey at the temples of his

carefully combed dark brown hair makes him look more like a banker than an oil explorer.

"I'm glad you're so satisfied, because I have an ulterior motive for inviting you tonight." TJ stroked his moustache. "I would like to ask you a favor and I'm not entirely sure how to do it."

"Just ask," Jack said. "You've been so great to me for all these years, I'll be happy to help if I can."

"Well," TJ said, "I need both of you to agree, although it's really Ronnie's favor."

Ronnie's head popped up, her blond hair brushing her shoulders. "Me?"

TJ sighed. "Let me explain. First of all, I hope you don't mind that Jack has told me about your delightfully original relationship."

"Of course not. Jack and I are not ashamed of our lifestyle." Ronnie stroked Jack's hand lovingly. "We love each other and have fun as well." Jack winked one grey eye and nodded.

"You two seem to have figured out something that works for you and you know how much I like you both."

Ronnie rested her elbows on the table and studied the older man. TJ, who had recently been promoted to executive vice president of American Oil, had been Jack's first boss. The two men had hit it off almost immediately, and as TJ climbed the corporate ladder, Jack climbed with him. Several years earlier, when Jack formed his own geology consulting firm, TJ had given him moral support and had seen to it that American Oil put him on retainer. Jack and Ronnie owed him a lot.

In addition to their business relationship, the two men had become friends. In the early days, TJ and Jack had traveled together on oil drilling expeditions, often spending weeks at a time in the field, living in a tent, and actually wielding a pick and shovel. In the years since TJ had become office-bound, Jack and Ronnie had dined occasionally with TJ and his wife Alice, most recently one evening the previous summer on the Sorensons' new forty-foot sailboat.

When TJ seemed at a loss as to how to continue, Ronnie said,

"Whatever is bothering you can't be that terrible. Why don't you just come out with it?"

"Right." He sipped his cognac. "It's my son. You met Tim last summer on the boat. What was your impression of him, Ronnie? As a woman. And be honest."

She remembered TJ's son. He had been on his way somewhere but had paused for a moment to make small talk. She recalled an awkward young man who seemed uncomfortable with her. "He's a nice-looking guy, as I remember," she said, hedging. "How old is he now?"

"He's twenty-four. Tell me what you think of him as a person."

"I hardly spent any time with him," Ronnie said. "But he was charming, seemed to know the right thing to say but I guess he seemed a bit distant, a bit difficult to get to know."

"He's shy with women because he's had a few bad experiences. And now he's much worse. He was engaged, you know."

"No," Ronnie said. "I didn't know. You said *was?*"

"I did. The bitch did a number on him. I think she was more interested in my money than in Tim. Anyway, about a month ago, when he seemed to be losing interest, she lost her temper at our dinner table one evening. There were several other couples, their friends and ours, and Clarisse had been drinking. Something snapped, I've no idea what. But whatever caused it she read him out and, among other things, told him he was a lousy lover. I think her exact phrasing was that he couldn't give a nymphomaniac an orgasm."

"Oh shit," Jack said. "He must have been devastated."

"He was. Fortunately Tim and I have an honest relationship and we've talked at length since then. He doesn't want anything to do with Clarisse, but he admits that she might have a point about his sexual prowess. He told me that he feels inadequate and awkward as a lover. I told him that good sex takes two and that maybe he and Clarisse just weren't compatible, but he's really down on himself. We talked about finding a prostitute to, you know, teach him about women and sex, but he didn't want anything like that. Too impersonal, too clinical."

"Am I starting to see a plan here?" Ronnie asked.

"I hope so," TJ said. "I know and trust both of you and I need someone to teach Tim about women. Ronnie?"

"I'm flattered and I'd like to help. But I won't do anything without his knowledge," Ronnie said.

"Of course not." He looked from Ronnie to Jack. "If you two agree, I'll talk to him. I mentioned you recently and he remembers meeting you last summer. As a matter of fact, I think he was impressed, said you were a knockout, as I recall. I don't know whether that's the good news or the bad."

"I think it would be wonderful for Tim," Jack said, his charming grin revealing even, white teeth. "Ronnie's just the right woman to teach a young man about love and sex. She's terrific." He squeezed his wife's hand.

"So you're both willing?" TJ said.

"If Tim wants to, I'm certainly willing," Ronnie said.

Later that night, Ronnie and Jack lay in bed, naked, propped up on several pillows. "That's quite an assignment," Jack said, "teaching a young man about sex."

"I know," Ronnie said. "It's a bit daunting."

"Nonsense," Jack said. He tangled his fingers in Ronnie's hair. "Any man who looks at your full lips will want to kiss you." He pressed his lips against hers. "He'll want to use his tongue to play with yours." He opened her mouth with his tongue and stroked the inside. "He'll want to touch your face." He ran the pads of his fingers over Ronnie's forehead, cheeks, and nose. "And close your eyes with his lips." He kissed her eyelids.

"Maybe you should teach him," Ronnie said. "You do things so well."

As his hands made her skin burn everywhere they touched, Jack said, his voice hoarse, "Will you tell me every detail? Will you demonstrate to me everything you taught him?" His breathing was rough as his hands found her wet center.

"I may not share exactly what we do because that seems very private. But I'll make up something delicious," Ronnie said, wrapping her legs around her husband's waist. "But for right now, just fuck me good."

They were both so hot that their mating was frantic, tangling their bodies in sheets and pillows. He pounded into her hard and screamed when he came. Her orgasm wasn't far behind.

Tim called Ronnie about a week later. "My dad told me about your conversation," he said without preamble. "I'm really embarrassed about all this."

"I'm a little uncomfortable too, Tim, but I gather that this type of thing is common in Europe. The older woman educating the younger man."

Tim's hollow laugh echoed through the phone. "That doesn't help and anyway, you're not that much older."

Ronnie laughed. "It doesn't help me either, but I'd love to spend time with you, if you'd like. We could talk and do whatever you want, nothing more."

Ronnie heard Tim take a deep breath. "I think I would." He paused. "Maybe we could have dinner at that place Dad took you to. Like next Tuesday evening?"

Ronnie had been dreading a long dinner during which she and Tim would have to make pleasant conversation. It sounded awful. "You know, let's pass on dinner," Ronnie suggested. "Let me meet you at your apartment at about eight. We can talk and see what happens from there."

"I could pick you up." Ronnie could hear the hesitancy in his voice.

"I'd prefer to meet you, if that's okay." No long drive with awkward silences.

"Sure. Ronnie?"

"Yes."

"I'm terrified and mortified."

"Don't be. We'll only do what makes both of us comfortable. Okay?"

"I'll see you Tuesday." Tim gave Ronnie directions to his apartment.

"Okay. I'll see you at eight o'clock. And Tim, wear those tight, over-washed jeans you were wearing that evening last summer. I remember how good they looked on you."

"Yeah," Tim said, his voice a bit lighter. "Sure. I will." He hung up.

Ronnie drove to the apartment complex the following Tuesday and grabbed a heavy camel wool coat from the back seat. She wore a deep red, button front, man-tailored shirt and jeans, with her bare feet stuffed into soft leather loafers. She had on almost no makeup and had pulled her hair into a ponytail. Although she was in her early thirties she looked younger and less threatening. Only her lingerie was intended to tantalize, a dark red demibra and matching thong-style panties.

Her palms sweaty, Ronnie parked her car, found her way to Tim's apartment, and rang the bell. It took a moment before she heard footsteps.

"Hi," Tim said as he opened the door. Ronnie was surprised at how much he had changed in the few months since she had last seen him. Although he had been twenty-three that evening on the boat, he had still had some of the gawky teenaged angles and hollows to his body. No more.

"You've grown up," Ronnie said as she looked him over slowly and appraisingly, enjoying the way his body now filled out the navy blue knit shirt he wore. His shoulders were wide and his hips narrow. Lord she loved muscular shoulders and she longed to run her palms over his upper arms, feel them around her. That would have to wait, however. Right now Tim's fists were clenched at his sides and the open ingenuous smile that she knew could warm his ordinary-looking face was hidden beneath his nervousness.

Tim was terrified. When he and his dad discussed Clarisse's ugly comments, and Tim had reluctantly admitted that even before that evening he had begun to doubt himself. He'd been a normal teenaged stud, seducing several members of his high school class, then having several longer-term relationships in college. But with Clarisse it had been different. As the months of their relationship

passed, it took longer and longer for him to arouse her. He tried
to be considerate and give her the time she needed but after pro-
longed foreplay, once he finally got inside, he came so quickly
that Clarisse complained that Tim always left her unsatisfied. The
last few times they had slept together, he'd been unable to get an
erection at all. "Don't you have a clue about women?" Clarisse
had shrieked late one night. "All you want to do is fuck. Stick it
in and to hell with the woman." She'd laughed at him. "Now
you can't even get it up." His brain understood what was going
on, but his soul had doubts.

The scene at his father's dinner table had been a humiliation
for Tim and for several weeks he had gone straight home after
work and shut himself in his apartment. After almost a month
his father had showed up at his door and sat him down for a
serious talk.

At first Tim had been appalled by his dad's suggestion of hiring
a prostitute, but when Ronnie's name came up, Tim's interest had
been piqued and his body had reacted. Although he'd only met
her the one time on the boat, he'd spent many nights fantasizing
about her long blond hair and great body. TJ had explained about
Jack and Ronnie's unusual relationship, and Tim had agreed to
the outlandish plan.

Now Ronnie was here and Tim was panic-stricken. This was
all a terrible mistake. As Tim saw the corners of her mouth turn
up, he asked, "What are you smiling at?" Her eyes were roaming
all over his body, making his skin prickle. Was she going to make
fun of him and of this ridiculous idea?

"Nothing. It's just that you've matured and I enjoy looking at
you." She would tell him later, in detail, how hunky he'd become.
Instinctively Ronnie knew that he wasn't ready.

Tim was nice looking, with sandy brown hair and eyes the color
of toast. As Tim nervously ran his long, delicate fingers through
his hair, Ronnie thought about how those hands would feel on her
skin. Nice, she thought warming to her task. Very nice. And despite his nervousness, he had a sexy way of looking right into her

eyes that made Ronnie tingle. "May I come in?" she said, noticing that he had worn the jeans she'd suggested.

Tim stepped back and let Ronnie brush past him into his apartment. God, he thought, she smells so good. "I'm glad you came." His face reddened and he looked mortified as he realized his accidental double entendre.

"You know, Tim," Ronnie said as Tim shut the door, "we're going to drive each other crazy if we don't relax." She placed a light kiss on his cheek and dropped her coat on a chair.

"Yeah," he said with a sigh. "I've been jumpy as a cat all day." He rubbed his hands down the thighs of his jeans. "I'm not sure this was a good idea."

"It was a wonderful idea and we'll just talk for a while. Nothing you don't want. Okay?"

Tim looked at his shoes, then looked at Ronnie. God, she was so sexy. He nodded.

Suddenly Ronnie was completely comfortable. Tim was a genuinely nice human being. "There's nothing to be jumpy about. Have you got anything to drink? I think we could both use one."

"I've got a bottle of champagne."

"Great. Got any orange juice? We could make mimosas."

"Sure. Good idea. The OJ's in the fridge."

"Any brandy?"

"There might be a bottle in the closet to the right. Why?"

"To make the perfect mimosa," Ronnie said, crossing to the tiny kitchen, "you should add a shot of brandy." Ronnie retrieved a container of juice and rummaged through the liquor closet until she found a bottle of Triple Sec. "This'll do," she said. Returning to the living room, she saw that Tim had half-filled two champagne flutes with champagne. He quickly added an equal amount of juice, then she topped each off with a shot of Triple Sec.

"To the evening," Ronnie said, touching her glass to Tim's.

Tim stared into her eyes over the rim of his glass, unaware of the sensuousness of his gaze. "Yes. To the evening."

Not too fast, Ronnie told herself, tearing her eyes from his face. She wandered. "Nice place," she said. They stood in the large living room which was comfortably furnished with a cream-and-navy rough-textured sofa, a matching lounge chair, and modern wooden coffee and end tables. The walls were covered with photos, mostly landscapes, taken all around the world. One that particularly intrigued her showed a market scene of stalls stacked with merchandise and aisles filled with over-tired tourists. Although the photo was in black and white, it conveyed all the colors of the scene. "Where's this?"

"Cairo," he said. "I was there two years ago with my dad."

"And this?" The picture was of a river with houseboats littering its shores.

"Amsterdam."

"Wow," she said, honestly impressed. "Did you take all these pictures?"

"Yeah. Photography has been a love of mine since I was a kid."

"These are terrific."

"Thanks. I've converted my second bedroom into a darkroom and I do all my own developing and enlarging."

Ronnie walked slowly around the room studying the black-and-white photos. "These are really very good. Do you ever do portraits?"

"Sure." He pulled out an album and proudly showed Ronnie several skillfully taken photographs of women. He pointed to one, a slightly over-made-up woman in her early twenties with an expression that, despite the smile, seemed disapproving. "That's Clarisse, my ex-fiancée. I wanted to mount this photo on cardboard and use it as a dart board, but it's too good a picture. You know, it's funny. Now that I think about it, this was one of the few times I ever saw her smile when it wasn't for effect."

Ronnie laughed. "From what your father told me, the dart board idea sounds like a good one."

Tim hesitated, then joined Ronnie's laughter. "You're right. But it truly is a good picture of her." He studied the photo. "Actually, she's never looked that good."

Ronnie kicked off her shoes, settled onto the sofa, and patted the seat next to her. "Sit here and we'll talk." As he sat down, she asked, "Would you be interested in taking some pictures of me? I'd love to have a good portrait to give Jack for our anniversary."

"Sure. That would be great. I'd really enjoy it."

"Have you ever considered taking portraits professionally? The ones you showed me were really good."

"Do you really think I could do this for money?"

"You never know. Maybe the ones I have in mind will be the start of a new career."

While they made small talk Ronnie felt the alcohol warm her body and knew that it would be easing Tim's fears as well. When there was a lapse in the conversation, she slid down so that her head rested on the back of the sofa. She handed Tim her glass and asked, "Would you like to kiss me?"

Tim put their two glasses on the table and said, "I think I would."

Ronnie wrapped her hand around the back of Tim's neck and gently pulled him toward her. She framed his face with her hands as he touched her lips with his. Gently, teasingly, she moved her mouth over his, nipping his lower lip with her teeth. "Ummm, nice," she purred.

Tim sat back. "This is so awkward. I don't know what to do with my hands. Maybe this isn't such a good idea." He looked away.

"We don't have to do anything you don't want to," Ronnie said, "but I'll be very disappointed."

Suddenly annoyed with the whole thing, he looked at her and snapped, "I don't need charity."

Ronnie stood up, unzipped her jeans, and slid them to her knees. She grabbed Tim's hand and pressed it against the crotch of her panties. "What do you feel? Am I hot and wet for you? Does this feel like charity?"

Her heat warmed his hand and her wetness made his fingers damp. She wanted him. Really wanted him. He looked into her eyes and saw desire burning there. Oh Lord, don't let me back out, he prayed, both to himself and to Ronnie.

She pulled his hand away from her crotch and held it while she slid her jeans back up and sat back down on the sofa. "I want you," she said softly, her gaze never leaving his eyes, "but I'll stop if you really want me to." She raised his hand to her mouth and placed a kiss on the end of each finger. "Should I stop?"

"No," he moaned.

She flicked her tongue over the tip of his index finger. "Then let's pretend that this is your cock." She drew the tip of his finger into her mouth. "Can you feel it? Does it feel good?"

He certainly could and it was unbelievably erotic. Electricity sparked in his groin, hardening his penis. "It feels very good." The words came out as part breath and part groan.

"Good. Then close your eyes and let me suck you." Tim closed his eyes and let his head fall onto the back of the sofa. It would be all right. Millimeter by millimeter she pulled Tim's index finger into her mouth, licking and nipping at the tip. She moved to the second finger and sucked it, then the third and then the pinkie. She lavished attention on each finger of his other hand in turn, until heat radiated from his body.

"This is how much I want you," she whispered. She took his hand and rubbed the palm against one erect nipple. This was wonderful. She could use his hand to touch herself exactly the way she wanted. She pressed and rubbed, arching her back and reveling in the sensations caused by his hand on her breast. Despite her hunger, however, she went no further, wanting Tim to take some of the initiative.

Soon touching Ronnie's breast through her shirt wasn't enough for Tim. He wanted to kiss her, to touch and taste her. He licked his lips and stared at her mouth. "I want you." Hesitant to do anything to break the mood, yet unable to resist any longer, he leaned forward and brushed Ronnie's lips with his. Suddenly he needed to devour and be devoured. He moved his head so he could delve into her warm mouth. He couldn't get enough of her.

Ronnie had never been kissed so thoroughly. "Oh Tim," she

sighed, wrapping her arms around his neck. They kissed for a long
time, as Ronnie slowly stretched out on the sofa and pulled him
over her so that his body covered hers.

"Too many clothes," Ronnie whispered when they paused for
breath. As Ronnie removed her blouse and tossed it on a chair Tim
stood up and pulled off his shirt. His body was just as beautiful as
Ronnie had anticipated. When he stood and started to unbutton his
jeans, Ronnie stopped him. "Not yet." She stood up and moved so
close to him that her lace-covered breasts brushed the sparse hair
on his chest. Slowly she ran her hands over his well-developed
shoulders. "When you opened the door I knew your body would
look like this," she murmured. "So beautiful."

"I go to the gym a couple of times a week," he said, breathless.
"I lift."

"You certainly do," Ronnie said, sliding her palms over his
chest and down his back. "Your body is wonderful."

Tim unhooked Ronnie's bra and freed her breasts. "So is
yours."

Ronnie slid Tim's hands down her ribs. "Pick me up," she
said. "I want to feel you move."

With Ronnie's palms on his upper arms, Tim tightened his
hands on her waist and lifted. "I love the way your muscles move
under your skin," she said, kneading Tim's biceps.

"And I love your tits," he said, holding her so her breasts
were level with his mouth. He took one nipple and drew it into
his mouth.

Her hands roaming over Tim's smooth shoulders and back, Ronnie let her head fall back, exposing her smooth, white throat. Tim
took the invitation and lowered her slightly so he could nuzzle
her neck. Holding her easily with her feet inches off the floor,
Tim licked Ronnie's pulse points and nibbled at the tender spot
where her neck joined her shoulder. "You taste so good," he
moaned.

He set her down gently and continued kissing her neck and
shoulders. Soon neither of them could stand, so they quickly removed their jeans and underwear and stretched out on the sofa.

"This feels so strange," Ronnie said, rubbing her back against the rough texture of the sofa's fabric. "It's actually erotic."

Tim rubbed his arms over the material. "I'll never think about this sofa the same way."

"I want you, you know." Not giving the flash of panic she saw a chance to blossom, Ronnie reached for Tim's already-hard cock. She unwrapped the condom she had dropped on the table earlier and slowly unrolled it onto Tim's hard cock. "Cold?"

"Yes," he said. "And very exciting."

"Let me share it." She rubbed the end of his cold, wet prick over her wet pussy. "Ummm, it is cold. And I'm so hot for you." She positioned his erection between her inner lips and arched her back. His cock drove into her. "Hold still and let me," she said, squeezing her vaginal muscles and watching the pleasure clearly visible on Tim's face.

She turned and pushed him back so his head rested against the back of the sofa and he was half sitting and half lying. "Hold still and just feel." She sat on his lap and impaled herself on his shaft. She used her thighs to raise her body, then drop, over and over, altering the speed and depth to suit her desires.

"Oh Lord," he moaned. "I'm going to shoot."

"Not yet," Ronnie said as orgasm built deep within her. "Hold completely still and feel, but don't come." When she felt him twist, she snapped. "Don't move and don't come!" He opened his eyes and stared at her. Slowly a smile spread over his face and he nodded.

She settled in his lap barely moving, his cock deep inside of her. "I'm going to come and I want you to share it." She took Tim's hand and touched her clit. Waves of pleasure started at her toes and deep in her belly and washed over her body ending in her pussy. "Feel," she yelled.

Her orgasm clutched at his cock, drawing his climax from him. "Yes. Now!" she groaned. "Do it." He thrust upward once, twice, then came, hard. Almost without movement, their mutual orgasms continued for long seconds. Ronnie collapsed pulling Tim with her and they dozed, tangled together.

Later, Tim stretched. "That was amazing."

"It certainly was. You were perfect."

He sighed and smiled. "We were perfect. I never knew making love could be so wonderful. Can we do this again sometime soon?"

"As long as we don't get confused. I enjoy fucking you, and we're friends. But that's all. Jack and I have a special thing and I love him very much."

"I understand. I can keep everything in perspective. Okay?"

"Okay. And you'll take some pictures of me sometime?"

"I'd love to."

An hour later, Ronnie arrived home to find Jack waiting for her. "How did it go, love?" he asked.

"It was fabulous and I think very . . . how should I say it . . . educational. How are you?"

"You know, I'm surprised at how I am. I'm great, and horny as a goat just thinking about you with that boy."

Ronnie grinned. "Well, we could go upstairs and work off that excitement." She walked over to Jack's chair, knelt between his knees, and unbuckled his belt. As she unzipped his fly she brushed his hard cock. "Or maybe we could stay right here." She separated the sides of the fly in his shorts allowing his hard cock to spring forth. "What's your pleasure?"

"You're my pleasure," Jack said softly. "So much pleasure."

Ronnie made a tight ring of her index finger and thumb and slowly slid that ring down the length of Jack's cock. With her fingers tightly encircling the base of her husband's cock, Ronnie licked the tip with the point of her tongue. Then she kissed the tiny hole in the end. "Your cock is so hard—like warm velvet over steel." She sucked the end into her wet mouth and slowly slid the length of it into her throat.

Jack watched his wife's head bob in his lap, unable to control the frantic excitement bubbling inside him. His hips bucked and his hot come tried to rush through the tight ring of her fingers. "Oh babe, let me. I'm so horny."

"Let you come?" she said, letting her breath cool Jack's wet cock. "Release my fingers?"

"Yes."

She sucked in his cock and then pulled back. "Say please."

"Please, babe."

Ronnie released her fingers and took Jack's entire thick cock into her mouth, sucking and flicking her tongue over the tip. Almost immediately hot come filled her mouth. As fast as she swallowed, some thick liquid escaped from the corners of her mouth.

When Ronnie had licked all the stickiness from Jack's cock, she sat back and said, "Now, let's go upstairs and we'll make love nice and slow."

Jack grinned his agreement.

Three days later, Ronnie stormed to the door, waving an envelope, as Jack arrived home. "You'll never believe what came in the mail today."

Jack could tell she was furious. "Calm down babe, and tell me what happened."

"TJ sent me a check for three hundred dollars and a thank-you note for the evening I spent with Tim."

"So why are you so angry?" Jack said, dropping his briefcase on the hall table.

"I didn't do this to get paid. I feel like a whore."

"But he was going to pay a prostitute anyway. Why shouldn't you take the money?"

Ronnie released her breath. "I am not a whore."

"No one said you were."

"But doesn't this make me one? Sex for money."

"Stop being judgmental," Jack said walking into the kitchen. "You had fun, Tim had fun, and TJ was delighted with the way everything turned out. And Tim's a better person because of your help. Right?"

"Yeah, but. . . ." She was flustered.

"Don't but me. How can this be wrong when no one's been hurt?"

"But I'm not a . . ." Ronnie paused.

"Hooker, call girl, prostitute, whore?" Jack said. "Words. Just words with all kinds of bullshit behind them. Stop using labels and think. Was anyone hurt?"

"No."

"You performed a service, and did it well. Right?"

"Yes."

"So you should be rewarded. Of course, you could send the check back. . . ."

"I could."

"But you don't want to. So the end result is that you had fun and got paid for it. A dream job."

"I guess I never thought of it that way." She dropped into a chair. "God, I did have fun."

"And so did we that night, if you remember." He groaned loudly and pressed a hand against the small of his back. "Our acrobatics almost put me out of commission for good."

Ronnie laughed. "You're right, you know. I am being silly." She stared at the check. "Three hundred dollars for having a good fuck. Seems almost too good to be true."

"So buy yourself something extravagant. Buy some sexy lingerie and gift wrap your gorgeous body for me."

"I could squander this. It's like found money."

"Yes, it is. You know," he paused, "my clients are sometimes out-of-town visitors who need to be entertained. Dinner, a show, intelligent conversation, and afterward. . . well, that's between the client and his date. If you think you'd like to earn some extra money. . . ."

"Prostitution?"

"Fun and games and a little cash on the side. And only if you want to."

"How much cash on the side?" she said, amazed at how excited she suddenly was by the idea.

"I've never been involved directly, but from what I understand they pay anywhere from three hundred to one thousand dollars per evening. For adult entertainment."

Ronnie's eyes widened. "One thousand dollars???"

Jack nodded.

"I'm flabbergasted. For doing what we've been doing anyway. Would you be okay with it, me with other men?"

"Well, if you'll tell me afterward a little about what happens, the idea turns me on."

"I won't violate any confidences, you understand."

"Of course not." He saw the gleam in Ronnie's eye. "Interested?"

"I think I might be."

He took her arm. "This conversation has made me horny. Wanna practice for your new profession? Or I could conduct your preemployment physical."

Ronnie headed for the stairs. "Last one to the bedroom has to sleep in the wet spot."

Chapter 3

"And that was how this began," Ronnie told Carla. "Tim took these pictures of me, you know."

"He really does great work," Carla said.

"He does, doesn't he? He's got a few girlfriends now, and he's marvelous in bed. He loves women, and it shows in his photographs."

"I love happy endings."

"Me too."

"And this works for you, this call girl thing?"

"It does. I make a nice living and I meet fascinating people."

Carla had a thousand questions. "Have you ever had a bad experience? You know, someone who gets abusive and wants something you don't want to do, that sort of thing?"

"No one has ever gotten out of line. I screen my friends very well. They're all recommended by other friends. I never give out my address until I'm satisfied they're safe and I have a private, unlisted phone number. And I never answer that phone. I let the answering machine take a message and I call back or I hear who it is and then pick up. Our first date must begin with dinner somewhere nice. I can size someone up quickly and if I don't get good vibes we part right then."

"Have you ever had an evening go wrong?"

"I've had several men who wanted things I wasn't willing to do," Ronnie answered. When Carla raised an eyebrow, she continued, "One man wanted me to urinate on him as he masturbated and another wanted to give me an enema."

When Carla made an ugly face, Ronnie said, "Don't judge. These activities give them sexual pleasure and that's their business. And some of the things I enjoy would turn others off. But sometimes I have to tell a customer that his fantasy won't work for me." Ronnie's smile was warm. "The urination guy was a really nice man, actually, and he offered me more money. I explained that money wasn't the issue and I suggested that he find someone else. We finished our meal and spent a pleasant hour discussing movies and he paid for dinner. I never saw him again."

"Any others?"

"A man named Harry was recommended by an old friend. We had dinner and talked about his fantasies. He was heavily into control and he wanted to dominate me, run things, and spank me when I was naughty. That would have been very difficult for me, since I'm a dominant personality myself." She laughed. "I never play with anyone when I can't have some fun too."

"Control?"

"Lots of people have fantasies that revolve around power and control. This guy wanted to be in charge of all the action. Actually he had another interesting fantasy. He wanted to have me take a pretend pill that would render me incapable of resisting anything he wanted to do. And there's another man who wanted to tie me to a bed. Not my thing either."

Carla felt a jolt of electricity flow through her body and directly into her pussy. The control fantasies sounded wonderful to her. "From the look on your face," Ronnie said, "I think we've found something you'd enjoy. Should I give you a phone number? He'll pay a thousand dollars for one night."

"Holy. . . . Not yet," Carla said, realizing that she was more than a little interested in Ronnie's work.

"Hmmm. I don't have to be psychic to guess what you're thinking, darling," Ronnie said, "but you realize that this isn't for everyone. You have to have strong, good feelings about yourself and you have to enjoy sex. The money is just an extra added attraction. In my mind, the fact that the money is secondary is what makes me an entertainer, not a whore.''

"Listen," Carla said, glancing at her watch, amazed that it was already after three. "I have to get home and I have a lot of thinking to do. What day next week works for you?"

"I'll be away next week." Ronnie laughed. "A friend has invited me on a cruise. Delicious food, wine, dancing, cavorting under the Caribbean skies, the works." She winked. "And I get twenty-five hundred dollars for little old me."

Carla whistled. "Holy shit."

"Mmmm. And he's a doll. Really an interesting man."

"Why you?" How could she ask what she wanted to know without it sounding like an insult? "I don't mean you're not great, you understand, but why. . . . well, you know."

"He's got the funny idea that no 'nice girl' would like the kind of cavorting we do." She settled back. "Actually, the entire cruise is devoted to dominance. It's an annual event and there's a whole group going. We've taken an entire separate area of the ship. I will be his Mistress Ronnie for the week and he'll be my sex slave. I've got a bunch of special toys and outfits for both of us."

"Have you ever done anything like this before?"

"We met two years ago on this very cruise. Another woman and I swapped slaves for an evening and Bob enjoyed being with me so much that we repeated the trip last year and will again next week. We play during the year as well." She flipped to the photo of the grey-haired school marm in the sensible shoes and smiled. "Bobby's a very difficult student."

"I'm speechless." Ronnie shot Carla an understanding glance.

"Let's see. The following week the boys are home from camp and we're going to a lake in the Adirondacks with my folks."

"Then I'm away," Ronnie said. "Jack and I are going to Disney World, of all places, for two weeks in August. I've never been there and despite all the warnings about the heat I'm like a kid looking forward to the rides and the parade of lights. And we'll siesta after lunch, of course. Jack and me, an air-conditioned room, and a king-sized bed.''

"You and Jack have a good thing going, don't you?"

"Yeah, we do. It's just this damn *blasted* business of his. He's gone more than he's home. But we have two weeks of sun and fun to look forward to and I, for one, intend to make the best of it."

"It looks like we won't see each other until September."

"I'm afraid so. You know, I'll miss you."

"Me too."

Ronnie checked the tiny date book she kept in her purse. "Okay. How about the day after Labor Day? Lunch here."

"That sounds great." The two women bussed cheeks. "You're quite something," Carla said.

"So are you. And I'm so glad we found each other again."

"Me too," Carla said. "Me too."

During the month that Ronnie was away Carla did a lot of thinking. She was intrigued and titillated by the idea of Ronnie's business and the prospect of joining her was never far from Carla's mind.

With the boys in camp, Carla spent the first week at home, pretty much alone, cleaning and shopping and fantasizing about being tied to a bed with a handsome man standing over her, watching her useless struggles. One morning she lay in bed until after nine, dreaming about being under some man's power, letting him do whatever he wanted without being able to resist him. With that picture in her mind, she slipped her hand between her legs and rubbed her clit until she came.

She spent the second week in the Adirondacks with her three rambunctious boys and her parents. They had a wonderful time together, swimming, horseback riding, playing softball and frisbee, and eating everything in sight, while blaming their astounding appetites on the mountain air. And every man she encountered became the center of a fantasy in which she was a paid courtesan. Carla spent the entire vacation in a state of frustrated sexual excitement.

More than once she looked at her three high-spirited sons and thought about their future. All three were exceptionally bright and all would be able to select from the best colleges. The question was would she be able to afford it. There was money set aside, but would it be enough? Or was money merely an excuse to do what excited and intrigued her? What did it matter? She had made up her mind and she knew it.

Trying not to lie too much, she talked to her mother one evening about the possibility of spending more time with her grandchildren. "I've spoken about my old college roommate Ronnie," she told her mother one evening over coffee after their return to Bronxville.

"How in the world did you find Ronnie?"

"I literally ran into her." Carla told her mother the story of her accidental encounter with her old friend, reassuring her that the medical scare had been really nothing.

"And how is Ronnie?" Mrs. MacKensie asked. "I remember the vacation she spent with us. She was such a lovely girl."

"She's hardly a girl now," Carla said. "She's married and she owns her own business."

"Your father and I were always sure she'd go far. She seemed like such an intelligent girl."

Carla smiled to herself. "I wanted to talk to you about that. She wants me to join her business part time. It'll mean extra money and I could use it for the boys' college fund. The costs are getting astronomical." From upstairs, she could hear the laughter that always accompanied her father's efforts to settle the boys in bed.

"What kind of business?"

"It's a service business of some kind. Public relations. I don't know many of the details but it will involve entertaining clients in the city some evenings."

"That's wonderful dear," her mother said. "You need some other interests in your life besides your sons."

"It would mean that you would have to stay with the boys more often. A few nights a week and occasional weekends."

"Weekends? How come? Not that I mind, you understand."

"God only knows," she answered, "but Ronnie warned me

about some out-of-town stuff. I don't know how often, but from time to time."

"That's great," Mrs. MacKensie said, laughing. "Force me to spend time with the boys. Twist my arm."

Carla laughed as she always did with her mother. "Thanks, Mom."

"And maybe you'll meet someone nice at one of those meetings. Maybe your friend Ronnie knows a nice man for you."

Carla laughed harder. "Mother please." When her mother raised an eyebrow, Carla said, "Okay. Maybe she does. I'll keep my eyes open."

"And if a date keeps you in the city, like overnight. . . ." She winked. "Just give me a call and I'll see to the boys."

An early September heat wave baked New York City and the humidity that hung over the metropolis caused Carla's short-sleeved rayon blouse to stick to her back. She walked up the brownstone's front steps and rang Ronnie's bell. "Come on in," Ronnie called from inside. "It's open."

Carla walked into the foyer and heard, "Lock it behind you, will you? Then come into the kitchen."

"Sure," Carla called, throwing the deadbolt.

Carla walked to the back of the building and into the large, airy kitchen. Ronnie already had lunch laid out on the table: a green salad, a bowl of crab salad, and a cold pasta with basil. Crisp rolls nestled in a napkin-covered basket and a bottle of white wine stood opened beside two crystal glasses.

"Oh, Carla," Ronnie said, hugging her friend, "I've missed you."

"Me too. How was Disney World?"

"Sensational. The rides were a thrill, the lines were short, and the siestas were . . . athletic." She picked up a small package wrapped in silver paper. "I hope you don't mind, but I bought you a present."

"A present? I didn't think to get you anything, I'm afraid."

"I didn't expect that you had," Ronnie said. "But I saw this and couldn't resist."

Carla tore off the paper and opened the small box. Inside was a pewter figurine of a dragon with his wings spread, his head thrown back as if roaring. He perched on a faceted crystal globe, his talons buried in the transparent ball.

Ronnie watched Carla lift the four-inch-high dragon so that the light turned into rainbows within the crystal. "The dragon is for fantasy," Ronnie said. "And for dreams that can be made to come true."

"You know that I've decided to join you in your business don't you?"

"I knew a month ago when I watched your eyes light up. Actually, I probably knew when we met again that first afternoon. After all, we were roommates for three years and I knew you very well then." She poured wine into the two glasses and raised hers in toast. "To fantasy. And to making fantasies come true for everyone involved."

"To fantasy," Carla said sipping the crisp white wine.

Over lunch Carla told Ronnie about her week with her boys and her parents. "How are your folks?" Ronnie asked. "I've always loved your mother. And your dad's a stitch."

"They were always fond of you too. They asked to be remembered to you and want you to come up for dinner some time."

"I'll do that."

"And how was the cruise?"

"I'd rather tell you about the entire week some other time," she said. "It's a little early in your education for that story."

"Was it that shocking?"

"Not for me. Trust me for a few weeks," Ronnie asked and Carla demurred.

After lunch, Ronnie said "I think it's time for you to have a look around upstairs."

Ronnie and Carla put the dishes in the dishwasher, then climbed the lushly carpeted stairs to the master bedroom. It was softer and more romantic than the downstairs, done in pastel pinks and warm, spring greens. The lounge chair was upholstered in a pink-and-green floral with green piping to match the bedspread and drapes. The oriental carpet contained the same shades of green, and together with half a dozen plants, gave the entire room a warm and comfortable aura. "I entertain in here when romance is at the heart of the encounter," Ronnie said. "I also sleep here sometimes when I'm stuck in the city."

"This is a wonderful room . . . soft and loving somehow."

"That's exactly the way I designed it. We'll need to coordinate, but you're free to use it whenever you want, for whatever you want. I have a cleaning woman who comes regularly so you don't even have to tidy up."

"Are you sure about my using your place . . . this room?"

"Despite the homey feeling, this is my working space, not where I live. Let me show you what I mean." Ronnie opened the door to a huge walk-in closet. "On this side," she said waving one hand, "are everyday clothes, the usual suits, dresses, blouses, things like that. Shoes are underneath." She looked Carla over. "I would guess we still wear the same size, so take your pick whenever you need something you don't have. I try to keep the two parts of me completely separate so I don't wear my personal clothes during business. You might feel differently."

Carla admired the collection of expensive clothes. She didn't need to examine the labels to know that Ronnie only chose the best. "Isn't this overkill? So many outfits."

With a smile, Ronnie said, "I love clothes and now I can indulge myself. Anyway, I do a lot of entertaining and traveling. It's surprising how many men want a well-dressed, well-educated companion to decorate their arm at a luncheon or business dinner."

"You mean like in *Pretty Woman?*"

"Exactly. Sometimes without any sex at all." She turned and indicated the other side of the closet. "This is the evening stuff."

Carla was stunned at the number of designer dresses: chiffon, lace, sequins, and satin in a variety of colors and textures. Her fingers strained to pull each garment from its hanger and try it on. At the end of the clothes rod hung a deep rose silk jacket, a full-length black satin coat, and two faux furs. "You're ready for anything, aren't you?"

"You have no idea." Ronnie crossed the room and opened the door to a second closet. "Play clothes," she said. Inside hung an assortment of costumes. Carla recognized some of them from the photograph album Ronnie had shown her. The pink little-girl dress and the leather-and-chain outfit hung with a leopard-patterned leotard, three leather dresses with multiple zippers, and several see-through lace bodysuits.

"On each hanger," Ronnie explained, "are all the items necessary for that persona. Besides the clothes and underwear, I have coordinated jewelry, perfume, extra makeup, whatever's needed, all in a plastic bag on the hanger. With one or two there's even a wig, should you care to wear it. I love the wigs; they make me feel like a different person. Feel free to use anything, just put the stuff back in its place. Sometimes I need to dash into the bathroom and change quickly so I like to have everything ready."

Carla whistled, long and low.

Ronnie opened the drawers of the wide dresser and showed Carla dozens of slips, bras both with and without cutouts so nipples could show through, satin and lace panties, silk teddies in a dozen colors, and garter belts with stockings. "Try anything on and wear whatever fits your mood. Or you might want to wear nothing at all under your evening clothes. There are few things more arousing than telling a man that you're not wearing underwear, and then going out for an evening. But everything's replaceable so if anything gets torn or whatever," she winked, "we'll get new."

When Carla looked as though she didn't understand, Ronnie said, "Sometimes a man wants to tear clothes off or cut them off slowly and dramatically."

As Carla gazed into the drawers, she couldn't imagine a piece of lingerie that Ronnie didn't own. She picked up a cellophane package. "Panty hose?"

"Even panty hose," Ronnie said. "I have one friend who loves to pull them off of me, very slowly and lick each part he uncovers. Another friend likes to cut a hole in the crotch and have my legs— in the panty hose—wrapped around him. And, now that I think of it, I had a friend about two years ago who liked to wear them himself. He'd put a pair on before we went to dinner. He claimed they sweetened the anticipation and from the way he attacked me when we got back here, I don't doubt it at all.''

Carla tried not to be shocked. She had read about transvestites but she'd never thought to meet one. "Woman's clothes?"

"First of all, he wasn't a transvestite," Ronnie said, as if reading her friend's mind. "Several men I know like to wear satin undies under their business suits. The slippery fabric feels good against the skin and it's a sexy little secret.

"Secondly, don't judge. There's nothing wrong with an activity that consenting adults enjoy in private, or, for that matter, in selected public locations. I learned that first time with Tim that labels are for people with small minds."

"You're right, of course. And I'm not being judgmental, just naive."

"Fair enough."

On the side of the closet opposite Ronnie's costumes were outfits for men: a Robin Hood-style green vest and tights, a black outfit that looked like it was designed for a second-story man, a silver lamé top and pants that had been cut to resemble a knight's armor, and a white shirt and short pants combination. "For a naughty little boy," Ronnie explained. Carla struggled to not let her amazement show.

Eventually they returned to the living room. "I want you to go slowly," Ronnie said when the topic turned to Carla's new career. "I'd like to see you build your sexual and sensual awareness little by little. And I've got just the place to start."

"You have?"

"Um-hmm. Rick. I'm due to call him in," she glanced at her watch, "five minutes."

Carla looked a little flustered. "Now? Oh God. I thought I was ready for this," she said. "Suddenly I'm not so sure."

"Don't worry, I wouldn't do anything for your trial run that you couldn't back out of at any time. Nothing is mandatory. But Rick is the perfect place to start. I call him and we make love over the phone."

"Phone sex? Like 1-900-suck-me-off?"

"Something like that. And don't make fun of it. Talking about sex and describing lovemaking is very erotic, very exciting, and leads to some delicious orgasms." When Carla hesitated, Ronnie said again, "Trust me?"

Carla relaxed. "I do trust you. It's just that phone sex conjures up such awful visions. A sweaty body jerking off while some impersonal bimbo talks and files her nails at the same time."

"It's not like that with me. Not at all."

"Of course not," Carla said.

"Before I call Rick—or Mr. Holloway as I call him on the phone—let me tell you about him. Rick's a happily married man who's involved in some kind of financing business on Wall Street. Like so many of my friends, Rick believes that his wife couldn't be interested in the things we talk about. Every now and then I'm tempted to phone his wife and somehow get her to talk to him. I think he'd be surprised. But, of course, I wouldn't do anything like that. My friend's lives, outside of our relationship, are strictly off-limits. I've never even seen Rick."

"Never?"

"Nope. One of my friends suggested that he call me. He did and we talked in private for an hour. I discovered that he likes to listen to sexy talk, sexy stories, things like that. He'd tried those 900 numbers but never found one he really liked. He has now."

"I assume you get paid."

"Sure. He leaves a message for me once or twice a month. The message tells me what time to call him back. He'll be sure to be in the middle of the office where he's surrounded by people. After we talk, he sends me a check for a hundred and fifty dollars. Now, I'll call first, then I'll tell you to pick up. Yes?"

"I guess. But I don't want to eavesdrop."

"You won't be. Let me take care of everything. I know Rick very well and he'll enjoy this conversation immensely."

While Ronnie dialed Carla settled deeper into an overstuffed chair and tried to prepare herself for what was to come. As hard as she tried, she couldn't imagine what would happen.

"Good afternoon," an efficient-sounding female voice said, "Mr. Holloway's office."

"Mr. Holloway, please," Ronnie said. "Mr. Black's office calling."

"Thank you. One moment please."

Although she was on hold, Ronnie held her hand over the mouthpiece. "Okay, Carla, you can pick up now."

"Are you sure this is okay, Ronnie? After all the man's paying good money for this phone call. He's not doing it to expand my education."

"Not only am I sure it's okay," Ronnie answered as Carla picked up the extension phone and draped her legs over the arm of the chair, "but I'm going to tell him that you're listening."

"You aren't," Carla said.

"I know just what he likes. This plays right into his fantasies. Knowing that you're listening will heat things up for him. You can't imagine how much I enjoy knowing I can make him hot just by talking. He gets hot and so do I. I think you'll find it very erotic also."

"Mr. Holloway here," said a deep, resonant voice. Carla watched Ronnie curl up and tuck her feet under her.

"Mr. Holloway," Ronnie purred into the phone, "this is Mr. Black's office. Can you talk?"

"Of course not," Mr. Holloway answered.

"That's good. How many people are within earshot?"

"About six."

"Can they see you? I mean your entire body," Ronnie said, "not just your head."

"Just the upper levels," he answered.

"Than I want you to move. I want you to be where, when you get all hard and swollen, everyone could see if they knew where to look.'' When there was no sound at the other end of the phone, she asked, ''Have you moved?''

There were shuffling sounds, then he answered, ''I have.'' Carla could hear office noise in the background.

''Good. I have a little surprise for you today.''

''You have?''

''Say hello dear,'' Ronnie said, waving at Carla.

''Hello darling,'' Carla said, dropping her voice a full octave and letting lots of breath escape as she spoke.

''Who's that?'' the surprised voice said.

''That's Snow White,'' Ronnie said. ''She's listening to everything we say. And she's never heard anything like this before. She's going to listen as you get excited. You won't be able to hide from her.''

''Snow White?'' he whispered. ''Oh shit.'' His voice trembled as it resumed its normal timbre. ''What's your associate like?''

''Oh, she's beautiful. Would you like to hear about her?''

''That's a fine idea. Let's discuss that.''

''Well,'' Ronnie said, closing her eyes. ''She's tiny, only about five feet tall, and she's got wide, sky-blue eyes and lots of long red hair. Her skin is like a soft ripe peach and her mouth is painted with bright red lipstick.''

''That's fine,'' the business-like voice said.

''Her hands are tiny but she has long fingernails. You know how they're painted?''

''Of course.''

''Certainly you do. They've been polished so they're shiny and bright red, like her lips. And she's wearing a white dress, cut low across her bosom so the tops of her nipples are just hidden beneath the lacy edging. Her cleavage is so deep and inviting that your hands itch to bury themselves between her large breasts. The dress is tight over her ribs and there's a full skirt with a dozen stiff petticoats. She's wearing very high-heeled sandals that are held to her feet with lots of tiny straps.''

''That sounds like a fine arrangement,'' Mr. Holloway said.

Carla was blushing listening to Ronnie's description. She was also getting very aroused.

"And she's wearing long white gloves," Ronnie continued. "Her fingers aren't covered so you can still see her red fingernails, but white satin starts at her palms and extends up way past her elbows." She paused. "Can you see her?"

"Certainly. I need to know more about how the deal will proceed."

"Well, she's listening to me and getting very excited."

Carla was surprised at how excited she really was becoming as Ronnie described this imaginary Snow White. Her body was responding. She wanted to loosen the jeans that constricted her.

Carla could hear movement at the other end of the phone, together with the clack of keyboards and the occasional jangle of a telephone. "Is that true?" the man's voice said.

"Yes," Carla said, strangely no longer embarrassed. "I'm very excited. My thighs are open and I'm getting wet." Ronnie opened her eyes and nodded her approval.

"Wonderful," Rick said. "It sounds like the arrangement is working well."

In the distance, a woman's voice interrupted. "Mr. Holloway. Can you take Mr. Malone on line two?"

"Not right now," Rick said. "Tell him I'll call back."

"You mean you can't take another call right now?" Ronnie chuckled.

"Not a chance," Mr. Holloway said. "Our business is more important. Where were we?"

"You'll have to refresh my memory," Ronnie teased.

"Shit," the voice whispered. "Okay, we were talking about the irrigation project."

Carla laughed. "Yes we were. I was telling you how wet I am."

"Snow White is just waiting for you, Mr. Holloway. Are you hard enough for her?"

"Certainly. What about the rest?"

"Well, Snow White is wearing pantalets trimmed with white

lace. They're getting wet in the crotch as her pussy gets hotter. Should we have her take them off?''

"A fine idea," Mr. Holloway said.

"Take off your pantalets, Snow White," Ronnie said. "Hold the phone so Mr. Holloway can hear your clothes come off.''

Carla raised an eyebrow and Ronnie nodded. Carla stood up and pulled off her jeans, holding the phone so the man at the other end could hear the rustle of each leg as she pulled her feet through. "Did you hear that?" Carla said. She heard the man's breathing, then continued, "I'm now naked under my dress, but I'm pulling my skirts down so you can't see or touch. . . . yet.''

Ronnie made an okay sign with one hand. Carla was continually surprised at how easy and enjoyable this was. And Ronnie got paid for this?

"It's about time you got to the meat of the proposal," the man's voice said.

"Honey," Ronnie said, "it's your meat I'm proposing.''

Holloway's deep laugh echoed through the phone line. "I'm not used to this kind of work being amusing. I guess that's why I like doing business with you," he said.

"Does a laugh make your cock any softer?" Ronnie asked.

"Of course not," he answered.

"Good. Now, where were we? Oh yes, Snow White is sitting on her throne, one leg draped over each arm, her skirts pulled down between her spread legs. Can you see her?''

"Uh-huh.''

"She reaches down and dips her red-tipped fingers into the sweet valley between her breasts and pulls first one, then the other, out of the bodice of her gown. Her nipples are sensitive and deep pink. She pinches them so they're hard, like large pebbles. She tweaks at one with her nails and rubs the satin palm of her glove over the other. Tiny pains and satiny pleasure. She switches pinching and stroking, going back and forth until her tits are aching.''

Carla massaged her breasts, feeling exactly what Ronnie was saying that Snow White felt.

"Is your cock aching too, Mr. Holloway?" Ronnie asked.

"Most assuredly."

"Is anyone looking at you right now?"

"As a matter of fact yes. Just a moment please." The two women heard Mr. Holloway shift the phone. "What is it?"

"I need your signature so I can get this into Express Mail by three o'clock."

There was some shuffling, then Mr. Holloway said, "That's done."

"Your poor cock," Ronnie said. "It must be hurting. Your balls too. And you can't do anything about it or everyone will see."

There was a barely audible groan.

"Wonderful," Ronnie purred. "Now, as Snow White sits on her throne, her pussy gets so itchy that she had to reach down and touch it. Can you see her? She's sitting with her legs spread wide apart. She slowly pulls up her skirt and slides her fingers up the inside of her creamy thighs. Do it, Snow White," Ronnie said, looking at Carla. "You know you love to have people watch you."

Carla stroked her pussy through her panties. She was soaking wet. She knew that if she caressed herself just right she would climax immediately but she found that she wanted to wait and continue to amuse Mr. Holloway. And, amazingly enough, she liked the fact that Ronnie was watching her.

"Mr. Holloway?" Carla said softly.

He cleared his throat. "Yes?"

"I'm right here, scratching the insides of my thighs with the tips of my long red nails. Now I'm using one nail and touching my clit, just brushing it, flicking it. It's so good."

"I bet if you play with it, you'll come," Ronnie said. "Right Snow White?"

"Oh yes," Carla groaned. "I want to come."

"That sounds acceptable to me," Mr. Holloway said.

"Stroke your cunt, Snow White," Ronnie said. "Put the phone near your cunt and let Mr. Holloway hear your fingers moving."

Carla held the phone close to her pussy and slid her fingers under the crotch of her panties. She knew just how to touch herself because she'd done it so many times in the past five years.

"Yes," Ronnie said. "I can see you with my eyes and Mr. Holloway can see you in his mind. Rub it harder."

"Yes," Carla whispered, panting. She was so close. Just another moment.

"Rub it faster, Snow White," Ronnie said. "Can you hear her, Mr. Holloway? Hear how close she is to coming? Hear her breathing, how fast it is? She's going to come . . . right now!"

Carla let out a low moan as she spasmed. She held very still and reveled in the waves of pleasure that washed over her body.

"Does your cock hurt, darling?" Ronnie said into the phone as Carla slowly recovered from one of the best orgasms she'd had in a long time.

"I think that will work out nicely," Mr. Holloway said. "I have to go now."

"Are you going into the bathroom to take your big hard cock in your hand and massage and fondle it until you spurt hot come all over?"

"I think that will be enough for now," he said, laughing. "Otherwise it won't go well for any of us."

"Right," Ronnie said, laughing too.

"Thank you darling," Carla said into the phone, her breathing not yet back to normal. "That was wonderful."

"I'll speak to you soon," Mr. Holloway said. "And thank you for your help in this matter. I'll handle it from here." As he hung up, everyone was laughing.

Chapter 4

"Oh, Lord," Carla said, curling up in her chair. "If that's what it's like all the time then I'll be both exhausted and delighted." Strange, but she wasn't embarrassed by Ronnie watching as she came.

"It is if you want it to be. You understand most of my rules and know that I stick by them, no matter how much money is involved."

"Spell them out again."

"I never do anything I don't think I'll enjoy and I make it clear to my friends that I always have the right to call things off at any time, as do they. That's part of the reason for having dinner with a new acquaintance before our first encounter. Doing what I do takes trust. Everyone must have the right to say stop and we always agree on a safe word."

"Safe word?"

"I usually use 'popcorn.' At any time, if anyone says that word, everything stops. Immediately. And if I can't trust my friends to obey if I say it, and to say it if they want to stop, it's no deal."

"Why is it important that they say it too? You're the one who needs a way out."

"Not really. Take men who enjoy being dominated. If I can be sure they'll use the safe word, I can do anything that takes my fancy. I describe what I'm going to do if it's the first time and I don't have to worry about going too far. The safe word is there

so they can yell, 'Please stop,' and know I won't, but be sure I'll
stop when that's what they really want.''

"That sounds reasonable,'' Carla said, still catching her breath
after the phone call.

"Also, no heavy drinking, although a glass or two loosens
things up. No drugs of any kind and, as you know, I insist that
my friends use condoms. He can have seventeen blood tests or
whatever, but condoms are mandatory. Period.''

Carla nodded. Everything that Ronnie said seemed, if anything,
overly cautious.

"You're still interested, aren't you?'' Ronnie said.

Carla took a deep breath. "After that phone call,'' she said,
"more than ever. But I'm a little apprehensive about where to
start.''

"I have a suggestion,'' Ronnie said, stretching out on the sofa
and crossing her long legs at the ankles. "An old friend called
me a few weeks ago. His name's Bryce and I've known him for
over a year.''

Carla had learned in college that Ronnie's particularly delightful, slightly mischievous smile meant that she was deeply
involved in hatching an inventive plot. When Ronnie didn't continue, Carla said, "And. . . .''

Ronnie picked up the glass of wine from the table next to her
and took a sip. "He's had an ongoing fantasy about wedding
nights and seduction. He's heavily into romance, music, wine, all
that.'' Carla could see the dreamy look in Ronnie's eyes. "He's
also into a bit of control, which I think you'll find irresistable.
And he's dynamite in bed, a deliciously creative man who gets
his satisfaction from giving as well as taking pleasure. We've
spend some memorable nights together.''

"He sounds too good to be true. Is he married? And if he is,
why does his wife let him out of her sight?''

"His wife died several years ago and part of the reason he
plays with me is that he's surrounded with matchmaking friends
who bombard him with suitable women. I think that, when he's
with me, he's comfortable. We have wonderful times together,

great sex, and there are no strings, no commitments." Ronnie smiled. "I hope you don't mind but we talked about you."

"You knew that I was going to do this, didn't you."

"You're not expert at hiding your feelings, and I know you pretty well."

Carla smiled and pulled on her jeans. "You certainly used to, and after that game we just played with Rick Holloway, you know me even better."

Ronnie laughed. "True. Anyway, I think he'd be a wonderful first time for you. He'd love it and, I can guarantee, so would you."

"It sounds like he's *your* friend."

"He's a special man, but he's just a friend. And I think you'd enjoy being together."

"But. . . ."

"Listen, Carla. I don't know whether you should do this at all. I understand myself and I've been doing what I do for almost four years. I love it."

"I know you do. I've given this entire situation a lot of thought and, well, it titillates me. I've told you that I don't know much about off-center sex, but I know that I want to find out more."

"And, of course, you can call things off at any time and go back to Bronxville and sell real estate," responded Ronnie. Each woman wrinkled her nose.

The phone rang and Ronnie and Carla listened as the answering machine picked up. "This is Black Enterprises. Please leave a message at the sound of the beep, and thanks for calling."

"Hi, Ronnie and Snow White, this is Rick Holloway. You're probably both listening right now so I wanted to tell you that I feel great. I'm in my private office right now and I'm sending you a check for three hundred dollars. I hope to talk to you both again soon. And Ronnie, thanks for knowing exactly what would increase the fun even before I did. Take care." He hung up.

"He really liked it," Carla said, still surprised at the power of the spoken word.

"He sure did. And you had a lot to do with that."

"I thought he usually paid a hundred and fifty dollars. He said he's sending three hundred."

"He's paying double. I guess he's sending half for me and half for Snow White." Ronnie pulled out her wallet and handed Carla three fifty-dollar bills. "That's your share."

Carla stared at the money in her hand. "This has to be immoral, illegal, or fattening. Maybe all three."

"Well, it's certainly not fattening and, as far as I'm concerned, it's not immoral. I don't think you can have a crime without a victim and none of my friends is ever a victim." She sighed. "Actually, some claim that what we do together makes them better lovers at home, either more creative or less demanding. However, it is prostitution and that's illegal . . . but what the hell." She sipped her drink and gave a mock salute. "Anyway, Bryce would love to spend an evening with you—your virgin experience, as it were."

Carla's hands trembled. "Now that I'm actually going to do it, half of me can't wait and half is scared to death."

"That's exactly the fantasy that Bryce wants. He loves the scared little girl and the initiation part of this. And you can say stop at any time. Bryce knows the rules. So, if you're sure. . . ."

Carla took a deep breath. "I am."

"Good. I'll give you his number and you can call him, make your plans. He'll take you to dinner, dancing, then to a hotel room."

"Not here?"

"You know you can use the house any time, although we'll have to coordinate carefully. But Bryce likes the idea of neutral territory. He's got oodles of money and he can afford the best. By the way, as a present to him, I think we should forgo the fee for this one night."

Carla chuckled. "I'm glad. Somehow it seems more honest for my first time." As she lifted her wine glass, her hands shook. "I'm nervous."

"Good." Ronnie handed Carla a piece of paper. "Here's his

number. Call him right now, while you're in this mood. Use the phone in the spare bedroom.''

Carla stood up and looked at the paper in her hand. "Bryce McAndrews—555-6749.'' She walked into the spare bedroom, picked up the cordless phone, and settled on the bed.

With shaky fingers, she dialed the number.

"Hello.''

"Is this Bryce McAndrews?''

"Yes.''

"This is Carla.''

His voice was suddenly soft and warm. "Ronnie's friend?''

"Yes.'' She had no idea what to say.

There was a warm laugh and Bryce said, "Are you free Friday evening?''

"Yes.'' Shit, Carla thought. Why am I so tongue-tied?

"I'll pick you up at Ronnie's place and we'll have dinner at an intimate restaurant I know. They have a small dance combo. I hope you like to dance. Leave everything to me. Just be ready about seven. Okay?''

"Okay.'' Her voice shook and Bryce was intrigued.

"You have no idea how I'm looking forward to meeting you, Carla.''

"Me too,'' she said softly.

Bryce's laugh was infectious. '' 'Til Friday,'' he said, then he hung up.

"Until Friday,'' she repeated into the silent phone.

For the next few days, Carla was a wreck. She drove her children to and from cub scouts and swimming lessons. She cooked dinner, watched TV, and visited with her parents, all the while quaking inside with a delicious excitement that she was amazed no one noticed.

Thursday, on a whim, she had her nails done. She'd passed Plaza Nails often and had occasionally thought about treating herself to a manicure. Always before, however, the cost had stopped her. If I want to stay home with the boys and not work full time, she had told herself as she walked passed the door toward the supermarket, I've got to be a little careful.

As she drove past the mall on the way to Little League Thursday afternoon she gave in to temptation. It's an investment in my career, she told herself. Anyway, I have Rick's three fifties in my wallet.

So while the boys were at practice, a manicurist named Micki, who didn't stop talking for an hour, lengthened Carla's nails with linen wraps and glue then polished them in a soft lavender shade called "Lilacs in the Spring." As Carla left, Micki told her to come back in a week for a glue manicure, whatever that was.

"Hey Mom," said Mike, her youngest son in the car going home. "You've got stuff on your nails."

"I decided to have them polished," she said, glancing at her nails for the dozenth time. "Looks snazzy, no?"

"I guess," Tommy said, "but it'll be hard to make pizza dough." Practicality was Tommy's hallmark. "They'll get all ookey. We are having your pizza tonight, aren't we? You promised."

"Of course. I promised."

Thursday evening after pizza, Carla spend several hours standing in front of her closet debating exactly what to wear. After her call to Bryce, she and Ronnie had rummaged through Ronnie's closet in the brownstone, but nothing in Ronnie's wardrobe made just the right statement. As the boys did their homework and watched TV, Carla put on, then took off at least a dozen combinations, selected then reselected like a schoolgirl preparing for her first date. "I'm an idiot," she muttered, throwing a beige, summer knit dress on top of the growing pile on her bed. She picked up the phone and started to dial Bryce's number to call the whole thing off. "God, this is really stupid." Then she put the phone down. "I can always call it off during dinner."

She hung everything back up, then closed her eyes and pulled a blouse from its hanger, coordinated it with a linen suit and stuffed all three garments in a tote bag to bring with her. Then she sat on the bed, pulled the items back out, folded them neatly, added a pair of low-heeled pumps and put everything back into the bag.

She gazed into the mirror, brushed her shoulder-length hair and shook her head slowly. Should I go down to the city early and have my hair done? she wondered. Somehow that didn't feel right. She had no idea why her nails should look better than her hair but it seemed wrong to have some fancy hairstyle. "Shit," she said aloud, "this is ridiculous. I'll worry myself to death at this rate." She stuffed a strand of hair behind one ear and went to tell the boys that it was bed time.

The following afternoon Carla packed an overnight bag for each of her boys.

"Are we staying at Gramma's?" her 13-year-old asked.

"Yes. For tonight."

"Got a hot date, Mom?" BJ asked as she packed.

"Where did you get that idea?" she asked, taken aback.

BJ put his fingers to his temples and closed his eyes. "I see all and know all," he chanted. When Carla raised an eyebrow he continued, "Well, Mom, new nails, an overnight visit Gramma and Grampa. I'm not a kid, you know. I watch TV." When she continued to stare at him he continued. "It's okay with me. Mothers need some fun. Oprah and Donahue say so. I'll be nice to Gramma and watch Tommy and Mike."

Her kid was watching talk shows and telling her that mothers needed fun. She playfully swatted his bottom, then stuffed Mike's PJs into his bag.

On her way into the city, Carla stopped at a local mall on a whim and bought a pair of large pearl-drop earrings that matched her outfit perfectly but differed from anything she owned. With the new jewelry in her purse, she arrived at the brownstone at about five. Since Ronnie was in Dutchess county Carla had the place to herself.

She wandered upstairs, filled the oversized tub, poured in a large scoop of bath salts and, while the water ran, put a Sinatra cassette into the tape player. While the crooner's familiar voice filled the room, Carla settled into the deep tub and leaned back, letting the light spicy scent relax her. She spent an hour in the water, adding hot whenever it became too cool. She fantasized about the evening and what Bryce would look like. She pictured him undressing her slowly, touching and stroking her. She could imagine him whispering in her ear, telling her how beautiful she was. She almost felt his hot body entering her and slowly loving her.

When she finally emerged from the tub her skin was soft and deep pink all over, and her nipples and pussy tingled. Part of her wanted to stimulate herself to orgasm, just to take the edge off, but she didn't. The edge fit right in with the fantasy that she and Bryce were creating.

At six-thirty, she put on a white, lacy bra and matching panty, an stylish white garter belt and stockings and a white satin half-slip. Then she slipped into the full-sleeved gold silk blouse and mid-thigh, off-white linen skirt she had brought and slipped her feet into her pumps.

She snapped on the earrings she had bought and looked at herself in Ronnie's mirror. As she had suspected, the earrings set off the blouse perfectly, but felt so alien to her that she pulled them off. After looking at her reflection for a moment she slowly put them back on. In for a penny, she thought, in for a pound.

She sat at Ronnie's dressing table and applied makeup, wishing that she knew enough about cosmetics to be able to do something different with her face. She examined her new long fingernails, then drummed them on the dressing table just to hear them clack. She brushed her brown hair until it shone and pulled it back behind one ear with a gold comb. She stood and stepped back so she could see herself in the full-length mirror. Not bad, she thought, not bad.

Ronnie had told her that if and when Carla wanted, she could have a makeover session with an old friend but Ronnie had also assured her that Bryce would prefer the natural Carla. Ronnie had several spray bottles of scent on her dressing table and Carla selected Opium, dabbing it sparingly on her neck and in her cleavage.

Trying to shake off her nervousness, she looked at herself one last time, grabbed her jacket and carried it downstairs, arriving in the living room just as the doorbell rang.

She took a deep relaxing breath, dropped her jacket on the back of the sofa, and opened the front door.

With a lazy gaze, Bryce looked Carla up and down. "You look splendid."

Carla stared at Bryce and for a moment was unable to move. Carla was dumbstruck. He was gorgeous. Tall and slender, Bryce McAndrews had carefully styled iron grey hair and deep hazel eyes that made Carla shiver as they took in her entire body. His charcoal grey suit was carefully tailored to show off his broad shoulders and flat stomach and his light blue shirt perfectly matched the small design in his Italian silk tie.

Bryce's full lips slowly curved upward indicating that he appreciated what he saw. "I've been looking forward to this evening ever since Ronnie told me about you," he said, "but now that I've seen you. . . . Well let's just say this is going to be a some evening."

Carla stepped aside and Bryce walked to the sofa, picked up her jacket, and held it out for her. As she slipped her arms into the sleeves, he leaned down so his lips were beside her ear. "You smell sensational. This was worth waiting for," he whispered. He placed a feather-light kiss in the hollow below her left ear, then stepped back. "Let's go."

His shiny black Porsche occupied a no-parking zone in front of the brownstone. He opened the door for Carla and, as she climbed in, he gazed at her long shapely legs and the shadowy cleavage between her breasts. "Ummm," he murmured. "Nice all over."

During the drive to the West Side, Carla learned that her date had four sons, all grown. She and Bryce talked easily about their children. It was so comfortable and Bryce was so charming that occasionally Carla forgot the purpose of the evening and where they were going to end up.

"It's just like a real first date," Carla said hesitantly as Bryce drove.

He softened his voice. "It certainly is. And I like it like that. Relax and let me make it good for you."

"I'll try," she said, startled that she had voiced her feelings.

"Are you really nervous?

"Yes," Carla admitted, clasping her hands in her lap to stop them from shaking.

"Good. A little scary expectation is just the right spice. Let me tell you about our evening. We're starting at a little restaurant called the West Side Club. They have great food, a fantastic wine list, and a three-piece combo for dancing. You do dance, don't you?"

"I used to love it," Carla answered honestly, "but I haven't danced in a long time."

"Like good sex, it's something you never forget." Giving her no time for a rejoinder, Bryce deftly pulled the black two-seater into the space in front of a long maroon awning. Immediately a uniformed doorman rushed around to open Carla's door. "Thank you, Marco," Bryce said, "but I'll assist the lady." Marco stepped aside as Bryce rounded the car.

Carla took Bryce's extended hand and, as she climbed out of the car, felt Bryce scratch her palm with one fingernail. Shivers skittered up and down her spine and the area between her legs grew warm. She looked over at her escort but he was busy giving his keys to Marco. Hand in hand, they walked into the depths of the darkened restaurant. "Ah, Mr. McAndrews," the maitre'd said unctuously. "I have your table all ready."

Without a word, they were led to the side of the room. Because of the expert placement of potted plants and lacy screens, each table seemed to be in its own private alcove. Bryce seated her. Almost immediately the waiter brought a cooler with a bottle of white wine already chilling. Proudly he showed Bryce the label.

"I hope you don't mind," Bryce said, "but I made a few arrangements in advance. Of course, if you'd prefer a mixed drink, or red wine, the waiter can bring you whatever you want."

"White wine will be fine," Carla said.

"Good. This is a Portuguese Vino Verde that I particularly

like.'' The waiter poured a sip for Bryce, who tasted it and nodded. "Don't freeze the poor wine,'' he said as the waiter poured for Carla. "Take the cooler away and just leave the bottle on the table.''

"As you wish, sir,'' the waiter said.

Carla sipped. "This is excellent,'' she said. "I've never had a Portuguese wine before. You have great taste.''

Bryce gazed into Carla's eyes over the rim of his glass. "If you put yourself into my hands for the rest of the evening, you'll see what good taste I really have.''

Bryce ordered dinner for both of them. Through fresh asparagus and thin slices of Smithfield ham, poached salmon with dill sauce and tiny boiled potatoes, they talked about inconsequential things from the music they enjoyed through books and movies to vacations. Since Bryce had traveled extensively both for pleasure and business, he regaled Carla with tales of the sites he'd seen. With Carla's agreement Bryce ordered lemon sherbet and Irish coffee for dessert.

As she finished her sherbet and sipped the heady brew, Carla realized that she hadn't had such an enjoyable evening in many years.

Music began. "Dance with me,'' Bryce whispered. He took Carla's hand and guided her to the tiny wooden dance floor. He held her gently, his right hand placed correctly in the small of her back. Carla realized immediately that he was a sensational dancer, gliding effortlessly across the small space. Several other couples joined them and, as the floor became more crowded, Bryce held her closer, his mouth against her ear, his left arm pressing lightly against the side of her breast.

"You're so graceful,'' he said, rubbing his forearm against the side of her bra and the flesh underneath, "like an angel in my arms.''

Carla swallowed hard and remained silent. Although she knew that this was to be her initiation into the world of recreational sex, she felt like a woman on her first date with a dangerously attractive man.

"I love holding your body close," Bryce whispered. "Your breasts are so full and your hips fit perfectly against mine." His breath on her ear caused a tingling at the base of her spine. "You're so responsive," he continued, "that I'll bet you're getting hot already."

For some reason, Carla needed to deny what he was saying. It was like a seduction, not an assignation, and somehow it was important not to be easy. When she took a breath to deny her feelings, Bryce interrupted, reading her thoughts. "You can deny it all you want but your body radiates sexual heat." He flicked the tip of his tongue in her ear, then nipped at her earlobe.

She shuddered, telling him about herself as accurately as she could have with words.

"Yes. You want me," he whispered. "But resist as well. It makes it all the sweeter to know that later I will hold you in my arms, naked and open. I'll overcome all your resistance and control your body with your own hunger."

He put his finger under her chin and lifted her face so she had to look into his eyes. "You'll want me so much that you'll beg for it." He tucked her against him and continued dancing, holding her close. No one else on the floor could possibly know about Bryce's erotic whisperings but Carla felt as if everyone was watching her.

They danced for a few more songs. Carla felt Bryce's hand sliding over her silk blouse. "I want your body to know exactly what's to come." His hot breath tickled her ear. "We're going to leave in about fifteen minutes. One or two more dances should be just right."

Carla realized that Bryce's planning and take-charge attitude would turn some women off, but the control that Bryce was exercising was driving her crazy. After the first few years of marriage, she had called most of the sexual shots. Bill would have been content with quickies, but Carla had wanted more. Frequently she would wear an alluring nightgown or a teddy and, when Bill responded, she would tell and show him what she wanted. She had enjoyed the sex, but would have preferred not to be in charge.

"I want you to do something for me," Bryce said a few minutes later. "Go into the ladies' room and take off your bra. I want to dance with you and feel your unrestrained breasts against my chest. I want to be able to look down the front of your blouse and see your nipples. Do it for me, Carla. Do it because I want you to and because it will make you a little less secure."

They walked to their table and Bryce gave Carla a tiny push toward the ladies' room. "Please," he whispered. The wine and the Irish coffee made her brave and daring. Not giving herself time to think, Carla walked to the bathroom, closeted herself in a stall, and removed her bra. She put the bit of silk in her purse and rebuttoned her blouse. She looked down, then smiled and unbuttoned the blouse's top two buttons.

She walked out of the stall and checked her appearance in the large mirror. Nothing showed from the front or side but, as she looked down she could see her full breasts and her hard, erect nipples. She smiled and walked back toward the table, enjoying the sway of her breasts and the brush of her nipples against the silk of her blouse.

"Nice," Bryce said as he watched her approach. He met her on the dance floor and took her in his arms. As they danced, he looked down. "Your breasts are magnificent," he whispered. "Your nipples are a dark, dusky pink. Are they so hard that they hurt?"

Carla had never been asked such sexual questions by a man before. She cleared her throat, unable to speak.

"Tell me. I insist." When she remained silent, he repeated, "I insist. Say to me, 'My nipples are so hard that they hurt.'" He slid his hand into her hair and turned her face up. "Say it, angel."

Certain words were hard for her to say; they always had been, even with her husband. Talking directly about sex and the anatomical parts involved had always been difficult for her. "I do hurt for you," she murmured.

"What hurts?" he said. She was silent. "The word 'nipple' is difficult for you to say isn't it? I can tell from your body's reaction. Your palm is damp and your hand is shaking." She tried to look down, but his hand remained tangled in her hair. "I don't care whether you want to or not," he said, his lips almost touching hers. "You will do as I say. Say 'My nipples hurt for you.'"

"Oh God. My nipples hurt for you." Carla could barely stand. The thrill and humiliation of saying that word made her knees weak. Fortunately Bryce held her tightly, supporting her.

"Oh yes. I like this. Let's continue this discussion somewhere else." Quickly he paid the check and guided her to the door. They walked a block in silence, the cool air clearing Carla's head a bit. They climbed the stairs to the door of an undistinguished building and Bryce unlocked it. "A very private place," he said as they went inside. "It's owned by good friends of mine who let me use it when they're away, which they are for the entire month of September."

Carla was aware of little as Bryce put her jacket away and guided her to the stairs that lead to what she assumed was the master bedroom. They stopped about three quarters of the way up. "Take off your blouse," Bryce said. "Right here."

She looked at him. Shouldn't he undress her? Removing her own clothes seemed so forward. Remembering why she was here, she realized her feelings were ludicrous, but they were her feelings none the less.

"Do it," he said, softly. "Be what they used to call a brazen hussy for me because I tell you to."

Slowly, Carla unbuttoned her blouse and pulled it off. "Yes," he said. "Your tits are magnificent, so hungry for my touch." He saw that the harsh language made Carla's hands shake and he smiled. "Tits. Say that word. Say 'My tits are so hard for you.'" He could see the muscles in her throat working as she swallowed. When she hesitated, he made it sound like an order. "Say it, Carla!"

"My. . . tits. . . . are hard for you."

"That's a good girl," he whispered. He walked up a step so that his mouth was level with her chest. "Hold your beautiful tits so I can suck them. Hold them for me."

It was both scary and liberating for Carla. Bryce was making her do things she wouldn't do herself, and she felt both compelled and freed. She slid her hands beneath her heavy breasts and lifted them so that the swollen nipples were level with Bryce's lips.

"Good girl," he purred. He flicked the tip of his tongue up and down over Carla's left nipple. Then he bit it, gently. "Is that good?"

"Mmmm, yes," she murmured.

He moved from side to side, from nipple to nipple, licking and biting until both breasts were swollen and reaching for his mouth. He turned her, urged her up the stairs and into the large bedroom. He moved to the bedside and turned on a small lamp, bathing the bed with soft light. "Your skin glows," he said.

Carla stood and dropped her blouse, watching Bryce watch her. Suddenly she realized how good it felt to have someone look at her naked body the way Bryce was looking at her. She was a sex object, and glad of it.

Bryce flipped the covers aside, sat on the edge of the bed, and leaned back on his elbows. "Strip for me, slowly."

Carla smiled and slowly unzipped her skirt, a bit less embarrassed knowing how she was pleasing him. She stepped out of her shoes, pulled her skirt and slip down and let them fall around her feet. She stood, wearing only her garter belt and matching stockings and her sheer white panties.

"Take off the panties," Bryce told her, "but leave on the rest. I want to see your pussy-fur surrounded by white lace."

Words like pussy made her tremble as she removed her panties. She stood and watched Bryce's gaze wander slowly over her body. "Nice?" she asked.

"Lovely," he said. "But you're a little too calm. You're getting too comfortable. Let's heat things up a bit. I want you to massage your breasts while I watch. Pinch your nipples."

When she did as he asked without much hesitation, he said, "Exhibiting your body doesn't make you shiver the way I want you to. What seems to tantalize you is saying those words." As he watched her blush he knew he'd found the way to make her hotter. "Say to me, 'My pussy is wet for you.' " When she remained silent he laughed. "You'll need to learn to say those things so I'll have to train you. Walk over here."

Bryce sat up as she walked to the side of the bed. When she started to sit down, he said, "Not yet. I want to make it difficult for you to stand up." She sighed and stood between his knees. "Now," he said, "when you're a good girl and do as I say you'll get your reward." He slid his finger into her wet pussy, touching her erect clit, then pulled his hand back.

"And when I don't?" Carla asked.

"You'll have to just stand there and wait. Understood?"

Carla nodded.

He leaned forward and blew cool breath through her pubic hair. She shivered and he said, "Good. Now say, 'Play with my pussy.' "

"Oh God," she said, feeling her juices soak her crotch. "It's so good when you touch me."

"Like this?" He caressed her clit again.

"Yes."

He pulled his hand back. "Then ask for it."

"Touch me."

"No. Not good enough," he said. "I told you what to say."

"Play with my . . . . pussy."

"Good girl." He slid one finger between her swollen lips. He could feel her muscles react to his touch. "Do you want more?"

Her hips were moving involuntarily. "Yes. I want more."

"Then say, 'Put your fingers into my pussy.' "

She was going crazy. She wanted everything. "Put your fingers in my pussy," she said.

When Bryce saw that Carla was shaking so much that she was about to fall, he said, "Lay down and spread your legs so I can see your beautiful pussy."

She stretched out across the bed and parted her legs. "Aren't you going to take your clothes off?" she asked.

"Not yet, angel, not yet. We're not finished with your lessons yet. We have to continue to increase your vocabulary. You've learned to say 'pussy' too easily. Say 'cunt.' Yes. Say 'Finger-fuck my cunt.' "

Oh God, she thought. I can't say those words. She swallowed hard and shook her head.

"Such a bad girl," Bryce said when she remained silent. He leaned over and roughly spread her legs wider. Then he blew a stream of air on to Carla's cunt and watched as her skin quivered. He flicked his practiced tongue over her exposed clit, then blew cool air again. "Say 'Finger-fuck my cunt.' "

It was torture. The alternate warm and cool sensations were driving her wild. She reached toward her pussy but Bryce grabbed her hands and held them at her sides. "Oh no. You can't relieve yourself that easily. Only I can give you what you want and you're going to have to ask for it."

She wanted his fingers inside her. Mindless with desire, she said, "Please. Finger-fuck me. Put your hand inside my cunt. Please."

"Oh yes, baby." He inserted first one then two fingers into her cunt and spread them to fill her. He pulled out, then rammed them inside. With his other hand he rubbed her clit until both of them felt the ripples of Carla's first orgasm.

"Don't stop," she screamed. "Oh God, don't stop."

"I won't angel," Bryce said, feeling the orgasm roll over her entire body. "Let go. Let it devour you."

"Yes, yes, yes." She spasmed for what seemed long minutes. When she calmed, he stood and pulled off his clothes. His large, fully erect cock stood straight out from his groin. Hungrily she watched his hand stroke the smooth, hard flesh.

"I love the way you watch my hands," he said. "Do you want to touch me?"

"Yes. Let me touch you. Let me take you in my mouth."

"Ahh," he said. "You like sucking cock. Tell me."

"Yes. I want to take you in my mouth." She sat up, watching his cock.

His hand slid over his hard penis, to the tip then pulling back to the root. "Say, 'I want to suck your cock.' "

Those words again. Carla could feel her body tighten. "I want to. . . ."

"Tell me."

"I want to suck your cock."

He leaned over and held his hard cock against her lips. "Open for me angel," he said. "Suck me into your mouth."

When she pulled him into her mouth he let his head fall back. She was good, giving him exquisite pleasure. Her mouth was slippery and hungry and her tongue slid all over his smooth flesh. She pulled back until the tip of Bryce's cock rested against her lips. "Say 'I want you to suck me'," she said, grinning.

He laughed, then said, "I want to fuck your cunt." He pushed her backward on the bed, slipped on a condom, and drove his large penis into her steaming pussy. Her stocking-covered legs wrapped around his waist and her hips bucked. Over and over he drove hard into her body.

"Yes, angel. Oh yes," he yelled.

"Hard inside me. Don't stop," she cried.

They came, first Carla, then Bryce. Still entangled, they rested for a few minutes.

"That was unbelievable," Bryce said later. "I'll tell you something you aren't going to believe. It's never been any better."

"Ummm," Carla said. "For me either."

"You're a desirable woman. And from what Ronnie told me, you're going to get to channel your charms into a productive business."

"Yes, I am. And I now know that it's going to be okay. I had almost forgotten how much I love fucking." She laughed. "I can even say 'fucking' now, thanks to you."

"Next time we'll have to find something else to play."

"Next time?"

"Certainly. I'm not letting something as good as you get away. And next time I'll happily pay for your attention."

"You don't have to pay me. This is too much fun."

"If you intend to go into business, your first lesson is not to give it away," Bryce warned. "And I hope you'll enjoy it every time with every man you're with. Especially me."

Chapter 5

Carla and Ronnie had lunch together the following afternoon in Ronnie's living room. "From your contented look," Ronnie said, swallowing a bite of grilled mushroom, "I assume Bryce did right by you."

"He sure did. It was wonderful."

"I'd love to hear all the details," Ronnie said, "But I don't want you to tell me anything that makes you uncomfortable."

With a laugh, Carla said, "That's very funny coming from you and considering the business we have in mind."

"You still have the right to be uncomfortable about things. You give up no rights here."

"I know, and thanks." Carla proceeded to tell Ronnie about the previous evening, chapter and verse.

"This tendency you have to be submissive could be a profitable addition to our business. You know that I tend to be the dominant one and I have many friends who enjoy playing with me. But lots of men like to be the master. Well," Ronnie said, spearing a shrimp with her fork, "we'll figure that out as time goes on. First, I'd like you to think about changing your appearance. Making yourself look more sophisticated. I'd love to get you an appointment with Jean-Claude."

"The Jean-Claude? The one who works with all the stars?"

"That's him. And he's done pretty well for himself since he and I first met," Ronnie said. "He did a makeover for me a long time ago, when he was still a hairdresser named Jimmy and I was still relatively monogamous. He did my hair, taught me how to use makeup, how to select the most becoming clothes, the works. I recommended him to my friends. He'll do wonders for you.''

"Am I that bad?"

"You are perfect for the supermarket and the PTA but not quite right for men who want to take you out and show you off. Like last evening. In addition to how it will make you feel, it makes a man feel potent if the woman he's with makes other's heads turn.''

"I guess you're right." Carla crossed the room and looked at herself in the antique mirror that hung over the maple desk. She lifted her long brown hair and turned left and right to study her face. As usual she wore only rouge, grey eyeshadow, and lipstick. Her earrings were simple gold hoops. "Do you think Jean-Claude could do something with me?''

"You bet." Ronnie looked sheepish, then said, "As a matter of fact, you're due at his studio in about an hour.''

Carla's laughter was immediate. "You were so sure?''

"What woman could resist putting themselves in the hands of a talented, gorgeous Frenchman with the soul of a lover.''

"Does he know about you and this?" Carla said, waving her arm around the lavish room.

"Actually he's a good source of referrals," Ronnie said. "He works around celebrities and he occasionally meets someone who wants discrete company.''

"You've entertained celebrities? Here?''

Ronnie sighed. "Russell Street was here just last month.''

"I'm impressed," Carla said. "Russell Street.''

"Don't get star struck. Eventually you may entertain someone famous, but what they want as much as anything else is a companion who'll enjoy cavorting without the trophy-collecting mentality that groupies are known for.''

"Well," Carla said, "if I'm due at Jean-Claude's, I'd better take a quick shower and wash my hair. Are you coming too?''

"I wouldn't miss it for the world.''

Jean-Claude did wonders. He cut Carla's hair short so it formed a soft frame around her face and rinsed in a slight reddish highlight. He and Ronnie spent an hour showing Carla how to put on her makeup and select clothes that would best accentuate her lovely figure. Together they tried earrings and necklaces on Carla to see which complemented the shape of her face and her large brown eyes. Jean-Claude's manicurist did her nails in a bright shade that Carla thought of as hemorrhage red.

Finally, when she studied herself in the mirror, Carla was thrilled. Her eyes appeared larger and her cheekbones seemed higher. Dangling gold earrings made her neck look longer and the teal scarf Jean-Claude had draped around the collar of her white blouse brought out the pink in her cheeks.

"Remember when we . . . uh . . . ran into each other that morning last summer?" Ronnie said with a wink. "You described yourself as medium brown and average, average, average?"

"I did, didn't I."

"And now?"

Carla gazed at herself in the mirror. "Well, I have to admit that I'm not half bad."

"Not half bad indeed."

When Carla arrived home late that afternoon, her boys just stared. "Hey Mom, what's with the new hair and stuff?" Tommy asked.

"I had a makeover. My friend Ronnie suggested it. Do you like?"

"Heck no," Tommy said. "You look like a model or something, not like a mom."

"Yeah," her youngest chimed in.

"I think I'll take that as a compliment."

"Cut it out you guys," BJ said. "Mom's looking for a man. It'll be good for her, dating and all." He patted her on the arm and Carla suddenly realized that her thirteen-year-old son was almost as tall as she was. "It's okay, Mom. If you find a nice man, I'll explain it to these guys."

"Thanks, BJ," she said, completely nonplussed, "but I'm not

looking for a man. I just want to look nicer for my business meetings."

"You know as well as I do," BJ said, "that grown-ups need a partner. Hormones and all that."

"Oprah again?"

"Yeah. And we learned about that in sex education."

Carla tried not to laugh.

"Will you still cook and stuff?" Tommy asked, his eleven-year-old mind not yet taking it all in.

"Of course. If you'll let me get into the kitchen we'll do Barrett-burgers for everyone."

Three days after Carla's session with Jean-Claude, Tim Sorenson maneuvered his station wagon into the parking space that appeared unexpectedly when a van pulled out from right in front of Ronnie's door. He sat for a moment, thinking about his assignment: to take photos of Ronnie's friend Carla for an album like Black Satin. Ronnie had told him a lot about the woman he was about to meet and he was confident that he could do a professional job.

Since his first evening with Ronnie, Tim had come a long way. He'd managed to tell his father that his working life wouldn't revolve exclusively around the oil business and, to his dad's credit TJ had taken the news just fine. Although he still worked at American Oil and Gas Products with his father, Tim now also viewed himself as a photographer. His work had appeared in several photography magazines and two of his views of the California coast were appearing more and more frequently in photo stores. Clients wanting Tim to do portraits had to book him three months in advance.

More important, thanks to Ronnie, Tim had discovered the joy of sex, to borrow a famous phrase. His new vibrancy showed in his work. Women seemed more beautiful, men more robust. His first serious photographic assignment had been the nearly two hundred pictures he'd taken of Ronnie for her album. During that photo session they'd made love in ways Tim hadn't dreamed of and they'd been together several times since. He now considered himself a sexual sophisticate. And he loved it.

He climbed out of the driver's seat and unloaded cases from the back of the wagon, stacking lenses, camera bodies, and video equipment. He also pulled out a nylon bag filled with goodies he'd gathered after his long conversation with Ronnie about Carla. He walked up the steps and rang the doorbell with his elbow.

When Carla answered the door she saw a wholesome, appealing looking young man standing on the stoop, his hands filled with black leather cases. Tim held the handle of a blue nylon gym bag with his teeth, which muffled his words. "Catch the top one," he mumbled. "It's going to fall."

The case toppled from the stack and Carla neatly caught it, tucked it under one arm, and snatched the bag from his teeth. "You certainly come prepared," she said.

"Over prepared, one might say. May I come in? This stuff's heavy."

"Sorry," Carla said, stepping away from the door and holding it open with her foot. "Come on in."

As if familiar with the house, Tim walked directly into the living room, dumped the cases on the leather sofa, and extended one hand. "Hi. I'm Tim, as you already know, and you're Carla."

Carla shook his hand and was charmed by the warmth of both his grip and his open smile. As Tim sat on the sofa and unsnapped his cases, Carla settled next to him and curled her feet underneath her. "Nice to meet you, Tim."

"Me too. I've talked about you with Ronnie and I've got some dynamite ideas about this shoot."

"You and Ronnie talked about me?"

"Sure. She helped me get a handle on what kind of pictures you want. I hope you don't mind."

"I don't. What did she tell you?"

"Just that this is your first venture into this . . . uh, business . . . and that you want shots for your album. I've got ideas about that but, if it's fine with you, I'd like to keep them to myself for the time being. Anyway, what do you think of Ronnie's album?"

"Impressive." Carla thought about the erotic photos of Ronnie and wondered whether she'd be comfortable enough with this stranger to pose like that. She twisted her fingers in her lap. "Ronnie looks so great."

"Yeah, they did turn out well. But I had a good subject." Tim studied his new subject more closely and muttered aloud as he thought. "Great eyes, fabulous cheekbones, great skin so there'll be no problems with closeups."

Carla squirmed under Tim's scrutiny, glad of the job that Jean-Claude and Ronnie had done with her. She ran her fingers through the cap of soft waves and nervously licked her lips. Tim's smile was warm and understanding and since his manner was both professional and friendly, she began to relax.

"I'm sorry you're nervous," Tim said. "I think you'll find the nervousness wears off quickly once we start."

"I hadn't realized how anxious I was about this. I really don't know exactly what to do."

"Don't worry about that. It's my job. Would you stand up?"

Carla stood, her hands hanging awkwardly at her sides.

"Relax," Tim said. "You're going to be great." Long legs he thought. A great body, magnificent breasts. He decided to take a risk. Either he was going to get terrific, sexual pictures or he was going to blow it before he even took one shot. "I can see your nipples through your shirt," he said softly. "Any man would want to suck them." He watched her body react and knew just how to get the attitude he wanted.

Carla was a bit surprised by the language coming from this stranger, but excited too. Although they shocked her, she realized his raw words also aroused her.

"Can I get you a drink or something?" she asked.

"Actually I'd like to get started, if that's okay. This light is wonderful and I'd like to get a few head shots right here before we do anything else."

Carla used the mirror over the desk to touch up her makeup. "Where would you like to start?"

Tim shoved a chair toward the window, adjusted its position

several times and said, "Sit here and let's see." Carla settled into the chair but Tim shook his head and pulled her to her feet. He moved the chair slightly and sat her back down again. "Yeah. That's nice," he said finally.

Heeding Jean-Claude's advice, Carla had selected a simple kelly green tank top and black palazzo pants. She added a gold chain with large open links and oversized gold earrings. As she settled in the chair, she fluffed her short hair and Tim watched the sunlight coming through the window catch the reddish highlights. She had used three shades of eyeshadow, liner, and mascara as Jean-Claude had shown her and, with the addition of rouge and lipstick, she had been pleased with the results.

"You look smashing," Tim said. "Now turn your head this way and tip your head." He spent several more minutes peering through the lens of his camera and adjusting the tilt of Carla's head and the angle of her shoulders. He also set up a video camera on a tripod, aimed at her chair.

"Video?"

"Sure. You'd be surprised how many men will enjoy watching you on tape, knowing that you're in the room with them, naked and willing."

"I never considered that but I'm getting an education quickly. Does Ronnie have a video?"

"Several. I'll shut it down if you don't want it."

Carla stared into the video camera's eye and found that being on display was exciting. Go the whole way? she asked herself. Who am I fooling? Damn straight I will. "Leave the camera running. It's fine."

When Tim had her positioned to his satisfaction, he said, "Now close your eyes." When she did, he said, "Picture yourself lying stretched out on your back on a blanket in a secluded clearing in a forest. The sun is beating down and heating your face. Can you feel it?" When she started to nod, he said, "Don't nod, just tell me. Is the bright sun hot on your skin?"

"Yes," Carla said softly raising her chin to the warmth.

"Now open your eyes." When she did, Tim snapped off several

pictures, capturing the soft, dreamy look he'd wanted. "Close them again. You're still lying in that clearing in the forest but now you're naked. You can feel the sun on your entire body, on your shoulders, your belly, your breasts." He paused and watched her face. "Open your eyes." He snapped several more pictures. "God, the camera loves you," he murmured.

"More?" Carla said, her voice husky.

"Close your eyes." She complied and he continued. "A man walks out of the forest. You can't see him because your eyes are closed, but he's tall and very good looking, with a great body and soft hands. He's wearing a pair of faded blue jeans and nothing else. You don't have to open your eyes to know that he's looking at your body, but you're not nervous. The heat of his gaze adds to the heat of the sun. He's staring at your breasts and he can see that your nipples are getting hard. Although you're pretending to be asleep, he knows, Carla. He knows you're excited. He knows that he's making you excited." When Carla opened her eyes, Tim snapped again, then told her to move one arm and retilt her head and took several more shots. With the sound of the clicking in her ears, Carla stretched and extended her arms over her head, making love to the camera.

"Close your eyes. It's important that the man believes you're sleeping, so when he stretches out next to you on the blanket you stay still and keep your body relaxed. He just stares at you for a moment, then brushes his fingers through your pubic hair just touching your love button. You remain motionless, wanting him to continue.

"Although you don't move, he knows how wet you're getting." Tim picked up a different camera and snapped a few shots of Carla with her eyes closed. He didn't know whether it was her expression or the line of her body, but she was radiating sex and he wanted to capture it. "You want to move your hips to deepen his touch, but you don't want him to know how he's affecting you, so you remain absolutely still, pretending that you're still asleep."

Carla was there, in the clearing in the woods. Tim's voice had transported her and she could actually feel the sun on her body, feel fingers probing and exploring the secret places of her body. God, she thought, he's really turning me on. I'm going to explode.

"Keep your eyes closed and pull off your tank top and your bra," Tim said.

Carla removed her clothes without hesitation. She was no longer nervous or embarrassed. Both Tim and the cameras seemed erotic and right.

When Carla was naked to the waist, Tim repositioned her in the chair so shafts of sunlight illuminated her shoulders and breasts. Her eyes were still closed as Tim moved back behind his camera lens. "Beautiful. Let your head fall back against the chair." He kept snapping as she moved, each pose a sensual invitation. "Now, he's still touching your clit and you're still pretending to be asleep. His fingers caress each fold and part your lips. You're so wet that his finger slides easily into your body."

Tim watched Carla's body react to his story. He knew that she was having a difficult time holding her hips still and he smiled as he watched her through his lens. "He adds a second finger, then a third, filling you completely." He saw how puckered her nipples were and added this to his story.

"Your nipples are so hard and tight that you think you'll die if his mouth doesn't take them. You slide your hands up your ribs and hold your magnificent tits out for him to suck. Offer them to him, Carla. Don't speak, but offer him your hard, tight nipples."

Carla's body tightened and she did as Tim asked. She flattened her hands against her belly and slid them upward, lifting her full breasts and offering their rosy tips to the camera. When Tim asked her to open her eyes, she still envisioned an attractive man lying next to her on a blanket in the sun.

"So good, Carla," Tim said, trying to resist the lure of his own sensual story. He wanted to take the breasts being offered into his own mouth, but he knew that would come later. For the moment, he kept repositioning her, snapping pictures as the video camera hummed in the background. He finished his second roll of film and changed to a third while Carla stood up and removed the rest of her clothes.

Ronnie had told Tim a lot about Carla and he had come prepared. He took a large piece of satiny soft leather from the nylon bag he'd brought and spread it on the chair. "Sit back down," he said, "and close your eyes again. Feel the leather against your skin." As she moved her naked body against the soft surface, Tim knew he'd been right. Leather would take Carla to the next level of sensuality. "Feel it, smell it. Fill your senses with it. Put your right leg over the arm of the chair and slide your ass forward. . . . Yes, that's right." Her pussy was wide open and shining.

Carla was in a sexual daze. She'd never dreamed that the smell and feel of leather could arouse her so. She felt she was going to climax, but everything about this experience was soft and gentle. She didn't understand it, but then she didn't have to.

"Go with it. Fly with the feelings. The blanket in the forest is made out of leather, soft, black, fine-grained leather. It's becoming warm from the sunshine and the heat of your body, and the man is rubbing a corner of it over your legs, your arms, your belly. There's no sound, except the rustle of his movements. You're unwilling and unable to move. You just lie there in the sun absorbing the sensations. Open your eyes." Carla opened her eyes, and Tim snapped several more pictures.

"He's stroking your clit faster now. It tightens your lower belly." Tim watched Carla's body and saw the tiny movements he'd been waiting for. "Do you want to touch your pussy, Carla? Are you so hot that you want to rub yourself while the man watches, while the camera watches?"

Carla had never wanted anything more in her life. "Yes," she whispered.

"Then do it," Tim said. "Touch your pussy. Make yourself come."

Carla touched herself, one hand on her breast and one in her pussy. She rubbed and probed until the tightness in her breasts and her pussy became almost pain.

"Rub it just right," Tim said. He moved around, snapping pictures of Carla's hand on her breasts, her fingers working in her cunt, her face as she strained in pleasure.

Carla heard the click of the shutter and felt Tim's movements around her. To her surprise, it added a new dimension to her excitement. She opened her eyes and watched the camera as it watched her. She moved so Tim could get a better view.

"You're close now, and you want to come," Tim said, taking the video from the tripod and aiming so it captured Carla's body and hands. "You like the camera watching you. You love it that I'm watching you. I can see everything. I'm going to record you as you come. Anyone who sees the pictures will see you getting off. Tell me when you're going to come. Tell me, Carla."

"Now," she said. "Oh yes. Now! I'm going to come right now! Watch me come." Waves washed over her. She moved her fingers around her pussy touching the right places with exactly the right rhythm. She drew the orgasm from her body, bit by bit, savoring every spasm, making it last as long as she could. Tim alternated between the video and his still cameras, taking dozens of pictures and long moments of tape.

While Carla recovered, Tim fused with his camera equipment. "Unbelievable," Carla said. "I was really nervous about this, but you're amazing. You've come a long way since you and Ronnie met."

Tim chuckled. "She told you about that?"

"I'm sorry. I hope that doesn't embarrass you."

"Not at all. That was the opening to a whole new world. She's wonderful, you know."

"I know." Carla sighed.

Tim handed her a glass of water and she took a long drink as her breathing returned to normal. "If you're recovered, why don't we go upstairs and try on some of the costumes for your album photos." He picked up the piece of leather and threw it over his arm. "And I think you should use a black leather cover on your book. Leather seems to turn you on."

Carla nodded her agreement. "I never realized it, but you're right."

Naked but unembarrassed, Carla climbed the stairs with Tim behind her. "You've got great legs," he said, "and a nice tight little butt. I like the way you walk around nude. You don't parade, yet you don't hide either.''

"I used to walk around without clothes a lot but with three inquisitive boys, I don't get much chance to anymore.''

Tim squeezed past her and shot a few snaps of her walking up the stairs. "God, you've got a great body,'' he said. "I love taking pictures of you.''

She put her hands behind her head and raised her elbows.

"You've got the most beautiful tits I've ever seen,'' he said.

In the bedroom, Tim opened a closet and pulled out an evening dress. It was a column of royal blue silk with classic lines and a high neckline in the front. "I've seen Ronnie wear this and I'd like to see you in it,'' he said. "You should wear primary colors, bright greens and blues. Red would look terrific on you, and black and white of course. Stay away from too much yellow and orange. It won't go with your skin.''

"You've got quite an eye,'' Carla said, selecting a pair of tiny bikini panties from a drawer. "That's exactly what Ronnie and Jean-Claude said.''

"I hope you don't mind if I pick out a few things for you,'' Tim said, flipping through the dresses.

"Not at all.'' She looked at the high-necked dress hanging on the closet door. "But isn't this a bit tame for our photos?''

"Wait until you see it on.''

As Carla reached for a bra, Tim shook his head. "No bra. You don't need it.''

"You're the boss,'' Carla said. She pointed to a large jewelry chest that stood on the makeup table. "What do you suggest with this dress?'' While Tim rummaged through the extensive collection of costume jewelry, Carla picked up the hanger and took a better look at the gown. From the front it looked almost demure, but the dress had no back. It was cut low enough to reveal the line between her cheeks. As she slipped it over her head, she said, "I'll have more cleavage in the back than in the front.''

"That's the idea. That's the first dress I ever photographed Ronnie in.''

"It isn't in the album," Carla pointed out.

"I know. I kept that picture for myself. I have it in my bedroom. I may keep the one I'm about to take too."

"Do you have fantasies about her?" she asked, fluffing her hair.

"Not any more. I did for a long time after our first meeting. Now we're just good friends. We fuck now and again and I take her to an occasional party, but that's about it." Tim had selected a pair of large silver-and-diamond dangle earrings and he handed them to Carla.

"They look like chandeliers," she said.

"Try them."

Carla stood in front of the mirror and clipped on the oversized earrings. Tim was right again. They accented the dress perfectly. "Change your makeup," he said. "More eyes and a darker lipstick."

Carla quickly adjusted her makeup as Jean-Claude had taught her to and suddenly she was a seductive woman of the evening. "Brilliant," she said.

"Brilliant is right," Tim said. He posed her with her almost-naked back to him, looking seductively over her shoulder. He snapped several pictures. "Now we come to album photos," he said, opening Ronnie's other closet. "Which of these says you?"

"I don't know. Which do you think I should wear?"

"Not my decision. For the album you need pictures of fantasies that you would enjoy acting out with a friend. That's a very personal decision." He reached into the closet and took out the pink little-girl dress. "This fantasy is about the older man who likes to make love to virginal little girls. You wear white socks and mary-janes, white cotton undershirts and underpants."

Carla smiled as she put it on. Tim photographed her sitting on the edge of the bed with her hands folded in her lap and knees locked together, looking a bit scared.

"This," he said, holding a short wedding dress and a veil, "is a similar fantasy, deflowering a wedding-night virgin." She dressed and Tim snapped that outfit as well.

They continued for over an hour, with Carla portraying a cheerleader, an aerobics instructor, a bikini-clad nymphet, and a harem girl. When Tim suggested the stern teacher costume, Carla demurred. "I don't think I'm the dominant type."

"Ronnie is," Tim said, "and I have some very sexy shots of her with a whip in her hand and a man wearing nipple clamps licking her pussy."

"I never saw those."

"She has some particular pictures for special friends."

"Should I have a special album? I can't see myself with a whip."

"I know that. But I have a different idea. Come with me into the other room," Tim suggested.

"What other room?"

"Ronnie's playground. She told me she hasn't shown it to you, so let me."

"Should I wear anything special?" Carla asked removing her costume, a nurse's uniform with a starched cap.

"Just your beautiful skin."

Tim opened the door to the other bedroom and let Carla precede him. As she entered the room she gasped. Almost cave-like, it was darkened with wood-paneled walls and heavy velvet drapes. As Carla looked around she saw that the room resembled a dungeon with eyelets, chains, and bondage equipment proudly displayed on every wall. There were three differently shaped wooden benches with hooks and straps attached and two cabinets filled with items Carla didn't recognize. A huge brass bed dominated one end of the room. As shocked as she was, Carla also realized that she could hardly breathe.

Tim walked in behind her and wrapped his long fingers around one wrist, holding her tightly. "Exciting?"

"Yes," she whispered.

"Ronnie thought as much. I took several rolls of film in here with Ronnie dressed all in leather brandishing whips and paddles. But I don't think that's you, is it?"

Carla shook her head. She was picturing herself held down or chained, restrained and helpless with a man standing over her enjoying her vulnerability. Tim took her other wrist and held her arms against her sides. He put his mouth close to her ear. "The word is 'popcorn,' " he breathed, rubbing his fully clothed body against her back. "Say the word and I'll stop whatever I'm doing. And let me give you some advice. Never play in here without a safe word. And never play with anyone you don't trust to honor it. Understand?"

"Ronnie and I discussed that. I understand."

"Say 'popcorn.' "

"Popcorn."

Tim released her hands and moved away. "Now, stand here and look around the room while I get my camera. While I'm gone, picture yourself strapped into each piece of equipment, unable to escape. From now on, don't speak unless I ask you a direct question. And don't move!"

The last was an order, one that Carla had no intention of disobeying. She looked around and studied each device. She imagined herself restrained in a few but she had no idea what many were for or how they worked. She didn't care. Her palms were sweating and she was struggling to get air into her trembling body.

"Good girl," said Tim reentering the large room. "You're so excited, you're ready to burst. That's very good. Come here." As Carla walked across the thick dark grey carpet her feet sank into its soft lushness. "Give me your arm." Carla held out her arm and Tim fastened on a tight leather wrist band. He looped a ring attached to the band over a hook on the wall and took a picture of her hand and arm.

"You know you can unhook yourself any time you want." Tim's voice caused a heat wave to wash over her. "But you want to stay there. You want me to restrain you. That's excellent." He fasteneded an identical strap around her other wrist and one around each ankle. The rings attached to additional hooks on the wall so her arms were held out from her shoulders and her legs were spread about two feet apart.

As the camera snapped, Carla imagined how she looked, fastened to the wall, controlled and helpless. God she was hot. If she could just touch herself. . . . But she wouldn't move, couldn't move.

Tim walked over and kissed her full mouth. Then he slid his finger across her hip until it was against her clit. "You want to come? Just like that?" He stopped. "No. Not yet. I want to play a while." He put the camera down. "After Ronnie and I had been together a few times, we discovered that we both have a love of dominance. I want to be in control. I want to be able to tease. I want to do anything and everything without any protest. Do you want to play with me?"

Carla nodded. At that moment she wanted to be dominated by him more that she'd ever wanted anything else.

"Do you remember the safe word?" he asked.

"Popcorn," Carla said.

"That's good. Now, a few questions. And I want honest answers. What if I hurt you, just a bit?" He pinched her nipple and twisted it hard.

It was so sudden that Carla cried out.

"Good or bad?"

Carla paused, then admitted, "Good."

Tim grabbed a handful of her hair and dragged her head back. He kissed her mouth, grinding his face against hers. She responded, pressing against him as much as her bound body would allow. "A true playmate," he said, unhooking her limbs from the wall. He pulled her over to a wooden bench, adjusted the length of its legs, and laid a leather spread over it. "This has been a fantasy of mine for a long time, but Ronnie is too dominant herself to really enjoy this. Lie down on your back."

Carla did, feeling and smelling the leather. "Inhale," Tim said. "Smell your own aroma." Carla breathed deeply and knew the scent of her arousal. She was so hot that she doubted it could get any better, but each time Tim spoke, it did.

"Here's something else for you to enjoy." He slipped a leather blindfold over her eyes.

The darkness was total. Being unable to see made her more aware of her other senses. She heard the rustle of Tim's clothes as he moved around the room. She smelled leather and sweat and sex. She rubbed her hands over the leather, appreciating its rich texture.

"Don't move," Tim said. Carla could hear the camera and imagined this scene as it would appear to those thumbing through her own 'special' pictures.

"Now slide up until your head hangs off the end. There's a pillow that will support your neck and let your head hang down gently." She slid along the leather until her neck rested on the pillow and heard snaps as Tim fastened her arms and legs to the bench. "These aren't hooks, they're padlocks," he said. "I want you to struggle to get free."

Carla experienced a moment of panic as she pulled at the locks. She had to test Tim's words. "Popcorn," she said.

Tim fumbled with the first lock until her right arm was free. "Refasten it," she said. "It's all right."

"I was afraid that I'd gone too far," he said. "I was seriously disappointed."

"Don't be. I just needed to be sure."

"Of course you did."

Tim quickly relocked her wrist. "Now struggle. I want to see your body strain, unable to get free."

She pulled at her arms and legs. The bindings didn't hurt at all, but she was, nevertheless, completely helpless.

"Beg me to let you go."

She heard the hum of the video camera. "Please." She knew that she could say popcorn at any time and he would let her go. She could also beg and plead and know he wouldn't release her. Her head angled downward was making her a little light-headed but it was fantastic. "Please let me go. Oh god, please."

"Oh no, baby. Not a chance." Then his hands were on her face, gently feeling around the blindfold. He slipped a finger into her mouth and she sucked as he worked it in and out.

"I want you to understand exactly what I'm going to have you do," Tim said. "This bench is at just the right height." What had to be his naked cock slid over Carla's cheeks. "You're going to

suck me good.'' He withdrew the finger from her mouth and replaced it with his hard erection. Carla gasped as Tim forced his
large member into her mouth, but she quickly started sucking as
he fucked her mouth. "Too good, too fast," he said, pulling away
from her greedy mouth.

She again heard a rustling then a buzzing. "Hear that?" he
said. "That's a vibrator and I'm going to make you come with it.
I'll be in control of your body. You won't be able to resist. You'll
come when I want you to and only when I'm ready.''

Carla jumped when she felt the buzz against her nipple. Jolts
of magic electricity bounced around inside of her, stabbing her in
the breasts, the belly, and in her hungry pussy. She wanted nothing
more than for Tim to fuck her, any way he wanted, but she sensed
that her resistance was part of his fantasy and she wanted him to
have it all. She knew instinctively what to say.

"Oh stop," she said, "please stop. It's torture.''

"It's exciting to beg, isn't it? And to know you can't sway me.
And I love to hear you plead for mercy, but there will be none.''
He placed the tip of the vibrator deep in her armpit.

Carla was afraid it would tickle, but it didn't. It just excited her
more. "I can't take it. No more, please.''

"There's so much more," Tim said. He moved the vibrator
until it was rubbing the insides of Carla's thighs. "Want it against
your cunt?''

"No. Don't.''

"I will. And what's more you want me to. It's so embarrassing
to admit that you want me to fuck you with this vibrator, this
artificial buzzing cock that can give you such pleasure.''

"Oh god, no.''

Tim was in heaven. This was his favorite fantasy and it was
better than he had dreamed it would be. And he was taking it as
far as it would go. "I think you'd better ask me to fuck you.''

"No.''

He teased Carla's cunt, touching her swollen lips, then stopping.
Sliding the vibrator through her thick wet juices, then moving it

back to the inside of her thigh. "I can make you crazy with wanting. Admit that your pussy needs to be fucked. Say it."

"Yes, do it," Carla said, slipping out of character. "Fuck me good."

Tim inserted the penis-shaped vibrator into Carla's pussy and strapped it in place with a piece of leather that was connected to the bench. "Now suck my cock," he said, walking around to the head of the bench and laying his cock against her mouth.

Carla became pure sensation. She sucked and lapped as the buzzing filled her demanding cunt. Tim came quickly, unable to resist the pull of Carla's mouth. She swallowed as he pumped until he thought he would never be able to come again. He pulled his exhausted cock from Carla's mouth, knowing that she hadn't come yet. "Do you want to come now, baby?" he asked.

"Please. Help me."

"Of course," he spoke reassuringly. He knelt between her legs and flicked his tongue back and forth against her clit. "Yes," she screamed. "Don't stop."

He didn't and Carla climaxed, shuddering and bucking against the straps holding her wrists and ankles. Tim pulled the vibrator from her sopping pussy, unfastened the straps and carried her to the bed.

"I've never experienced anything like that before," Carla said.

"It was great for me too," Tim said. "Maybe when I've developed the pictures, we could get together again to look them over . . . and whatever."

"Yes," Carla sighed. "Lots of whatever."

Chapter 6

Carla stretched languidly on her bed and, knowing her friend would still be up, dialed Ronnie's number in Dutchess County from the private phone she'd had installed in her bedroom. It was not quite eleven in the evening and, once the boys were in bed, Carla had soaked in a hot tub for almost an hour. Despite the predictable romance novel she had read, she had been unable to relax. She was confused about the following evening, her first with her new black leather album.

Wrapped in an old velour robe, socks, and a pair of Garfield slippers that her boys had gotten her the previous Christmas, she listened to the phone ring.

"Hello," Ronnie answered.

"Hi, it's me."

"Hi. What's up?"

"Well. . . ." Originally it had felt odd to discuss the business of sex with her three boys sleeping just down the hall, but after a few late-night phone sessions with Ronnie the whole thing felt almost normal. "A man named Max called and I called him back. He says he got my number from you."

"He did. When my friend Bert called and told me he had a friend, I suggested you. You've got to get your feet wet at some point, so to speak. I hope that giving him your number was okay."

"Oh sure it was. He left a message on my answering machine.

95

And now I'm excited, but also nervous. What if I'm not good enough? What if he doesn't get his money's worth?''

"He will. I assume you two talked and you feel comfortable with him.''

"Of course. He sounds nice and he's never been with a ... someone like me before.'' She giggled into the phone. "I think he's more nervous than I am.''

"He probably is. You'd be surprised how anxious some men get. But that can add to the anticipation.''

"I know. Part of me is so keyed up I'm ready to come if someone looks at me crooked. But part of me is worried.''

"You'll be fine. And if something feels uncomfortable, just tell him. If he's unwilling to do anything else, give him his money back and say good night.''

"He says he wants to see my album. He's obviously heard about yours.''

Ronnie snuggled deeper under her covers. She had been watching TV in bed, naked, and now she slithered over her satin sheets, feeling the smooth fabric against her skin. Talking about sex always made her horny. "Is your album ready?'' she asked.

"I met with Tim yesterday and we looked over the pictures he took. He does marvelous work. Some of those photos made even me hot. I bought an album. It's black leather.''

"Great. Satin and leather.''

"Max said he's looking forward to a creative evening. How do you broach the subject of fantasy?''

"It's different each time,'' Ronnie answered. "Some men just want straight fucking and you don't have to use the album at all. Most men who call me, and who will call you, have been referred by someone else, someone who's enjoyed the fantasies that I've created. Let's face it. I'm expensive and you will be too. Someone who just wants a good lay can get that for a lot less money. So our kind of friends, or clients as you call them, want something out of the ordinary, something that they can't get at home. I guess creative is as good a term as any.''

Carla shifted the phone to a more comfortable position on her shoulder. "But how, exactly, should I begin things? I can't just say, 'Want to act out a story,' can I?"

"You probably won't have to. Most of the time new friends will know about your album from whomever recommended them. They may even have decided on a fantasy. Some, will never have thought about role playing, and those are the most fun for me. Once you get past a man's initial shyness, play-acting can be the grestest sexual turn-on there is. Gets them outside themselves. They can do anything, be anyone, and no one's judging or censoring."

"You're still not answering my question. How do you start things happening?"

"Okay. Let's take the first man I played with after I put together my album." Ronnie shifted the phone to the other ear, settled back, and stared at the ceiling, remembering Tory Palluso.

Ronnie introduced herself to the maitre d' at La Bon Nuit and he efficiently guided her to a quiet section off to one side of the busy restaurant. As she slalomed between tables of two or four expensively dressed diners, she had a moment to look over Mr. Palluso who, she saw, was sitting on a chair opposite the ban-quette, hesitantly sipping a glass of red wine.

Tory Palluso was about forty-five, Ronnie guessed, with a receding hairline and wire-rimmed glasses. To his credit, his dark hair wasn't combed over the top to disguise his balding pate, but was neatly trimmed and styled. From several tables away, he didn't appear to be a good-looking man. His granite-hard profile and pointed chin, heavy black eyebrows and matching moustache seemed overwhelming.

As Tory looked up and saw her moving toward him, Ronnie smiled and nodded. He looked straight at her and she was struck by his eyes—so bright blue that if not for his glasses she would have thought he was wearing colored lenses. Both his smile and his unusual eyes made his face surprisingly appealing.

As he watched the beautiful woman making her way to his table Tory thought, she doesn't look like a call girl. But Frank had assured him she was the best. If she was as good in bed as she looked, she was going to make him regret that he only got to New York two or three times a year.

"You're Ronnie," Tory said.

"Tory," Ronnie said, extending her free hand, "I'm so glad to meet you." The maitre d' pulled out the table and Ronnie settled herself on the banquette. She set the package she was carrying down next to her.

"Wine?" he asked. When she nodded, he asked, "Red or white?"

"Red."

"I looked at the wine list and they have a nice Burgundy, if that's okay."

"That will be fine," Ronnie said. She had barely gotten comfortable when the waiter brought the wine. When Tory nodded the waiter opened the bottle and nearly filled her long-stemmed glass. "To an eventful evening," Ronnie said, lifting her glass toward Tory.

"Eventful," Tory said as his glass touched Ronnie's. "A superb way of thinking about things." He sipped. "You're lovely."

Ronnie smiled. She had selected a soft chiffon scoop-necked dress in a shade best described as cantaloupe and worn it with a triple-strand pearl necklace and pearl drop earrings. A matching triple-strand bracelet and a gold watch showed off her long, slender fingers. On a whim she'd had her nails done that afternoon in a frosted shade the exact hue of the dress.

"Thank you," she said softly, and raised an eyebrow. Tory's dark suit was carefully tailored to hide the slight paunch she had noticed as he stood up and he wore a monogrammed white on white shirt and conservative paisley tie. Everything about him bespoke pride in his appearance and money enough to indulge it. "You're not bad yourself."

Through a savory vegetable pâté, a crisp green salad with a peppercorn vinaigrette dressing, veal with capers served with a wine, lemon, and butter sauce, and julienned vegetables, they talked about business, family, and other ordinary things. Over an apple tart with a delicate, thin crust they discussed politics. They agreed more than either had expected.

Over napoleon brandy and espresso, Tory finally broached the reason for their dinner. "We have a mutual friend," he said, suddenly hesitant. "Frank Morrison."

"I know," Ronnie said. "He gave you my phone number."

"Right."

When the silence became awkward, Ronnie said, "Do you want my company for the rest of the evening?"

"I enjoyed our dinner. You're a highly intelligent and knowledgeable woman, for. . . ." He stumbled over the end of the sentence and swallowed hard.

"For a hooker." Ronnie laughed. "Don't be embarrassed. I'm not. I love what I do and I love fulfilling men's fantasies, which, I gather, is what you want."

"My wife is a wonderful lady, don't get me wrong."

Ronnie interrupted. "Why don't we agree not to mention her for the rest of the evening. Tonight is for a little adult entertainment. Maybe, one day, you'll see fit to share some of your desires with her. I'll bet she'll be more receptive than you'd imagine, but that's neither here nor there. Let's discuss you."

"I want something unusual. Frank said you and he played out a fantasy of his. He wouldn't tell me about the specifics. 'Too personal,' he told me. But from the grin on his face, he must have enjoyed it tremendously."

"Do you have a fantasy in mind that you want to act out?"

"Not really. Frank said you'd have suggestions."

"I have something here that may help you decide." The tables on either side of them had long since been vacated, so Ronnie motioned for Tory to sit beside her on the banquette. She picked up the package she had carried into the restaurant and placed it on the table. From a large black-satin drawstring bag, she withdrew a photograph album with a black satin cover and placed it in front of Tory.

She placed her hand on the closed book. "In here are fantasies, scenes that we can play together. Look through the book and I'll

describe each fantasy.'' She handed Tory a flat, black-satin envelope about four inches square, with a black tassel tied to one
corner. ''When you find something you'd like, put my fee in the
envelope and use this bookmark to hold the page. Then we'll go
back to my house and play.''

Hands trembling with expectation, Tory took the envelope and
opened the cover of the album. The first photo was of Ronnie
dressed in a black satin bustier with matching garter belt and
stockings. ''That's Marguerite, the stripper,'' Ronnie explained as
Tory gazed at the first picture. ''She'll strip very slowly for you.''

He turned to the next photo. Ronnie was dressed all in green.
''That's Maid Marian. She's been in love with Robin Hood for
months, but they've never had time to be together.''

Tory lifted the album page and turned to the next photo. ''Nita's
a harem girl. You were very brave in battle and saved the sultan's
life. He's allowed you to pick one girl from his harem and she's
yours for the evening. She's been very well trained in the arts
of love.''

She continued as Tory turned pages. ''That's the Princess Melli-
sande. She's not allowed to have intercourse until her marriage,
but she satisfies herself, and most of the guards in the castle, by
masturbating while they watch, then bringing them to climax with
her mouth.''

The next shot was of Ronnie in her bed, dressed in a nightgown,
holding a sheet up against her breasts. ''And that's Bethann. She
was asleep in her bed when a burglar broke in. At first, he wanted
to steal her jewels. Now he just wants her body.''

He turned the page again. ''That's Miss Gilbert. She's the head-
mistress at an exclusive boy's school and, if you want to meet her,
she'll explain your punishment for being a naughty boy in class.''

For picture after picture, Ronnie explained fantasies to Tory.
The last dozen photos in the album were explicit pictures of Ronnie, guaranteed to ignite the most selective viewer. Ronnie stood
as Tory turned back to the beginning to review the photographs.
''I have to use the ladies' room. I'll be a few minutes so look

through the book and select. Of course, you could make up your
own fantasy or we could just go back to my place and make love.''

"Not on your life. I've never had a chance like this.''

When Ronnie returned from the ladies room, Tory had her coat
over his arm. He helped her into it, then handed her the book.
She opened to the page he had selected and removed the satin
envelope. "Nita will please you in every way,'' she whispered as
she slipped the five hundred-dollar bills into her purse.

The ten-minute cab ride was the longest Tory could remember.
Ronnie's stocking-covered legs were just inches from his and he
longed to run his fingers up the inside of her sweet thighs. He
held himself back. This night was going to be something extraordinary. He was going to let Ronnie dictate the speed. And he would
savor every minute.

Ronnie had initially been reluctant to use her brownstone, wor-
rying that one of her friends might get out of hand, either during
an evening of pleasure, or afterward. But she quickly realized
that her customers had more to lose than she did if the police
became involved.

The cab let them off in front of her house and they quickly
made their way inside, then up to the bedroom. "There's a bottle
of champagne in the fridge,'' she said, pointing to the small wet •
bar in the corner of the room, "and glasses just above. Pour some
for each of us and make yourself comfortable. I'll just be a moment.'' She took a hanger from the closet and disappeared into
the bathroom.

Five minutes later Ronnie emerged from the bathroom. "Sir
Knight,'' she said softly, "I'm Nita. The Sultan has told me of
your bravery and I'm honored you picked me for your evening.''

Tory just stared. Her halter top was made of light-blue gauze
so sheer that it allowed glimpses of her nipples. A veil of the
same material covered the lower part of her face. Matching harem
pants rode low on her hips, flared at the legs and gathered tightly
at the ankles. Through their sheer fabric Tory saw a dark triangle
of hair at the junction of her thighs.

Nita's feet were bare, and she wore long earrings and bracelets on her wrists and ankles, all with tiny bells that tinkled as she moved. Her head was bowed and her long blond hair was covered with a soft blue, gauzy veil. A golden chain hung around her bare midriff. Covering her navel was a dark blue jewel.

"I hope I please you," she said softly. "You have only to indicate how I may serve you and your wish will be my command." She crossed to stand in front of him and slid her hands up his silk shirt, sliding her jacket off his wide shoulders.

"Will you dance for me?" he asked.

Ronnie put a tape in the player and the room filled with rhythmic, exotic music. Sinuously, Nita undulated around the room, turning down lamps, and lighting candles and sticks of incense. As she twirled, she removed the veil covering her hair and slid its soft folds across Tory's face. At one point, she stood in front of him, placed the veil over his head and kissed his lips through the sheer fabric, the bells continually tinkling.

When he reached for her, she danced away, trailing the veil over his skin. She held the transparent fabric under her breasts and lifted so the unrestrained twin mounds stood out from her chest and jiggled as she moved, covered only by thin layers of gauze. She thrust her chest into his face but, when he went to kiss one nipple, she danced away.

Near then far, close, yet not quite close enough. The fragrance of her eastern perfume filled Tory's head and he longed to taste her mouth. When next Nita danced close, he grabbed the scarf that covered her face and wrapped it around her body, trapping her swaying bottom.

Nita leaned over and licked Tory's upper lip with the tip of her tongue. Back and forth, her tongue danced over his mouth as her bottom swayed against the imprisoning scarf. Each time he would have pressed his lips tightly against hers, she moved slightly away, allowing only the lightest of touches of mouth against mouth.

"More," he growled. "Kiss me, woman."

Nita's mouth was so close to Tory's that her breath cooled his wet lips. "Your wish," she breathed, "is my command." She pressed her mouth against his and her tongue requested entry.

Greedily, he opened his mouth and swirled his tongue against hers. For long moments, their lips and tongues joined in fiery combat, plunging, then drawing back.

While they kissed, Nita opened the buttons of Tory's dress shirt and tugged it from his body. She removed her mouth only long enough to pull his undershirt over his head and finally she ran her hands across his chest so the hair slid between her fingers. She scraped one nail down his skin.

He was on fire, yearning to devour this woman who was his for the evening. When he let go of one end of the scarf she slipped away, teasingly moving around the room. She turned her back, then took off her top. Naked to the waist, Nita held up a scarf and twirled. Tory got quick glimpses of her full breasts, their large darkened nipples standing out from the soft white skin.

Without taking his eyes from her body, Tory stood, removed the rest of his clothes, and tossed them aside. "Your staff is fully ready, my lord," Nita said, staring at his erect cock. "Shall I take it in my mouth and show you how much pleasure I can give you?"

He dropped into the chair. "Oh yes, Nita, but just a little. I will have better uses for my staff."

She knelt on the floor at his feet and brushed her hair across his loins, combing her hair with his cock. The sensation was so exquisite that he was afraid he would come without her ever really touching him. When she finally placed a light kiss against the tip of his erection, it took all his concentration not to climax right then.

Nita flicked her tongue over the end of Tory's cock, licking the sticky pre-come fluid. Then she pursed her lips and sucked his purple cock head into her mouth. She took it in as deeply as she could, then pulled back, her head bobbing up and down in his lap.

"No, not yet," he growled. He stood, put on a condom, grabbed her around the waist, and pulled her harem-pants down. He turned her so she was facing away from him, bent her at the waist and plunged his cock into her wet pussy from behind. Over and over he drove into her until he moaned with his release.

Ronnie hadn't actually climaxed, but she was strangely satisfied, sharing Tory's pleasure. She reached between her thighs and cupped his testicles, squeezing and milking all the thick fluid. His body bucked as the last of his orgasm flowed into her.

When Tory collapsed, Ronnie got a warm, wet face cloth from the bathroom and leisurely washed his penis and testicles. She squeezed his cock and satisfied herself that there was, at least for the moment, no arousal left in him. She never left anyone unsatisfied.

He stood up, stretched, and looked at the clock beside the bed. "That was great, but I'm afraid I have to go now," he said.

"You have my number," Ronnie said, "and there are many other pictures in my album."

"I don't get to New York often," he said sadly, buttoning his shirt. "But when I do, you can be sure you'll hear from me."

Ronnie shifted the phone to the other ear. "I see Tory two or three times a year," she said to Carla, "and he's very generous." Carla heard Ronnie's short laugh. "Last time, in addition to paying me, he brought me a magnificent gold bracelet with a tiny bell on it."

"Do you always play the same scene with him?"

"Not always, but we come back to Nita more frequently than any other fantasy."

"Thanks for the story," Carla said. "That makes it much easier for me to deal with Max."

"Well, good luck tomorrow night," Ronnie said. "And most important of all, have fun."

"I will. Believe me, I will."

When she first saw Max, Carla had to smile. He looked like the stereotypical mountain man, about thirty-five, with almost black hair, a rugged build, and a full, bushy beard and moustache. "You're a great looking woman," he said without preamble. "Nice body, good bones."

"Thank you," Carla said, her nervousness quickly disappearing. "And you're very handsome yourself."

He fluffed the beard that was long enough to cover the first two buttons of his open-necked shirt. "You mean this," he said as she put her napkin in her lap. "I think it's ridiculous that a man spends ten or fifteen minutes each morning scraping a dangerously sharp instrument over his face. When I graduated from high school, I stopped shaving."

"I guess that means that you don't work in the grey flannel world of corporate America."

His laugh was as booming as she had expected. "You're right. I'm a maverick and proud of it. I own my own business, Sheridan Plastics. Hell, I am Sheridan Plastics. Built it myself from the get-go, you might say. Now some guys in pin-striped suits want to buy me out for an amount of money that has more zeros than I had dollars when I started. And I can sell or I can tell them to go to hell. It doesn't matter to me."

"Are you married?"

He saddened. "Unfortunately, just when life was getting good, Marie died. Auto accident. It was real fast so at least she didn't feel anything."

"I'm sorry."

"It was almost eight years ago. Now I just like to have fun. Nothing serious, mind you. Just fun. What do you want for dinner?" Max asked.

"You selected this place and you seem to know your way around. What do you suggest?"

"I love a good steak and this restaurant serves the best in town."

"Sounds great to me," Carla said. Recently her life seemed to be a gustatorial war between nouvelle cuisine and peanut butter and jelly. She looked up as the waiter held his pencil poised. "Sirloin, medium rare with a baked potato and a salad."

"Good choice," Max said to the waiter. "Do that twice. And let's have a bottle of Chateau Margeaux. I think you have a 1964 hidden away." He turned to Carla. "The Margeaux is a bit light for a steak, but it's excellent."

"Very good sir," the waiter said.

"You're full of surprises," Carla said. "I would have taken you for a beer type of guy. Or even bourbon."

"I was—still am—but I've learned to appreciate a good wine. I also enjoy ordering the most expensive bottle on the menu."

Carla laughed loudly. She found she really liked this unusual man.

"I understand you have children."

They spent the next hour in pleasant conversation. As the meal neared its end, Carla considered the problem of how to bring up her album but, as Ronnie had predicted, Max saved her the trouble.

"I'd like to see your pictures."

Nonplussed, Carla reached down and opened a black leather attache case that sat near her feet. "How did you know about the album?" she asked as she placed the book on the table.

"I guess that's called Black Leather. Bert told me about Ronnie and her book, Black Satin. I assumed you would have some photos too. That's why I called you. Now, be a good girl and get lost. I want to look at this in private. Oh and take off that bra. I like tits that jiggle."

Carla burst out laughing. "Anything you say." She went into the ladies' room and, inside a stall, took off her bra. She was glad she had worn her teal-blue knit dress and only a half-slip. Max would be happy at the way her breasts bounced. When she arrived back at the table, Max was looking at a picture of a woman in a slinky negligee. "I want to wear something like this," he said, not the least embarrassed. "And I want you to fuck me in the ass with a dildo."

"You certainly know what you want," Carla said, completely surprised by the nature of the request.

"I most certainly do. Can we play?"

"Of course." Ronnie had told her that she had lingerie in larger sizes and had shown her the love toys. "I can't guarantee that exact outfit, but I'm sure I have something you'll like."

"That's okay. And by the way, you have great tits."

Max dropped a handful of bills on the table and almost dragged Carla to a taxi. In the bedroom of the brownstone, Carla put her coat and Max's away and went through the bureau drawers. She pulled out a black nightgown with a deep vee front and back and thin straps over the shoulders. She placed it across Max's lap. "How about this?"

His huge, calloused hands slid over the delicate fabric. "It's beautiful."

Carla found another, a peach-colored satin lounging set with feathery trim. "Or this?"

Max held the black gown in one hand and the peach in the other, rubbing the slippery material between his fingers. In another drawer Carla found a bright red teddy that had long attached garters and panties to match. As she handed the pieces to Max, she saw his eyes light up. "Do you have stockings?" he asked.

"Of course." Seeing Max's expression she said, "You've obviously selected this one?"

"Definitely." He stood up and quickly removed all his clothes.

Carla tried not to think about how much hair Max had all over his body and how the undies he had selected would look. She was afraid she would giggle. When she looked at his face, however, she quieted. He was mesmerized and his body showed clearly that he was extremely excited. Anything that excites a man like this can't be bad, she thought.

"Will that thing fit around my waist?" Max wondered, pointing to the bustier.

"Well, let's try." Carla stretched the silky red lace teddy around his waist and threaded the laces through their eyelets.

Max let his head fall back and closed his eyes as the silk caressed his skin.

Carla fetched a pair of thigh-high red stockings. "Sit on the edge of the bed and I'll help you put these on." Max sat and Carla scrunched one nylon on her thumbs. "Raise your foot," she said, kneeling on the rug. Slowly, she took his foot in her hand and slid the nylon up the arch. Inch by inch, the sheer red material covered first his ankle, then his calf, his knee, and his hairy thigh. His cock was rock hard as Carla fastened the stocking to the garters.

Max held his breath and trembled as the second stocking inched up his leg and Carla snapped the garter in place. "Soft," she said, sliding her hand down his nylon-covered leg. "Very smooth."

He lifted her hand from his leg. "Not yet," he said through gritted teeth. "I want to feel the rest of the outfit."

"Of course," Carla said. She slid the bikini panties over his large feet and up to his knees. "Now stand up." Agonizingly slowly, Carla pulled the panties over his engorged cock, then stroked his body through the cloth. Up and down his legs, across his chest, up and down his cock. Her hands were everywhere, their touch muffled by the various fabrics.

Max's breathing was ragged. This was better than it had ever been for him. He stood, his eyes closed, his body quivering, as he tried to retain control. He realized that Carla was no longer touching him. He opened his eyes and saw her, still completely clothed, holding a slender penis-shaped dildo in her hand, stroking its length.

"You know what I'm going to do now, don't you?"

He could no longer remain standing. He collapsed, curled on his side, on the bed. "I know."

Carla sat behind him and applied a generous amount of lubricant on the flesh-colored rod. "You know where you need this?"

"Yes."

She pulled the panties to one side and slid the dildo easily into Max's ass and replaced the nylon. "Now, that's done and held in place firmly. Stand up."

"I don't know whether I can."

"You can and you know it."

Max stood up, almost unable to control his body. It was taking all of his strength not to come. But when she milked his cock with one hand and rotated the end of the dildo with the other he was done. Semen soaked the front of the panties, drenching Carla's hand. It seemed hours and still he came, Carla handling his cock in front and twirling the dildo in back. When his body was empty, Max dropped back onto the bed.

Carla sat beside him until his breathing had almost returned to normal. Then she withdrew the dildo from his body, washed it and put it away in the toy drawer.

"That was marvelous," Max said, turning on his back and watching Carla move around the room. "Just marvelous." He sat up. "Help me off with this stuff."

Carla carefully removed the clothing, then slid a new pair of red satin panties up Max's legs and over his limp penis. "Leave them on under your slacks and think of me as the material rubs your cock."

"Hell, Carla, you'll have me hard all the time."

"That's the idea. Your cock will be hard and you'll remember me."

With a quick laugh, Max pulled on his slacks over the red panties. "I just hope I don't have to pee before I get home. Someone in a men's room might see this red stuff and get the wrong idea."

"Or the right one."

"You're quite something, lady," he boomed. "I'll be calling you. And I've got a lot of friends. I hope you're not overly booked."

"I'll make room. Any friend of yours will become a friend of mine."

As Max left, Carla noticed that he was walking just a bit differently, enjoying the slither of the red silk under his slacks.

About a week later Carla received a note in the mail. "Max told me about you. The plumber will be at your apartment at six o'clock on Tuesday evening the 27th." The note was signed "Gene." The only other thing in the envelope was five hundred dollars in cash. Later, Carla got a phone message from Max saying that a friend of his named Gene would drop her a note soon.

Carla was at the brownstone at six on the selected evening, dressed in a pair of tight, white denim pants and a snug-fitting plum-colored polo shirt that accentuated her bralessness. When the doorbell rang, she opened the front door and faced a muscular, if slightly overweight, man of medium height. He wore a pair of stained coveralls and carried a toolbox. "I'm Gene," he said, "and I'm here to fix your kitchen faucet. Max said your plumbing wasn't usually a problem."

Carla almost giggled. "My plumbing is usually fine," she said. "But that kitchen sink has been giving me a terrible time recently."

"Let's check it out." Gene followed her the kitchen and proceeded to actually dismantle the faucet while she watched. "Okay, lady," he said, "I'm going to need some help here."

"What can I do?"

"Most things, I'd imagine," he said, grinning. He had disconnected the faucet and fastened a huge pipe wrench around some connection at the back of the sink. "But right now I need you to hold this wrench."

Carla replaced his hairy hands on the wrench with her own. "Now pull hard," he said, "and hold tight. If you let go, we'll have water everywhere."

Knowing nothing about plumbing, Carla had no idea what this man had done, so she pulled on the wrench with both hands. "Don't let go," he warned again. As he stood up, he brushed against Carla's breasts which, since she was bent over the sink, were hanging heavily against her shirt. "Nice melons, lady," he said, squeezing one of the heavy globes.

"Hey," she said, "cut that out."

As she started to straighten, he said, "Don't let go of that pipe or it'll make old faithful look like a garden sprinkler."

"Shit," Carla said. She had no idea how much of this was fantasy and how much was reality. Not ready to take a chance with Ronnie's kitchen, she held onto the wrench.

"I'm glad you understand," Gene said. He squeezed her breast, weighing its fullness in his hand. "Nice big tits," he said, nodding. "Fill the hand, and then some. I love titties that are more than a handful."

"Will you let go," Carla snapped.

Gene backed up and, behind her, Carla heard tools banging

around in the toolbox. "Here we are," Gene, the plumber, said. Carla heard a loud snipping sound. Suddenly her polo shirt was being cut up the back and across the shoulders. With a yank, she was naked from the waist up. "That's better," Gene said.

"Now wait a minute," Carla said but Gene silenced her with a pinch of one of her swollen nipples. "Ouch."

"Be a good girl," Gene said, "and don't let go of that pipe." He leaned over and bit her earlobe. "If you say 'Uncle,' I'll stop. Understand?" he whispered. Carla nodded.

With both hands holding the wrench tightly, Carla tried to wiggle away from the plumber's hands, but she had almost no room to maneuver. He pressed his body against her back and his rough palms cupped her heavy breasts and pressed them against her ribs. As he held her, he thrust her lower body against her buttocks, jabbing her with what felt like the largest cock ever.

"That's for later," he said, his laugh warm, moist waves against her ear. Again he backed up and rummaged in his toolbox.

Suddenly Gene draped heavy, cold lengths of chain over her shoulders and wrapped it around her ribs and under her breasts. "That's cold," she shrieked, as he fastened the chain in the back.

"And this is warm," he said, leaning into the sink and sucking one nipple into his mouth.

The contrast between his hot mouth and the cold chains was tantalizing. She started to relax and loosen her grip. "Don't let that go," he said. "I mean it. It'll drown us both."

"Shit," she hissed again.

Gene pulled one nipple while he nursed on the other. He moved around to the other side and exchanged his hand for his mouth. He was rough and both his mouth and hands were painful, hurting yet exciting and soothing all at once. "Am I hurting you?" he asked, pinching her left tit hard.

"Ouch! Yes, you're hurting me." Carla looked down and saw a bright red mark. She knew that she would say 'Uncle,' but she wasn't anywhere near needing to. Quite the contrary. She felt wonderful.

"Good," Gene said, unzipping her jeans and pulling them

down. Automatically Carla lifted her bare feet so he could pull the pants off, leaving her dressed only in her panties and several lengths of chain. Gene slid his hand down her belly and into her panties. "You're hot for me," he said, his fingers pulling her wet pubic hair. Carla couldn't deny what was obvious to the touch. "I have just the right tool to use and it's not the one you think."

He pulled something from his toolbox and Carla felt something slender, cylindrical, and cold wiggle into the narrow crevice between her legs. "The right tool for every job," Gene muttered. He slid the dildo deep into Carla's pussy. In and out he fucked her with it, moving the slender object around so it touched every inch of her insides.

Her knees weak, Carla had to be reminded not to let go of the pipe. "Hold on to that wrench, lady. Hold on." He pulled her panties back up to keep the dildo in place while he undressed. Since she couldn't let go of the wrench that held the disconnected pipe, Carla backed up as far as she could and arched her back.

She worried about how to insist on a condom without ruining the fantasy, but, as if he had read her mind, she heard the telltale ripping of the condom wrapper. "Don't you worry about a thing. I wouldn't do any job unprotected."

Gene held his large cock in one hand and moved aside the crotch of Carla's panties with the other. With little warning, he pulled out the dildo and rammed his huge cock into Carla's soggy pussy. He was enormous, stretching Carla's body almost to the point of agony. But not quite. The sensation of being so full drove Carla to climax quickly. With a loud scream she came and soon thereafter Gene spurted come deep into her.

When his breathing was more normal, Gene took the wrench from Carla's hands and disconnected it from the sink. No water spurted out. As she dropped on a kitchen chair, Carla watched Gene efficiently reassemble the faucet.

"Nice plumbing," Gene said, packing his wrenches in the toolbox and gazing at Carla's body. "Very nice plumbing."

"And the tools you used were absolutely perfect for the job," Carla said, still puffing.

"I'll be back if you have any more trouble."

"Any time," Carla said. Gene zipped up the front of his coveralls, picked up his toolbox, and left.

Chapter 7

Over the next few months, Carla and Ronnie established a routine. Carla didn't want to be away from her sons any more than was necessary, so she limited her encounters in the city to Tuesday and Thursday evenings and the occasional daytime frolic that didn't keep her from being home when the boys arrived from school. Ronnie used the brownstone other evenings and occasionally on weekends. Every Monday Ronnie and Carla met for lunch, sharing stories and deepening their friendship.

By Thanksgiving Carla had developed a clientele consisting of about a dozen men who regularly perused her album and played out their fantasies with her. A special favorite, her first customer Bryce McAndrews become a regular visitor to the brownstone on 54th Street. At least twice a month, he and Carla got together, ate at a four-star restaurant, and attended a Broadway show or a concert at Lincoln Center. Once they had spent an hour at a Benjamin Britton concert that they both hated. They left after the first selection, when they discovered their mutual dislike of any music composed in the twentieth century. Most evenings they ended up in the paneled room, although occasionally they parted without making love at all.

One afternoon in mid-December Bryce called and told Carla that he wanted to act out an especially elaborate wish of his. He'd make all the arrangements for the following Tuesday and he asked her to leave the brownstone at seven-thirty that evening, setting a key beside the front door, then come back at exactly eight o'clock.

Carla left at the appointed time, had a cup of coffee at a little restaurant on Second Avenue, then returned to the house filled with mounting expectation. Bryce seemed to understand her desires more and more and their appetites matched perfectly. She walked into the front hallway and heard his familiar voice. "Up here," he called from the second bedroom.

When Carla walked into the room, the entire atmosphere had changed. Bryce had replaced the dim lighting with strong, 100-watt bulbs and all of the exotic equipment that could be concealed was out of sight. Bryce wore a white lab coat and had a stethoscope draped around his neck. "Thank you for being so prompt, Miss Barrett, and I'm sorry you haven't been well."

It took only an instant for her to slip into the part and only slightly longer for her to be wet and trembling. "It's been a difficult time," Carla said trying to suppress her growing flush.

"I understand completely." Bryce handed her a light blue paper smock exactly like the one she had worn at her last doctor's appointment. "Step into the bathroom and put this on. I'll be ready for you in a moment."

As she took the smock from him, Carla noticed a narrow, padded table covered with a strip of plain white paper, set up in one corner of the room. Her knees wobbled. Did he know about her "playing doctor" fantasy or was this his own erotic dream? It didn't matter.

In the bathroom it took Carla only a moment to strip off her clothes and put on the smock. "Nothing but the smock," Bryce's voice said through the bathroom door, "and have the opening in the front. I'll need to examine all of you."

Timidly she walked from the bathroom. She realized that the room smelled of antiseptic. "That's a real doctor's examination table," Carla said.

"Of course," Bryce grinned. "And this is a real doctor's office. Now, Miss Barrett, lie down."

She stretched out on the table and the doctor put a pillow under her head. "I hope you're comfortable," he said. "Are you nervous?"

"Maybe a little," Carla said. Barely covered by the scratchy paper gown, she felt exposed, despite the fact that Bryce had seen her nude a dozen times.

The doctor picked up a pencil and pressed the point gently against her upper arm. "There," he said. "I've given you something to relax you. Now let's discuss your symptoms. Any loss of appetite?"

"Unfortunately none that I've noticed."

Bryce ran his hands down her sides. "You've nothing to worry about, Miss Barrett. You have a beautiful body. Any difficulty sleeping?"

They continued bantering for a few moments, then Bryce said, "Are you less anxious? I hope so. That injection I gave you should thoroughly relax you. Your arms should feel very heavy."

The sound of Bryce's voice flowed through Carla's body like warm honey. Although he'd used no real medication on her, she felt almost liquid as she melted into the table. "My arms are very heavy."

"And your legs too. As a matter of fact it's getting very hard to move at all. It's a nice, floaty feeling, but you know you can't move. Close your eyes."

Carla did, slipping further and further into the scenario Bryce was enacting.

"Good girl," he said. He took out some cotton and a bottle of alcohol. He soaked the cotton and pressed it against Carla's upper arm.

The cold was surprising and the smell was enough to transport Carla more deeply into the scene. "That's cold," she whimpered.

"Yes," Bryce purred, "it is. And you want to move away from the cold but you can't. As a matter of fact you can't move at all." He moved the still-wet cotton to the inside of Carla's calf. She wanted to pull away but she couldn't break through the haze of the fantasy. Or she didn't want to.

"You're not frightened, but you can't move. The medicine I gave you is a special blend of exotic drugs. You can see and hear and feel, but you can't move, can't speak, can't resist anything I want to do to you.

"First, your breasts." With almost medical objectivity, he pressed and prodded at her flesh and pulled at the nipples. "Your tits get firm," he said. "Good reaction to stimulus." He used a pair of tweezers to pinch one erect nipple. As Carla's body winced, he said, "That must hurt a bit. It's too bad you can't move. And you can't move, can you?" He used the tweezers to lightly pinch tiny pieces of skin all over her body, nodding as her body reacted. "Very good," he said.

Carla gazed at Bryce but said nothing.

"Next is the temperature test." He reached behind him and picked up a glass full of ice. While Carla watched, he picked up a cube and held it so the icy water dripped on one breast. As the drop trickled down her white skin, he licked up the water with the tip of his tongue. Drip, lick, drip, lick, he alternated ice water and the heat of his tongue. She became accustomed to the routine and closed her eyes. Suddenly the frozen cube pressed firmly against her left nipple. "Owww," she yelled, her body jerking.

"Don't try to move," Bryce said. "It's impossible to overcome the effect of the shot I gave you and it is very harmful to your body when you try to resist. Just hold still and I'll finish the temperature test." He dropped the cube back into the glass and placed the flat of his tongue against her almost-frozen dark-pink bud and held it there as the warmth seeped back into her skin.

"Good," he said as Carla's body relaxed, "you've done very well with this test." He opened the bottom of the gown and slid his fingertips up the inside of Carla's thigh until he reached her cunt. "So wet," he chuckled. "You are excited by these procedures. That's very interesting."

Excited by these procedures? Carla was certainly excited by these procedures, but it was humiliating to know that Bryce could reach between her legs and tell how aroused she had become.

"Let's see. What else excites you?" he said. "I know. Words excite you. Let's just test to see which ones exactly." Keeping one hand on the springy fur between Carla's legs, Bryce leaned close to her ear and whispered, "How about when I tell you that your pussy hair is so soft? Yes. Your cream is flowing so those words must work." He rubbed the wetness around, stroking her clit. "How about when I say 'Your titties are standing up, waiting for my mouth'?" He sucked her upright nipples and continued to agitate her cunt. "What if I tell you that my balls are heavy and my cock is hard, waiting to slide into your pussy? Soon I'll place the tip of my dick against the opening of your greedy slit and push it in ever so slowly."

Carla was lost in a sensual fog, her eyes closed, giving herself to Bryce, hearing his voice and feeling his fingers between her legs. Tremors began deep in her belly and she knew that his manipulation was going to bring her to orgasm.

"You're close to coming," Bryce said. "But I don't want you to just yet." He stopped and got another ice cube. "Let's cool you down a bit." He maneuvered the frosty cube over Carla's pussy lips.

"Oh God, stop," Carla said, forgetting that she supposedly couldn't speak.

"You know the word to use," Bryce said, removing the ice cube, "if you really want me to stop."

"Yes. I do, Bryce," she said, warmth flowing back into her chilled lips. Then she added, "Doctor, please don't do that."

"It's no use asking me to stop," he continued. "The doctor has to do these sexual tests. It's purely scientific."

He's making me crazy, Carla thought. "Please no more." But she wanted more. As much more as Bryce wanted to give her.

Bryce rubbed the cube lightly over Carla's clit, watching her arousal decrease. "Good girl," he said. "Your reaction to this test is excellent." He pushed the cube into Carla's cunt, then pushed two fingers in after it. "You feel hot and cold at the same time," he said. "The sensations must be driving you crazy."

"Ummm," Carla said. Cold water from the melting ice trickled down Bryce's fingers and ran from her cunt down over her ass.

"Maybe you're getting hot enough for the final test," Bryce said.

Final test?

With two fingers buried deep inside of Carla's pussy, Bryce took his other hand and explored the rim of her tightly puckered hole. Then, with both hands moving he leaned down and flicked his tongue over her clit. Fire blazed to and from all the sensitive places he was touching. Hot and throbbing, Carla released, screaming. Every muscle in her lower body spasmed.

"Your body is clenching my fingers," Bryce said, his face buried in her pubic hair. "Come baby," he purred, his hot breath restoking the fires in her pussy. "Keep coming." He drew his fingers from her cunt and quickly moved around the foot of the table and parted the sides of his lab coat. He wore nothing underneath and his arousal announced itself.

As he stood at the foot of the table his cock was at the height of Carla's pussy. He slipped on a condom, then pulled her legs so she slid down the table. He parted her thighs so her soaked cunt pressed against the tip of his cock.

Her juices were still mixed with melted water from the ice. "Not too fast," he told himself, gritting his teeth against the desire to slam his body into hers. "Make this last." His body shook and sweat ran down his chest as he fought for control. He rubbed his sheathed cock against Carla's overheated flesh, then pressed just the tip into her.

She was more excited than she had ever been, yet, because she had already climaxed once, she was able to experience all the nuances of Bryce's body. She could hold herself at a level just below climax, slipping into the ecstasy whenever she wanted to. He opened her inch by inch with his cock, slowly filling her. Occasionally she squeezed her inner muscles and smiled as Bryce shuddered.

When he was fully inside, Bryce stood still for a moment savoring the sensation of being encased in pulsating velvet while the tip of his cock was slightly cold from the remains of the ice. Carla wrapped her legs around Bryce's waist, then pushed her cunt against him driving Bryce's cock still deeper. He could hold still no longer. With panting breaths he clenched his ass muscles and let his body thrust into the slick heat.

"Oh yes," he cried as hot bursts of semen exploded from his penis. "Oh Carla yes." He collapsed, his upper body lying across hers, both breathing hard and trembling. She shuddered as her muscles pulled at him.

Long minutes later they were calmer. "Oh doctor," Carla said with a giggle, "your tests are so educational."

"Zertainly," Bryce said, imitating a thick German accent. "Ve try to be zo zientific." They lay together until Carla's leg began to fall asleep. She moved slightly and Bryce's satisfied cock slipped from her body. As Bryce stood up, he said, "Okay, last one to the shower has to scrub the other, all over."

They made love again in the shower, steaming water pouring over their soapy bodies as Bryce pounded into Carla's cunt from behind.

When he was dressed, Carla said, "You have no idea how much fun our evenings are for me." She stretched on the bed watching his eyes rake her naked body.

"Me too," Bryce said, kissing her on the tip of her nose.

As usual on their evenings together, Carla had arranged for her parents to stay with the boys so she could sleep in the city. "You could stay here tonight," Carla said, reluctantly. Although Bryce still paid her for their evenings together they were also lovers and she sometimes wanted to spend the night with him. But staying here together felt wrong, somehow. Too comfortable. Too married.

"No, but thanks. We both like things just as they are." He counted out five hundred dollars and put it on the table. "No strings."

Carla smiled. "Right," she said, playfully swatting his now-clothed behind. "Let me know when you want to get together again."

"Will do," Bryce said as he walked toward the bedroom door. "Call you soon."

The Village Tavern, known affectionately in Greenwich Village as the fat-factory, was not one of Carla's usual restaurants. It specialized in mammoth hamburgers, great steaks, forty-five varieties of beer, and desserts covered with real whipped cream. Patrons joked that an ambulance stood by at dinner time in case of a heart attack.

The two men who sat at the table in the back of the Village Tavern were not Carla's usual type of client. As she studied them she saw that, except for the fact that one man wore rimless glasses, they looked as alike as two men who weren't related could. Both men were of medium height and build with ruddy complexions and weathered skin. Both men appeared to be in their thirties, with well-muscled arms and upper bodies. Their heads were together and they were deep in conversation.

As Carla approached, the darker of the two obviously said something funny and both men roared. "Which is Dean and which is Nicky?" asked Carla dropping into an empty chair.

Both men looked at Carla, and looked and looked. Carla smiled easily, enjoying their frank admiration of her white cotton mantailored shirt, western vest, and tight-fitting, stonewashed jeans. She wore a multicolored zuni fetish necklace and matching earrings and had applied little makeup. The two men were silent for a long moment, then spoke simultaneously.

"He's Dean."

"I'm Dean." They laughed together, a warm sound that made Carla imagine how nice it would feel to be so close. "Timmy wasn't kidding when he told me you were a knockout," Dean said. "Until you got here, Nicky and I had been wondering whether this was a dumb idea. Now I think we've done real good."

"Tim told me that you two had some recent good luck," Carla said. Tim Sorenson had called Carla and told her that Dean Gerard and his friend Nicky Romano wanted to employ her for an evening. Except for vouching for Dean's character and setting up the meeting, Tim would tell her nothing else.

"We won fifteen thousand dollars in the lottery. Seventy-five hundred each."

"I've never met a lottery winner before," Carla said. "Congratulations."

"Thanks," Nicky said. The waiter arrived and Dean suggested a German beer that Carla had never heard of. When Carla nodded, Dean held up three fingers and the waiter disappeared.

"Tell me a little about yourselves," Carla said, aware that she was treating them like a pair rather than two individuals.

Dean did the talking. "We both work for the city department of sanitation. Sometimes we toss garbage cans and sometimes one of us drives a truck. In the winter we shovel and plow." No wonder they have such great arms, Carla thought. "We've been doing this for almost fifteen years and we met our first day on the job. Nicky and me are a team."

"Married?"

"Dean is, I'm not," Nicky said. "Not any more."

"And how do you know Tim?" Carla asked. "He told me almost nothing when he called."

Dean took a breath and pushed his glasses toward the bridge of his nose. "I've known Timmy for many years. We met in a beginner's photography class and we've kept in touch ever since." Dean looked at Carla. "I know, I don't look like a photographer but I've been into picture taking since I was a kid."

The waiter put their beers on the wooden trestle table in front of them and listed the specials of the day.

"I'll have the double lamb chops, medium rare, french fries, and a salad with roquefort dressing," Carla said. In for a penny. . . .

"A woman after my own heart," Nicky said. "Make that two."

"Three," Dean said and the waiter disappeared. "You know, this is all a bit strange," he continued, "so let me get to the point and explain what I have in mind. Timmy told me that you're a call girl."

"Dean, that's not a nice thing to say," Nicky said. He turned to Carla. "Sorry, Carla. This is kind of awkward."

"It's okay," Carla said. "I enjoy having sex and fulfilling men's fantasies and I do it for money. I guess that makes me a call girl."

"Fantasies," Dean said. "That's what Timmy said. And I've

had a fantasy for as long as I can remember. I want to direct a movie.''

"A movie?" Carla said.

"A movie. Just a short thing. Nicky's going to be the male star and we want you to be the girl star.''

Carla had a moment to consider the proposal as the waiter arrived with the most enormous chops she had ever seen. When he was gone, Carla took a bite. "Fabulous," she said. "Tell me more about this movie.''

"I love to watch X-rated movies and I've always wanted to direct my own,'' Dean said. "I want to do one that's better than the crap that's out there.''

"Don't get us wrong, Carla,'' Nicky said. "We don't want to sell it or anything. We just want to make it and then watch it ourselves.''

"I've never been in a movie,'' Carla said. "It might be fun. But I don't want to go to my local theater and see my name in lights or my naked body on the screen.''

"Of course not. That's not at all what we have in mind,'' Dean said. "Hey Nicky, can you picture the guys we know watching you naked.''

Nicky got a strange look on his face but Carla decided to go along with the idea. "If Tim says that you guys can be trusted, it's fine with me.''

"That's terrific." They spent the rest of the meal discussing the film's almost meaningless plot.

As the three finished gigantic pieces of apple pie with homemade vanilla ice cream, Dean reached into his pocket and withdrew an envelope. "For your time," he said. "I hope it's right. Timmy told us about your usual fee, but there are two of us and . . . well. . . .''

Carla put the envelope into her purse without looking inside. "I'm sure it's fine," she said. "Now, where to?''

"I've taken a suite in a hotel," Dean said. "Nicky knows where. I've set up lights and some fancy video stuff I rented but let me have one final check and get ready.'' He glanced at the dinner check and put a few bills on the table. "You two wait here for a few minutes, then follow along. Come into the room together and we'll take it from there."

Nicky raised his hand to his forehead in a mock salute. "You got it, boss, Mr. Director, sir." He turned to Carla. "I hope this works out."

Carla and Nicky talked for ten minutes then made their way to a suite in the Gramercy Park, an older hotel in the low twenties. As they approached the door, Nicky said, "You know what we're doing?"

"I guess," Carla answered. "It's a little loose."

"We'll fake it." Nicky knocked, then inserted a key in the lock and opened the door. Carla entered and saw the camera, filming their actions. She turned to Nicky, waiting at the door. "I had a nice evening," she said, working herself into the part she was playing. "I enjoyed myself a lot."

"Me too," Nicky said. They were supposed to be coming back from their first date. "Can I come in for a nightcap?"

"I'm kind of tired," Carla said.

"I won't be long. I just don't want the evening to end yet."

Carla and Nicky walked into the sitting room of the two-room suite that Dean had rented. It was done in cream and gold, with accents of light blue and grey. The heavy ivory drapes were tightly drawn and all the lights were lit, supplemented with two bright spotlights aimed at the sofa.

Nicky closed the door and leaned against it. "You know I want you," he said. "Your gorgeous body has been driving me nuts all evening."

Carla's character was supposed to be reluctant, but persuadable. "But we hardly know each other," she said.

"Do you believe in love at first sight?"

Carla laughed. "I believe in lust at first sight."

"Oh sugar," Nicky said. "Let me make love to you."

"Cut," Dean said. "That's great. Let's move to the sofa. Now Nicky, let's say that you and Carla have been making out. Kiss

her good, then show me how you get her to start undressing and
how you begin touching her.''

"This is really weird,'' Nicky said.

"It's kind of fun,'' Carla said. "I like being directed, told how
to act.'' She sat on the ivory upholstered couch, ruffled her hair,
and extended her arms. "Come here and convince me.''

Nicky looked at Dean, shrugged, and sat beside Carla. He kissed
her tentatively, brushing his lips against hers. He stroked her hair
back from her temples and kissed her forehead. "Hey, Nicky,''
Dean said. "I don't have endless film. Let's get serious.''

"This is making me really uncomfortable,'' Nicky whispered,
his lips against her cheek.

"I understand,'' Carla answered *soto voce*. "It can be weird
having to perform.''

"All right,'' Dean said, "cut. When you whisper I can't hear
you. Listen. I gotta take a leak. You two figure out the rest of the
show and I'll be right back.''

When they were alone, Nicky said, "This seemed to be a terrific
idea when Dean dreamed it up. Now, I'm afraid I won't be able
to . . . you know. Those guys in the movies are so well hung and
seem to get it up whenever. . . .''

"It'll be okay.''

"Oh it's not you. I just don't think I can perform on
command.''

Carla unbuttoned the top button of her shirt, took Nicky's hand
and stroked it softly over her breast. "I won't let you embarrass
yourself. I promise.''

Nicky slid his palm over Carla's erect nipple. "You're very
sexy,'' he said.

"Hey, I've got an idea,'' Carla said, sitting up. "Let's make
Dean tell us exactly what he wants. Move for move. We do nothing unless he tells us to. That sounds extremely sexy to me. And
no pressure on either of us.''

Nicky took a shaky breath. "You mean that he calls all the
shots?'' He paused. "Actually, that sounds sexy as hell.''

Dean had returned and overheard Nicky's last sentence. "You want me to tell you guys what to do?"

"Right," Carla said. "It's hard to pretend to be part of some story and get turned on at the same time."

"Hummm. Being the director for real. It sounds kinky. The audio will pick up what I say." He paused to think it through. "Telling you to suck and fuck . . . sounds hot."

"Not fucking," Carla corrected. "Making love. Touching, stroking, kissing, licking, you tell us everything. And remember that if we're not hot and ready to fuck when you say so your movie has no final scene and it isn't our responsibility."

"I love a challenge," Dean said. "Okay with you, Nicky?"

"Just so long as you understand that if I don't get hard, it's your fault, not mine."

"Okay. I like this. Let's go into the bedroom." Quickly, Dean moved his lights and video equipment into the bedroom. "Lie on the bed, Carla," he said, "and Nicky beside her." The two did as they were instructed, stretching out on the satin bedspread. "Nicky, kiss Carla on the mouth and slide your hand onto her tit."

Nicky leaned over Carla and gazed into her eyes for a moment. "This really is a turn-on," he said as his lips pressed against hers. He spread his palm over her right breast and kneaded the soft globe. He kissed her mouth, then moved his lips to her ear. "That's right, lick her," Dean said, and Nicky swirled the tip of his tongue into Carla's ear. As he licked, he hummed softly and Carla could feel the vibrations through her entire body.

She twisted, giving Nicky better access to her ear as his hand brushed back and forth against the fabric of the front of her shirt. "Unbutton her blouse," Dean said.

The remaining two buttons came undone easily and Nicky slipped his hand inside. "Pull the blouse open so I can see her undies. I love those shots of breasts in tiny brassieres." Carla was glad she was wearing a palepink lace demicup bra. They'd have their money's worth and more, as much as she could provide.

Dean moved around the bed, peering through the lens of the camera. "Yes," Dean exclaimed. "Beautiful. You've got such great nipples that I can see them through your bra. Don't you agree Nicky?''

"I certainly do." He rubbed her breasts through the lacy fabric.

"Suck one nipple through the lace and make it hard," Dean said and, as Nicky followed his instructions, Dean rounded the bed and crawled across to get a close-up of Nicky's lips on Carla's erect nipple. When he could resist no longer, Dean put the camera down and sucked Carla's other nipple. Two mouths on her breasts was unbelievably erotic.

A little shaky, Dean returned to his camera. "No, no. Mustn't lose my objectivity," he said. "I want to make this good so I can watch it over and over." He positioned himself at the foot of the bed. "Carla, I think you should take Nicky's shirt off, very slowly. And kiss and lick his chest as you do it."

She opened Nicky's shirt and rubbed her hands over his lightly furred skin. She kissed his flat nipples as she eased his plaid shirt from his shoulders. "And yours too, Carla," Dean said. As Carla shrugged out of her shirt, Dean sighed. "Great boobs. Shit, see how they overflow the cups of that tiny bra?" Carla heard the whine of the zoom lens as Dean came in for a close-up of her right breast.

Suddenly, Dean turned off the camera. "I just realized that we're missing a great opportunity here," he said. "Anyone see a TV?"

Seeing none, Carla said, "There must be one. Maybe it's in that wall unit. Why?"

Without comment, Dean found the large-screen TV and connected some wires from the camera to the back. "Now watch. Nicky, suck her nipple again." As Dean started the camera, the picture of Nicky's mouth appeared on the screen.

"Oh God," Carla said. "That's wild."

"Right. You get to star in your own X-rated movie and watch it at the same time. Nicky, feel up her breasts so she can watch your hands massage her."

Carla found it amazingly exciting, feeling Nicky's hands on her body and watching it happen on the screen at the same time.

"Okay, take the bra off." Nicky unclasped the bra and dropped it on the floor. There, in full color, were her breasts, with Nicky's dark-skinned hands covering them. "Suck and bite them. Lick them until the nipples are real tight."

Nicky's mouth covered Carla's breasts, softly pulling them to tight peaks. Carla watched the TV screen as Dean moved the camera around, getting different angles of Nicky's mouth and Carla's breasts.

"Cut." Carla smiled as she sensed Nicky's reluctance to stop what they were doing.

"Take the rest of your clothes off, Carla," Dean said, "so I can get some shots of your sweet pussy." She pulled off her jeans and panties and stretched out on the bed, with Nicky beside her. "Now, Nicky, get her wet." He turned his back to adjust his video.

Nicky ran his hand up the inside of Carla's thigh and tentatively touched her lips. "She's already soaked," he said, surprised.

"You make me horny," Carla whispered. She reached down and squeezed the ridge of hot flesh that pressed upward against his belly beneath his jeans. She winked. "You seem to be horny too."

Dean turned the camera back on and focused the lens on Carla's breast. "Spread her legs, Nicky. I want to see your hand on her pussy." The camera panned slowly down her ribs and belly until her cunt filled the screen.

Carla turned and looked at the TV. She had never seen herself like this, open and waiting, ready to be filled, with Nicky's dark, blunt fingers playing idly with her pussy hair. It sent a jolt of pleasure shooting into her depths. She saw Nicky's fingers slide toward her swollen lips and, when he touched her, she could both feel it and see it. It was the most intense sensation she could remember.

Without being told, Nicky pulled off his clothes while the camera watched. His erection was rigid and thick, jutting from a nest of black hair in his groin. Carla smiled. Arousal was no longer a worry for him. She reached out and wrapped her hand around the engorged organ and pulled it until Nicky was sitting on the bed beside her. She turned so her ass was in the air and her head was in his lap.

"I'm going to make you come," she said softly. "And you're going to watch. Look at yourself."

Nicky stared at the TV screen and watched Carla's mouth on his cock. He was both feeling and watching a beautiful woman kissing the head of his cock, then pursing her lips and sucking him into her waiting mouth. He closed his eyes and reveled in the sensations.

When Nicky started to lose control, Carla wrapped her fingers around the base of his erection and squeezed his cock and balls tightly, preventing him from climaxing. She wanted Dean to have great pictures, ones that Nicky would be proud of. Higher and higher Carla forced Nicky, her head bobbing in his lap, sucking his cock yet keeping him from coming.

Finally she looked at the camera and said, "Every good porno flick has a come shot and Nicky's going to be the star of this one." She breathed hot air on the end of his cock while she grasped the shaft with one hand and kept the fingers of the other around the base. "Are you going to watch your own climax?" she asked Nicky.

Dean panned to his friend's face and watched as Nicky's eyes opened and stared at the screen. The camera returned to his cock, covered by Carla's hands. "Watch, baby," she said. "Watch your cock as you shoot beautiful come on my tits." She licked the length of his erection, making the hard shaft shiny and wet. She rubbed just a bit more, then, as his semen boiled from his balls, she released her hold on the base of his cock and moved so his come spurted on her breasts. The camera recorded as thick gobs of goo covered her large tits.

"Shit, Nicky," Dean said as semen erupted from Nicky's cock. "I didn't know you were such a stud. Maybe we should show this to the guys." Finally, Nicky collapsed onto the bed, exhausted.

By the time Carla returned from the shower, fully dressed, Dean had returned all the camera equipment to the cases and Nicky was dressed. "We're going to watch the tape," Dean said. "Are you going to stay?"

"No, I don't think so. I already know how it ends."

While Dean fiddled with the VCR, Nicky walked Carla to the door of the suite. "Thanks," he said. "I doubt that Dean will be able to keep that film to himself and now I'll get some kind of reputation with our friends. I hope you don't mind if your face shows a bit."

"Not at all, as long as it's just your friends. After all, a stud like you should be able to show off a little."

As Nicky watched Carla walk toward the elevator, he said, "Hey Carla, thanks again."

Dennis Stanton was an old friend of Ronnie's and they had spent many enjoyable evenings together. Tonight, however, he had something very unusual in mind and since the evening's entertainment wasn't exactly her taste, Ronnie had suggested that he call Carla. When Carla heard about the engagement, and, of course, the fee, she agreed quickly.

A stretch limo arrived in front of the brownstone at exactly eight o'clock. Dennis helped Carla inside. A man of about fifty, Dennis had deep chocolate-brown eyes and dark hair with wings of silver at the temples. He wore a magnificently tailored midnight-blue tuxedo with a matching tie and cummerband.

"It's nice to meet you," Dennis said softly, sliding the partition window up to prevent the limo driver from overhearing. "It's a short drive to where we're going, so let me get right to the point. Ronnie said she told you what I want."

"She did, but explain again. I want to be sure I understand everything."

"I belong to a sort of unofficial sex club. There are about twenty of us, all men, some married, some not. Once a month we get together and indulge our shared passions. Some men bring women, paid or otherwise, and some don't. The women, of course, must be of a particular type."

"I know. Submissive."

"Exactly. And if you know Ronnie, you know that that's not her."

Carla smiled and nodded. She couldn't picture Ronnie bowing her head and submitting meekly while men used her body. To Carla, however, it sounded irresistible.

"Anyway," Dennis continued, "I've never brought a woman to one of our partices ... until tonight. If you're willing, of course."

"I am, as long as condoms and safe words are agreed to in advance."

"They are," Dennis said. "No whips or anything like that, except with the permission of the woman involved. The word 'Yellow' is a temporary safe word, in case you want to stop things for a minute, say if you're cold or your foot's asleep. 'Red' is an absolute stop and anyone disregarding it is asked to leave our club and is not allowed back." His soft smile made him look a bit like Cary Grant. "Every member values membership too much to risk banishment so should you say so, everything stops. Is that all right with you?"

Carla took a deep breath and nodded. It was hard to reconcile Dennis's handsome, open expression with the dark nature of the evening's entertainment, but as she thought about the sex party she was about to attend, she shivered.

"Good. From now on you will follow my directions without question. You will keep your eyes downcast and speak only when spoken to. Do you agree?"

Carla started to answer, then decided to begin her part immediately. She looked at the floor of the limo and nodded.

"Good girl," Dennis said. "Are you wearing the clothes I sent you?" When she nodded, he said, "Then take off your dress."

Quickly, Carla pulled off her navy knit dress. Beneath it she wore a tight, crotchless, dark blue satin teddy with openings at the front of each breast so her nipples were exposed. Old-fashioned dark blue-and-white lace garters held up her blue net stockings and she wore very high-heeled blue satin pumps. She placed her dress on the seat beside her, folded her hands in her lap, and stared at Dennis's shoes.

"Very nice," Dennis said, staring at her scantily dressed body. "Your clothes will be here waiting for you when we return." He looked her over carefully then continued, "You really are gorgeous and you seem to have the proper attitude." He pinched one of Carla's nipples hard and, although she winced slightly, she didn't make a sound or look up. "Yes indeed," Dennis said. "I will be proud to present you to my friends."

She knew it was silly but Carla found she was pleased that he thought her worthy of the evening's entertainment. "Now," Dennis said, "a few additions." He buckled a leather cuff with a large metal ring attached around each of Carla's wrists and ankles. A slightly narrower cuff went around her neck and Dennis turned it so the ring was in the back. He attached a short chain to the ring and let it fall, cold and heavy, down her back between her shoulder blades to her waist. "Now," he said, "remember 'Red' is the safe word." He took a small padlock from his pocket, drew her arms behind her back, and locked the rings on her wrist cuffs to the end of the chain. Carla wasn't in any physical discomfort, but, with her arms secured behind her she was awkward and off balance.

"Good," Dennis said, as the car pulled to a stop. He buttoned a long, full-length, royal blue evening cape around Carla's shoulders and, as the chauffeur held the door, they got out. Carla quickly realized that despite her immobilization, to a bystander she looked like any woman might, going to a formal function.

Her head lowered, she moved her eyes from side to side and realized that they were entering the lobby of a very exclusive hotel, although she wasn't sure which one. They entered the 'Penthouses Only' elevabor. Dennis said, "Only members and their ladies will be permitted up here. We've taken the entire floor for the evening."

The elevator doors swept open onto a small vestibule. Her eyes on the carpet, Carla followed Dennis through the only open door into a large living room.

"Ah, Dennis," a man said. "I see that you've brought a young lady for us. Wonderful."

Something about the gathering made Carla shiver with expectation. Although she'd read about them in magazines, she'd never believed that clubs like this really existed.

"Gentlemen," a man said, tapping a tiny hammer on a miniature gong, "now that everyone's here, the meeting will come to order. Bring the women forward."

Dennis propelled Carla to the center of the room where she stood, eyes downcast, with two others. One woman was a statuesque blond with light blue eyes and dark red lips and the other a petite black woman with very short fluffy hair and skin the color of taffy. The women were dressed in capes similar to Carla's, each in a different color. Carla looked around as best she could without raising her eyes and estimated there were about a dozen men, of varying ages and physical types, all in formal attire.

"Do the women know the corrrect forms of address?" the leader asked. He was of Mediterranean origin, with very dark hair and eyes and olive skin.

"Not mine, sir," Dennis said. "I felt it was your place to instruct her."

"Ladies," the leader said. "For tonight I will be your king and you will address me as 'your majesty' or 'sire.' "

"Yes, your majesty," Carla said. She heard the other woman say the same thing.

"All the other men will be addressed as 'my lord.' "

"Yes, sire."

"Obedience is your most important function. You will follow the orders of any man here, without question. The safe words are 'Red' and 'Yellow.' Have these been explained?"

Carla heard voices assuring the leader that the women had been told. "You understand that you must use these words if you feel any discomfort, either physical or mental. I emphasize the word must. If we find that you've been too polite to use the safe words when you should have, then everything will stop and you'll be escorted home. And that would be a shame."

"Yes, sire," Carla said.

"Now, will the gentlemen who brought our gifts for the evening please unwrap them.'' With a flourish, the capes were pulled from the three women's shoulders. Carla could see that the other women were cuffed and chained the same way she was and dressed in teddies, stockings, and shoes that matched their capes.

The leader started with the blond, whose cape and teddy were a soft rose. ''Vivian,'' he said, ''you're as beautiful as ever.'' The leader raised his right arm and slapped her hard on her naked ass.

''Thank you, sire,'' she said, a small smile playing around the corners of her mouth.

''For the two new men here tonight,'' the leader said, ''let me explain that Vivian likes her pleasure a little rough. Sometimes she deliberately disobeys commands and must be disciplined. Those who enjoy that type of play may want to stay with her for the evening.''

He moved to the tiny black woman. ''Shanna,'' he said, ''we haven't seen you for quite a while. And I see that you've cut your hair.''

''Yes, sire. I sincerely hope you approve.''

He tangled his fingers in her short fluff, dragged her head back, and kissed her hard. ''I do,'' he said finally. ''Down.'' Shanna clumsily fell to her knees despite her chains and pressed her forehead against the leader's shoe. ''As you see, Shanna is very well trained and will gladly do whatever she's told to. We are all happy to have her back with us this evening.''

He turned to Dennis. ''This one is new. Thank you for bringing her.'' To Carla he said, ''Do you have a name?''

Carla looked at Dennis from the corner of her eye and when he nodded, she said, ''Carla.''

''Carla what?''

She knew he wasn't asking for her last name. Softly, without lifting her eyes, she said, ''Carla, sire.''

''Very good. Very good indeed.'' He turned to the men gathered around. ''Blindfold them.''

Someone tied a soft cloth firmly around Carla's head. She heard the rustling and shuffling of people moving around, and the hum of lowered voices. Suddenly someone pinched her left nipple, which was proudly standing out through the opening in the front of her teddy. She gasped, but didn't move. "Nice," a voice said. Then several hands slid over her breasts, legs, and buttocks, the sensations heightened by Carla's lack of sight. "Very nice," another voice said.

Carla recognized the leader's voice. "Mark, I assume that you and Harry want to take Shanna." There was a pause, then he continued, "Good. Take her into room two. Paul, take Vivian across the hall."

"Thank you," a man's voice answered.

"I want to break in our newest guest myself," the leader said. "The rest of you," he laughed, "pick your pleasure. You have three lovely ladies from which to choose."

Carla was flattered at having been chosen by the leader. She had no idea how many other men were in the room. Someone thrust one finger between her legs. "She's very wet," a man said.

"Wonderful," the leader said. "She's a lovely piece, Dennis. You've done an excellent job."

"Thank you. Shall I undress her for you?"

The leader must have nodded because someone loosened the laces of the teddy and the garment fell from her body. Hands were everywhere, probing, stroking.

"She has the most fantastic boobs," a voice said. "May I have them?"

"I see no reason why not, Chet. Prepare her." Carla's hands were unlocked and a belt was buckled tightly around her waist. Her wrist cuffs were refastened above her elbows and then attached to rings at the sides of the belt. Her upper arms were now efficiently attached to her sides, leaving her lower arms free. Then she was pressed down until she was lying face up on a pad on the floor. Someone quickly spread her legs and fastened her ankle cuffs so she was held wide open. Hands checked to be sure that her blindfold was still in place.

"Thank you," the man called Chet said. Chet straddled her waist and squeezed her full breasts. "These are so big and full," he whispered. "I must have them." Hands rubbed something cool and slick all over her chest.

"Chet's in heaven," a voice said.

"If he's not careful he'll come before he's even started," the leader said, laughing.

"A hundred says he'll come in under two minutes." Carla heard a mix of voices.

"Hold them," Chat said, oblivious to what was going on around him. He grabbed Carla's wrists and pressed her hands against the sides of her breasts. "I said hold them!"

Carla had no idea what he wanted, but held her mounds the way Chet's hands showed her. Suddenly, she felt Chet's hard cock thrusting between her tits. He was fucking her breasts, driving his cock so hard that on each stroke it pressed against her chin. Now that she understood, Carla held her breasts tightly together, making a narrow channel for Chet's hard cock. He bucked against her breasts until he screamed and spurts of come covered Carla's chin and chest.

"One minute, forty-two seconds." There was a round of applause.

Almost immediately, Chet was lifted from Carla's body and damp cloths whipped over her chest and face. "You have great tits for fucking," the leader said. "How's your mouth?"

"I hope I am worthy, sire," Carla said, licking her lips.

"Open for me," he roared. When she did, he filled her mouth with his erection, pressing it all the way into her throat. The velvety length slid in and out of her mouth. She sheathed her teeth with her lips and tightened around his shaft.

"He'll come even faster than Chet," a voice said.

"Squeeze my balls, bitch," the leader snapped, and Carla did as she was instructed, tonguing and sucking until the leader came. She eagerly swallowed every drop.

"My Lord, she's a great little cocksucker," the leader said when he regained his voice. He rubbed her wet pussy. "And she's loving it all." Low voices said things that Carla couldn't quite hear. Then she heard the leader's voice. "Dennis. Since you brought her, you may play first."

Play?

"If you have no objections," Dennis said, releasing her arms, "I'd like to remove her blindfold."

"If you like." When the cloth was removed from her eyes, Carla blinked several times, then glanced around the room from where she lay on the pad. Her ankles were being held open by two men who sat so they had a full view of her wide-open pussy. Another man sat on a chair, intently watching her face. The leader lay near her hip, his head propped on his hand. She couldn't see Dennis until he walked around to her other side, something in his hand.

"Carla, darling," he said. "I have some toys for us to play with." Dennis opened a large black-and-red lacquered box and showed Carla the contents. Inside, a collection of dildos was arranged according to size. The smallest was about as slender as her pinky, the largest almost two inches around. "Let's see how much you can take." He inserted three fingers into her wet pussy, then selected the next to the largest dildo.

It looked too big to ever fit inside her, but as Dennis slid it into her waiting body Carla realized that she was filled completely. "Yes, that's just right."

Carla swallowed hard, trying not to lose control in front of all these men. She saw Dennis select a dildo about the size of his thumb from the other end of the collection. "How's your ass?" he asked.

"Virginal," was the only answer she could think of.

"Fantastic," the leader said. "Dennis, you're a lucky man."

As Dennis spread some lubricant on the dildo two men slid Carla's body forward so her knees were bent. One of the men rubbed cold, slippery gel around her rear hole, then Dennis pushed in the slender dildo until the flange at the base rested against her cheeks. Another man pulled a thin piece of fabric mesh from the belt in the back, and stretched it between her cheeks and across both dildos to anchor them securely in place. The mesh snapped to connectors at the front of the belt.

"How do you feel? Tell us, Carla."

"Strange. Filled, yet empty. Wanting. . . ."

"Ah, Dennis," the leader said. "A gem." There was a round of quiet applause, either for her or for Dennis.

Dennis reached into the box and pulled out a pencil-shaped rod. Suddenly, a humming sound filled the room and, as Carla watched, Dennis knelt on a pillow and inserted the wand through the mesh and into the dildo in her cunt. Shafts of pure pleasure coursed through her body and her hips bucked as much as her shackled ankles would permit. "Ahhh," she cried.

Dennis moved the dildo so the pulses touched every inside part of her. As one dildo pressed against the other, the vibrations flowed from her cunt to her ass. Dennis withdrew the rod, then slid the vibrating tip around her pussy, through her soaked folds. "Watch her," he said, "as I make her come."

"We will," the leader said. "I love it when a woman loses control."

Watch her come? It was humiliating, but erotic. She closed her eyes. "No," Dennis said. "Watch us as we watch you. I command your body and I can make you come whenever I want. All these men will be watching you and they'll know exactly when you lose control."

One man unzipped his pants, took his erect cock in his hand, and fondled his straining shaft. He caught Carla's eye and grinned, licking his lips.

"Are you ready, gentlemen?" Dennis asked.

"Ready, Dennis."

"Good. Carla, I'm going to make you come now, and you have no choice. We're all going to watch your hips buck and see your face as your climax fills your body. We will all know that you cannot resist."

Oh God, Carla thought. She was so hot that her entire body was quaking. Although it didn't feel right to want to be so controlled, she knew that he was right. She would come and Dennis knew it.

Dennis fitted the vibrator into the dildo in her ass and slowly moved it in deeper. "Now, Carla. Come for us." He rubbed her clit. "Keep your eyes open and watch these men come as they see you lose control."

She couldn't help it. She screamed as one of the strongest orgasms she had ever experienced took over her entire body.

"Oh fuck," a voice yelled. Carla looked up at the man stroking his cock and saw semen spurt from the tip and spatter on his hand and his pants legs.

Dennis turned the vibrator off, but left it inside Carla's body. He pulled down his pants and shorts and threw them on the bed. "Touch your pussy and make your hand wet." Carla did and Dennis took her slippery hand and placed it on his cock. "Hold your hand still so I can fuck it. Do it for me, Carla."

She held his cock in her hand and squeezed. Dennis moved his hips, forcing his erection through her tight fingers. Although she didn't move her hand, she tensed her fingers in rhythm, milking the come from his cock. "Oh that's so good," he said, groaning. "But it's too fast." Carla enjoyed rushing him, forcing him to come as he had forced her. She knew just where to press and squeeze. When he came she could feel the pulses throughout his cock.

The leader reached over, unsnapped the mesh, and pulled the dildos from Carla's passages. "Turn her over," he said, and the men quickly removed her shackles, turned her, then replaced her bindings so that she lay face down on the pad. The leader placed a pillow under her hips so her rear was in the air, then parted her cheeks with his fingers and rubbed more lubricant around her puckered hole. "So. You have never been fucked in the ass," he said, unrolling first one, then a second condom over his cock. Although he wasn't very large, Carla was afraid.

"No, sire," Carla said, tensing. She had always been a bit leery about anal sex and, so far hadn't been asked for it by any of her clients. Dildos were one thing, but she was unsure that she wanted to go this far. The leader watched her face as she considered.

"I won't come inside of you," he said, gently, "and I'm always very careful."

Although she had climaxed, Carla was still excited and intrigued by the idea of being fucked in a new way. She knew that she could call things off whenever she wanted so she deliberately relaxed her muscles and closed her eyes.

Sensing her agreement, the leader pressed his slick covered cock against her anus. As her body tensed and relaxed, he pushed, slowly forcing his hard penis into her rear passage.

"Oh, sire," she whispered. "That's so strange."

"It is good?"

She hesitated. "Yes, sire."

When he was as deeply inside as he could get, the leader took his index finger and rubbed her clit.

Blazing heat slashed through her body and orgasm took control again, her rear muscles clenching rhythmically on the leader's penis. "Yes! Yes!" Her orgasm went on and on, until she had no more to give.

"Ahhh," the leader said, pushing against her as she came. "Wonderful." He pulled his still-hard cock from her body, peeled off one condom, had his men turn her, and then he plunged his sheathed cock into her pussy, slamming it into her until he suddenly screamed, and spasmed inside her.

Later, when they had all cleaned up and were ready to leave, the leader kissed Carla deeply. "You were a marvelous addition to the evening's entertainment, darling. We'll be sure to let you know when we meet again. Please feel free to join us, whether Dennis can attend or not."

"Thank you, sire," she said, wrapping her dark blue cape around her naked body.

Dennis held her around the waist. "If she can be here, sire, you can be sure I'll bring her."

Carla smiled as she stepped into the limo.

Chapter 8

Ronnie and Carla were in the sunny kitchen of the brownstone finishing the last of a pint of chocolate-mint frozen yogurt. Falling snow created miniature drifts on the railing outside the living room window.

"Is something bothering you?" Carla asked.

"Jack's home."

"That's great," Carla said. Ronnie's husband had been overseas for the last month. "Isn't it?"

"Oh it's wonderful to see him, if only briefly." Ronnie put her dish on the coffee table and was silent.

"Come on, give," Carla said. "Trouble?"

Ronnie took a deep breath. "No, not really. Not anything I can put my finger on. It's just that, after what you and I do here, sex with Jack seems so ordinary."

"Ordinary?"

"You know. We fuck quickly and hungrily, and then he talks about business: oil, rock formations, three-dimensional computer models, helicopter surveys, whatever. We never talk about us, really. Our lives."

"That's part of the problem of being apart so much. You have so little day-to-day contact that you live in different places. Mentally, I mean. When my folks lived in Florida briefly a few years ago, my mother used to insist that I call at least once a week. She said that when you talk frequently all the everyday stuff is important, but when you only talk occasionally, it's hard to find anything worth mentioning.''

"That's true, I guess. It's also the sex.''

"No rushing across airports and fucking in the back seat of the car?''

Ronnie's laugh was warm and rich. "Lots of that. We're good together but it's just ordinary, somehow.''

"That figures.''

"Huh?''

"Of course sex with Jack is ordinary, unless you work hard at it. Everything we do here is exciting, first times with new people, new fantasies, toys, games, whatever. But it's just the same old Jack. Nothing new.''

"I guess.''

"Have you ever played fantasy games with him?''

Ronnie thought. "Not recently.''

"Well, take your own advice. Do what we always suggest that our clients do. Let your mind wander. You're one of the most skilled women I know at reading other men and their sexual desires. Read yours and his, for a change.''

"You know, you make a lot of sense.''

"Of course I do. I've learned from an expert. Do the two of you have time tonight?''

"Unfortunately, no. Not for a month or so. He's gone again.''

Ronnie looked so forlorn that Carla quickly changed the subject. "You know, I've had quite an education over the last three months so now I think it's time for you to tell me about that wild cruise you went on last summer.''

Ronnie licked the last of the yogurt from her spoon and dropped it into her bowl. "Yes, I suppose it is. Okay. You make coffee and I'll tell all.''

They wandered into the kitchen and Carla got the coffee from the fridge. While she set up the filter, Ronnie started her tale.

"It all began almost four years ago with Bob Skinner. He looked through my album and when he found the picture of me in that stern teacher outfit, he reacted immediately. We came back here and I disciplined naughty little Bobby who couldn't get his lessons right.

"A few weeks later, he selected the photo of me in that leather outfit holding the whip, and said, 'Would you be her for me, ma'am?' In that scenario, he calls me Mistress Ronnie. We've played both those fantasies frequently and he really gets off by being slapped around and made to do things."

"And that's what you did on the cruise?" Carla said, pouring water into the coffee maker. "Be Mistress Ronnie and whip him?"

"We discovered very early that it's not the pain that turns him on, although Bobby loves it when Miss Gilbert hits him with a ruler. Mostly he loves to feel powerless, to know that he must submit to all of my demands without question. He's hard all the time until I let him come. Some women don't let their subserviants come at all, but I make sure that Bobby climaxes every time we're together. Eventually."

"I'm so curious," Carla said, settling at the country kitchen table across from Ronnie, the room filling with the smell of brewing coffee. "Tell me about the cruise. How do they set it up? Aren't there other people on the boat?"

"Two couples started this group," Ronnie explained, "and they set up each cruise. We use the same ship, the *Atlantic Voyager* each year. It's small and they set aside a special area for just us, off-limits to the rest of the passengers: a private dining room, secluded deck space, and so on. And our cabins are in a roped-off area. The crew knows what we do and only those who've agreed to ignore what goes on work in our section." She sighed. "That caused an unusual situation this time, but I'll get to that later."

"How many people go on this cruise?"

"There are usually about thirty couples, most like Bob and me, a dominant mistress and her servant. A few are men with submissive women. We use common sense and rules, like you and I do with our customers. Everyone gives and gets pleasure and that's all that matters to any of us."

Carla nodded. Since she had gotten into power and control fantasies, first with Bryce and then with Dennis and the sex club, she had a much better understanding of the intense eroticism of dominance and submission.

"Some of the couples are into heavier activities than Mistress Ronnie and Bob. Some get into heavy pain and whips, shoe licking, and other things that Bob doesn't enjoy. But each of us knows our partner's tastes and we cater to them, and to ourselves. And we always use safe words."

"Are there many . . . professionals like us there?"

"Some are part-time relationships like Bob and mine, and some are married couples or partners who live together and are into dominant fantasies either full- or part-time. But both partners enjoy their roles and love the chance to submerge themselves in eroticism for a week."

"Okay," Carla said, pouring the steaming coffee into mugs. "Tell me everything."

"When we first arrived, Bob unpacked and put away our clothes while I wandered around our area of the ship. I ran into several women I remembered from the previous year and we sat on deck and discussed a few special activities we had planned. I have to tell you that talking about the upcoming week got me going. I couldn't wait to return to the cabin. When I arrived at our stateroom Bob was prepared."

"Everything's ready, Mistress," Bobby said as Ronnie walked back into the spotless cabin. He had arranged the closets carefully and Ronnie's clothes were all hanging or neatly folded. He had put his few outfits in a bottom drawer. He had set out two lightweight paddles on the small table. Several brown-paper-wrapped packages sat on the dresser where he had been instructed to put them. He had no idea what was inside but knowing Ronnie's creativity, curiosity made his cock hard.

"Very nice," she said and Bobby glowed with pride. "Are you ready as well?" Ronnie asked. She was dressed in a soft pink sleeveless blouse and a full deep blue peasant skirt. She wore

high-heeled sandals over her bare feet. Her toenails, like her fingernails, were painted deep red.

"Yes, Mistress," he said, staring at the floor. Ronnie circled
Bobby examining his outfit. He had changed since arriving on
shipboard and now wore only a pair of extremely tight black spandex shorts that enclosed his erect cock. He had fastened a leather
collar around his neck and he wore a green band around his right
bicep signifying his servitude. His feet were bare and he stared at
his naked toes.

Ronnie patted the giant bulge in the front of his shorts. "My
goodness. Have you been thinking about the mysterious packages?
Have you been wondering what's inside?"

"Yes, Mistress."

"Well, you'll find out." She patted his groin again. "And you'll
be glad."

"Thank you, Mistress. Is there anything you desire of me?"

"Yes. I think I'll let you pleasure me before dinner."

"Thank you, Mistress. How would you like me to do that?"

Ronnie glared at him. "You shouldn't have to ask. You should
know how to please me by now." She walked to a small chair
and sat down. "After you've done your job, you'll have to be
punished for your lapse of understanding."

Bobby knew that there was no way that he could have guessed
how to please Mistress Ronnie at that particular moment, but the
punishment was part of the excitement. And anticipating the punishment was another. But now he would give his mistress pleasure
and there was nothing better than that.

"Down," she said and Bobby got down on his hands and knees
and crawled toward her. "I need my feet massaged."

Carefully Bobby removed each of Ronnie's shoes and placed
them under the table in the corner of the room. Then he sat at his
mistress's feet and pressed his fingers deeply into her arch, which
he knew she loved. He massaged each foot and calf, then paid
careful attention to each toe until his fingers ached. Slowly Ronnie
relaxed. "Mistress, may I go further?" he asked, knowing better
than to look her in the eye.

"I think so," she answered, excited by Bobby's submissive behavior. "But first, take off my panties." When he reached for her undies, she added, "With your teeth."

He looked startled, but quickly addressed himself to the task. "Yes, Mistress," Bobby said. He rolled Ronnie's skirt up around her waist and, as he grasped the elastic of her bikini panties with his teeth, he could smell her musky aroma. She wanted him and that made him happy. He jerked at the elastic.

"Ouch!" Ronnie said, slapping him sternly on the shoulder. "Be gentle!"

"I'm sorry, Mistress." He pulled at the waistband gently, shifted to the other side, and pulled again. Ronnie moved her rear so he could slowly maneuver her panties over her hips, down past her knees, and off. Bobby picked up the wisp of dark blue silk with his teeth and placed it neatly on the bed. He gazed at Ronnie's cunt, newly shaved and now exposed for his viewing. There was something demanding about a shaved pussy and it excited Bobby so much that his cock became even more uncomfortable inside the tight shorts. But, of course, he knew that that was not Mistress Ronnie's concern.

Bobby massaged Ronnie's calves and thighs, reveling in both her relaxation and her building sexual excitement. "Mistress may I?" he asked, flexing his cramped fingers.

Ronnie shifted her hips to the edge of the chair and nodded. Bobby stroked the inside of each thigh, approaching but not touching her bare pussy. He brushed his mistress's outer lips with the tip of his finger, then with the tip of his tongue. "Please, Mistress."

"Please what?"

"Mistress, may I lick your clit?"

"All right," she purred.

Bobby knew how to please his mistress. He licked and sucked like a man possessed, his tongue and fingertips everywhere at once. He slid two fingers deep into her pussy and sawed them in and out. When he added a third finger and simultaneously sucked her clit, her muscles spasmed almost immediately. "That's so good," she moaned. "Don't stop."

He smiled. She knew he wouldn't stop until he had given her all the pleasure it was possible to give. He licked and stroked, adjusting his movements to her excitement level. Leaving his fingers quietly inside Ronnie's body, Bobby soothed her until she was calm, and then pulled his hands away.

"May I get you a glass of water?" he asked.

When she nodded, he opened a bottle of spring water he had placed in a bucket and poured her a glass.

"That was very good," Ronnie said, taking a long drink and patting Bobby on the head like a pet. "But there's still the matter of your punishment."

"Yes, Mistress."

"Since your tongue was so talented, you may pick the instrument you prefer."

"Thank you, Mistress," Bobby said, picking up a Ping-Pong paddle and handing it to Ronnie. "My pants, Mistress?"

"You may leave them on," Ronnie said.

Without another word, Bobby lay across his mistress's lap, his spandex-covered bottom ready for Ronnie's skillful application of the paddle. "Since I'm in a very good mood," she said, "I think ten will suffice for the moment."

"Thank you, Mistress."

The first three were light slaps and, with the covering of the tightly stretched shorts, Bobby felt only a general tingle. The next three were heavier, making his body jerk slightly with each one. Swats number seven and eight were harder still, stinging his ass and forcing his hard cock against Ronnie's thighs. Ronnie pulled the spandex down and administered the final two swats with all her strength on his bare cheeks. She pulled the stretchy fabric back up and patted his inflamed bottom.

"Mistress, please," Bobby said, his body quivering.

"Please what?"

"Please, I want to come. I'm so excited."

"Are you my good boy?" Ronnie asked, moving so her thighs rubbed his swollen member.

"Yes, Mistress."

"What if I say no?" She usually denied him any release for several hours. The women liked their slaves to be constantly erect, anxious to please in order to be allowed to climax.

"Oh sweet Jesus," Bobby said, sweat forming on his forehead.

Ronnie reached underneath him and squeezed him tightly. "Is that better?"

"Yes, Mistress," he said, although both of them knew it was not.

"You may come," Ronnie told him.

"My shorts?"

"Too bad. After you spurt they'll be all sticky inside." She smiled. "Of course, for the rest of the day, as you move, you'll be reminded of my generosity."

"Thank you, Mistress."

"Touch it yourself."

Standing in front of Ronnie's chair, Bobby rubbed the length of his rock-hard cock through the tight elastic fabric. When she sensed that he was almost ready to climax, Ronnie picked up the paddle and swatted his ass. He came, screaming.

For the rest of the afternoon, Bobby followed Ronnie around, sitting at her feet as she lounged with other women, fetching drinks and snacks for her and her friends, and watching the way the other women treated their slaves. He was so lucky, he realized, that Mistress Ronnie knew exactly what he liked.

That evening, at dinner, he cut Ronnie's meat and fed her, waiting until she was finished with her meal before he ate anything. The cruise ship staff discreetly ignored the goings on, although one busboy stared longingly at Ronnie.

After dinner, three of the women and their slaves put on a show. The men danced, slowly stripping, then one of the men was whipped by the other two under the direction of the women.

Bobby took part in a contest to see which of four naked men could hold out the longest against the sexual teasing of a woman who looked like an in-the-flesh Barbie Doll, with huge breasts and a tiny waist. The woman whose slave lost the contest and spurted semen all over the stage dragged the hapless man back to their cabin for what would undoubtedly be a long lesson in self-control. Ronnie praised Bobby for his ability to restrain himself and, as a reward, let him fuck her with a large dildo.

The following morning, Bobby unwrapped the packages Ronnie had brought. Inside one he found a flanged anal plug and in another a harness to both control his cock and keep the dildo in place. Ronnie lubricated the plug and filled his ass with it. Using the many buckles, she fitted the harness so that it held his balls away from his body, showed off his erect cock and held the dildo deep inside his ass. For the entire afternoon, he wore nothing else so that everyone in their part of the ship could examine his body and discuss his excitement level.

About four days into the cruise, Bobby was feeding Ronnie lunch when she noticed the busboy staring intently at her. He was in his late teens and of medium height with shoulder-length sun-bleached blond hair held with a rubber band at the nape of his neck and pale blue eyes that seldom left her hands. As she thought about it, Ronnie realized that he had been watching her since the week began. As he stared, she quite deliberately poured the contents of her water glass into an empty cup beside her and when Bobby tried to refill it, she waved him away.

"Young man," she said, pointing at the busboy, "I need more water." The other two couples at the table stared at her, obviously curious as to what was going on.

"Certainly," the busboy said, fetching the pitcher. When Bobby looked crestfallen, Ronnie said, "I know you like serving me but don't worry. You'll be rewarded later." She pointed to an area on the floor beside her chair and Bobby sat down.

As the busboy arrived with the water pitcher, Ronnie said, imperiously, "Pour very slowly and don't spill a drop."

"Yes, ma'am."

"You've been watching me," she said as the young man poured the water, his hand unsteady.

"Yes ma'am." The glass was about half full.

"Don't stop pouring," she said, unzipping the front of his black slacks. His hard cock sprung free, sticking out lewdly. She wrapped her hand around it and held tightly. The busboy's hand began trembling so much he spilled water on the table. "You spilled," Ronnie said.

"I'm terrible sorry, ma'am," the young man said.

"What's your name?" Ronnie asked, still holding his erection.

"Mike," he answered, gazing at Ronnie's filled water glass.

"Well, Mike, you've been very careless." Ronnie looked at the other two women and their subservients, all of whom were watching the scene before them intently. "What should we do with careless workers, Mike?"

"They should be punished."

"I agree," Ronnie said. "What are your duties for the rest of the afternoon?"

"I'm off duty at two and I don't have to serve again until dinner."

"Oh, you'll have to serve again before that." Ronnie glanced at her watch. Quarter of two. "Good. Report here to me at two-oh-one sharp."

"B-b-but I have to change out of my uniform. That will take at least five m-m-minutes."

"Two-oh-one. And I don't like to be kept waiting." She gave his hard cock a final squeeze.

Zipping his pants, Mike scurried away.

"May we stay and see the show?" one of the women asked.

"Of course," Ronnie said. The two women moved to the far side of the table, their men at their feet. Ronnie's heart was pounding. She particularly enjoyed the thrill of a first encounter with a man who wanted to be dominated. She looked at Bobby, sitting quietly at her feet. Since he was paying for the week, she had to be sure this was all right with him. "Yes?" she whispered. From the smile of his face, she knew it was fine.

Precisely at two-oh-three, Mike arrived in the small dining room dressed in jeans and a sweatshirt. His breathlessness was a result of either running from the kitchen or his excitement. Ronnie purposefully looked at her watch. "You're two minutes late."

"I did the best I could."

"Let's understand a few things. First, I am Mistress Ronnie and you will always address me that way."

Mike rubbed the palms of his hands down the thighs of his slacks and swallowed hard. "Yes, Mistress Ronnie."

"Good. Second, you will never look me in the eye. Your gaze must never be above my waist." Mike's eyes dropped. "Third, you will never wear anything from the waist up or the ankles down in my presence unless I expressly tell you to." When Mike didn't move, she added, "Is there any problem with that?"

"No, Mistress." As rapidly as he could, he pulled off his sweatshirt, kicked off his shoes, and dragged off his socks.

"I love the look of bare toes. Wiggle yours for me." He did.

"Have you ever been with someone like me before?"

"Yes, mistress." He hesitated and Ronnie motioned for him to continue. "Her name was Mistress Gail and she was my neighbor for a few months about a year ago. We were together only a couple of times."

"Good enough. Then you understand what is expected." Ronnie reached out and grabbed Mike's crotch. "Why me?"

Mike trembled. "You're very strong, and very beautiful. . . ."

"And . . . ?"

"And you treat your slave the way I'd like to be treated."

Ronnie removed her blouse and Mike stared at her bra, which had zippers up the center of each cup. "Unzip me with your teeth."

Hesitantly, Mike knelt down and took the tab of the left zipper between his front teeth. He pulled gently until one puckered brown nipple poked through the opening. "Bobby," Ronnie said, "the other."

Bob quickly complied. Ronnie placed one hand on the back of each head and forced one mouth to each breast. "Suck," she said, "and maybe I'll reward the one who does the best job." Ronnie leaned back, submerged in the sensation of two mouths on her body. "Nice," she said. "You are each doing a fine job."

Ronnie looked at the two other women who had been intently

watching the performance. Each of them had bared her breasts and had her slave servicing her nipples.

"Bobby," Ronnie said, waving the two men away, "you know how I like my pussy licked. Instruct Mike on the proper procedure." She slid forward on the chair until her hips were at its edge. When she parted her thighs, the two men saw that she wore no panties.

As Mike knelt between her spread legs, Bobby said, "See how wet she is. Doesn't she smell fantastic?"

Bobby showed Ronnie's newest servant how to stroke her inner thighs, flick his tongue over her swollen lips, and use his fingers to give her maximum pleasure. "Now," Bobby said, pointing to her clit, "rub her right there, just hard enough to make her feel it."

"Ummm," Ronnie purred. "So good."

To Bobby, this situation was unique, and incredibly erotic. He was not quite a servant, but not a master either. And he was anxious to show the newest slave how to satisfy his mistress.

"You're doing well," Bobby said, slightly jealous of Mike's ability to please. "She likes three fingers in her pussy if she is going to come." He hesitated. "Mistress. May I touch you as well?"

Ronnie nodded and Bobby took one nipple in each hand and pinched the swollen tips. With Bobby's hands on her tits, Mike's tongue lapping her pussy, and his fingers deep inside her cunt, Ronnie came. Her body jerked so hard that the two men had to struggle to stay connected.

"Oh, splendid," Ronnie said when her breathing returned to normal. She smiled at the two other women, each of whom was having her pussy serviced. "Are you very horny?" she asked her slaves.

"Yes, Mistress," they said in unison.

"Then strip. Quickly."

When they were naked, she said, "Face each other." The two men stood, close enough so that their erections were almost touching. "Now, hold each other's cock."

When they hesitated, Ronnie ordered, "Do it now!"

With a groan, each man reached out and wrapped his hand

around the other's cock. Ronnie remembered a conversation she had had with Bobby several months earlier when he had admitted to the dark fantasy of holding another man's cock and being held by him as well. She had decided to make it come true for him.

"Mistress, please don't make me do this," Bobby said. His body, however, said that, rather than stopping, he wanted to be forced.

"Quiet," Ronnie snapped, looking at Mike carefully. "And you, Mike?"

He bowed his head and whispered, "I will do whatever gives you pleasure. If it gives you delight to watch me do this, then I can only obey."

"Then, Mike, make Bobby come."

"Please no, Mistress," Bobby said.

Ronnie stared at him and raised an eyebrow.

"I'm sorry, Mistress," Bobby said.

"Good. Now you will both do as I say. Make each other come while I watch."

The two men stood, stroking each other's cock, watching their hands, their breathing hard and ragged. "Concentrate," Ronnie said and the men did.

"Cup each other's balls and fondle them. Use both hands!" As the small group watched, the two men acted out their hidden desire.

It took only moments until each man spurted semen on the other's hand. One of the women cried out her pleasure as her slave drove her to orgasm. The other climaxed silently.

"The rest of the cruise was delightful," Ronnie told Carla, sipping a fresh cup of coffee. "Mike spent each of the remaining afternoons with a different woman.

"How did you know about Bob's desire to touch another man?"

"He'd told me once, when I forced him to reveal his darkest fantasy, and his body language that afternoon was more than eloquent."

"You always seem to know how to find that extra bit of spice. How do you do it?"

"I've no idea. I guess I read my friends well." She tapped her forehead. "And I remember everything."

"I hope, someday, I'll be that good."

"You will," Ronnie said. "You will."

Jeffrey DeLancy III was an extremely dignified looking man in his mid forties with eyes that were almost navy blue and carefully trimmed, salt-and-pepper hair, beard, and moustache. A corporate attorney visiting New York, his three-piece suit was immaculately tailored and he wore a heavy gold ring with three channel-set sapphires on the ring finger of his right hand. When they met, Carla had commented on his well-developed body, and he had told her that he played racquetball and tennis as often as he could.

Now, as Carla returned from the ladies' room, Jeff was staring at the picture of the nightgowned woman clutching her bedclothes to her breast and staring, terrified, at someone just behind the camera. As Carla sat down he slammed shut the book. "Let's go back to your place," he said, picking up his coffee cup, then setting it down without drinking any. "This fantasy business is silly."

"We can go if you like," Carla said, "but I think there's something you want to tell me."

"I don't think so." He signaled the waiter for the dinner check.

"Jeff," Carla said, placing her hand over his, "tell me. That's what I'm here for."

"We both know what you're here for. So let's get to your place and do that."

"You don't have to tell me what's upsetting you," Carla said, "but I doubt that it's as bad as you think it is." Jeff sat silently staring into his coffee. "I saw which picture turned you on. That's Bethann and she was asleep when the burglar broke in. Do you know what he's going to do?"

Jeff's hand trembled under hers as she continued her story. "He's going to hold her down, feel her struggles, force her to bend to his will. She's afraid that she will be unable to fend him off." She was as excited by her recitation as Jeff obviously was.

"You're talking about rape," he said.

"Yes. But this is fantasy rape, not intended to actually hurt or do anything that Bethann's not willing to do."

"Fantasy rape, real rape. It's wrong however you define it."

"You know, nothing that goes on only in your mind is bad."

Jeff slowly raised his eyes and looked at Carla. "I wish I could believe that."

"You've got a fantasy. You want to rape a woman. Well not rape exactly. You don't want to really hurt her, just have her pretend to resist so you can subdue her. Force her. Right?"

The waiter arrived with the check, took Jeff's credit card, and disappeared.

"More people than you might imagine have rape fantasies," Carla continued. "As a matter of fact, I've always wanted to be ravished. Held down so that I couldn't move."

Jeff gazed into Carla's eyes. "You mean that, don't you?"

"I really do. While I was having that picture taken, I was thinking about the man who would tear off Bethann's clothes."

"Will Bethann fight the burglar?" he asked softly.

"She'll fight very hard."

"She'll know that he won't really hurt her, but she'll fight anyway? Struggle and try to get away?"

"Yes," Carla whispered. "Let's just be clear about two things. First, 'popcorn' is the safe word. If either of us says that, everything stops. And second, you'll use a condom even if it's out of character."

Jeff looked into her eyes, believing that this might actually happen. "Popcorn. Everything stops." He pulled out his wallet and slipped five crisp one-hundred-dollar bills into the black leather envelope. "I understand."

They traveled to the brownstone in silence and Carla motioned to Jeff to wait downstairs. She ran to the closet then back downstairs and handed Jeff some loose-fitting black sweatpants and a black turtleneck shirt. "When the light goes out, Bethann will be in bed, asleep. There has never been a burglary here, you know, but Bethann has always been worried."

Carla hurried back upstairs and pulled off her clothes. Knowing that many men have fantasies about ravishing a woman, she and Ronnie had adjusted several pieces of lingerie by clipping a few threads to make them almost fall apart if someone yanked. She slipped on a specially prepared kelly green charmeuse short gown, climbed into bed, pulled the sheets up to her chin, and turned out the light.

Minutes later she saw a dark form slip through the doorway. Light suddenly filled the room and a hand pressed across her mouth, forcing her against the mattress. "Don't scream," the voice hissed. His other arm snaked across her belly, pinning her down. "I just want your jewelry."

She struggled, trying to get free but he was too strong. But she had to be sure he understood the rules. "Popcorn," she mumbled. Reluctantly, he eased the pressure against her mouth and stood up. Carla stared into Jeff's eyes, deep blue against his black turtleneck. "You understand."

He nodded and she smiled. She slid across the bed, away from him. "Don't hurt me," she whimpered. "I'll tell you where all my jewelry is."

He watched her heaving chest. "I've changed my mind," he said in a menacing tone. "I've decided I don't want your jewelry. I want you."

"No, please," Carla said, getting into her part. Even pretending, the danger felt incredibly real and exciting. Her heart pounded as she grabbed the sheet and held it against her breasts.

Jeff crossed the room and theatrically closed the door. "You're not getting away," he said, "but you can try, of course."

"Don't hurt me," Carla said in a tiny voice.

"I won't hurt you unless you resist." He grabbed Carla's wrist and dragged her across the bed. He tangled his hand in her short hair and pulled her head back.

Carla's eyes widened. His hand in her hair hurt, but the discomfort excited her. She tried to twist her head to avoid Jeff's mouth which was slowly descending on her, but his hold in her hair allowed her almost no movement. She used her fists to pound on his chest, but it was like hitting a board. His mouth captured hers and molten heat flowed through her lips. Somehow it wasn't just a kiss, it was possession.

Jeff climbed onto the bed and straddled Carla's hips, effectively pinning her to the bed. He leaned forward, pressing his forearms on hers and holding her head with both hands in her hair. "You're mine," he growled, "whether you want it or not."

"Please, let me go. I won't tell anyone you broke in here." Real tears pooled in the corners of her eyes. "Please."

"Not a chance, lady," Jeff said. His mouth moved over her face, licking her eyelids and nipping at her earlobes. "I can do anything I want and you've got no way to stop me." He grabbed the front of her green nightgown and pulled. The fabric parted easily, leaving Carla naked.

She had to get away. She relaxed for a moment, then with a burst of energy, she arched her back and pulled her arms free. As Carla lay on the bed panting Jeff suddenly needed to get out of his clothes. He pulled the dark turtleneck over his head and tossed it on the floor. His pants and shorts followed and, erect and huge, he climbed back on top of his victim. "You've had enough time to contemplate what's going to happen."

Again Jeff grabbed her wrists and held her arms above her head. He devoured her mouth, forcing his tongue inside to duel with hers, rubbing his naked, lightly furred chest sinuously against her chest. "Nice," he rumbled. He released her wrists and held her head as he kissed her face and neck.

"No," Carla yelled, dragging her fingernails across Jeff's back. "Let me go."

"A regular wildcat," he said. He used the weight of his body to pin Carla to the bed, then slapped her hard across her thigh.

His handprint stung, but it also increased the heat in her groin. It was hard to fight against being raped when being possessed by him was exactly what Carla wanted.

Again and again he slapped her until his hand began to sting. "Had enough?" he asked.

Carla nodded, blinked hard. "Just don't make me . . . you know.

I'm a nice girl. I've never been with anyone but my husband. Don't force me. Please.''

"Ah," Jeff said, "but I will do just that." He slipped on a condom, then held his hard cock at the entrance to Carla's pussy. Sensuously, he rubbed it against her clit. "You say you don't want me," he said. "I'm a rapist, forcing you to accommodate me, but your body is wet. You must be very evil."

"I'm not wet. I don't want you." She struggled, dragging her fingernails down Jeff's back and across one shoulder. Bright red tracks appeared down his skin.

"Your body says different." He guided his turgid erection to her opening and pushed. "And you can't stop me anyway." He pressed his hips forward and drove his cock into her. "You're wet and wide open so I can fuck you." His fantasy was so real that he lost control, pounding into his victim until he arched his back and spurted semen deep inside of her in shuddering pulses. Panting, he collapsed on top of her.

Carla stroked his back and ran her fingers through his hair. "That was so good," she whispered.

"It was unbelievable," he said, his body limp and exhausted. The scratches on his back stung. He rolled to one side and Carla walked, naked, to the bathroom. She returned with some antiseptic and applied some to his back and shoulder.

He looked at the welt on one side of his chest. "I'll enjoy looking at that for days," he said, running one finger over the mark.

"I'm glad. I was afraid of doing damage."

"And I'm really sorry if I hit you too hard."

"You didn't."

Jeff put his clothes on. "Thanks for a fantastic evening," he said. "May I call you again?"

"Of course. Bethann will always be here, as well as any other women you want to be with."

"I'm glad. You'll be hearing from me."

As the winter waned, Carla and Ronnie spent one day every week sharing experiences, since they were the only ones with whom they could discuss their flourishing business. Each Monday Carla packed her boys off to school, tidied the house after the weekend, and then drove into the city. Ronnie discovered R & R's Gourmet Take-out and each week she picked up a luxurious luncheon, usually a pasta salad and one of the unusual breads for which R & R's was famous. When she returned to the brownstone, she selected a bottle of fine wine from the cellar and made sure that it was the proper temperature.

One Monday, after a particularly sumptuous meal of prosciutto and cantaloupe, rottini and mushroom salad, and crusty, hot sesame bread, Carla and Ronnie slipped off their shoes and stretched out at opposite ends of the living room sofa, their bare feet on the coffee table. "That was a particularly good Sauvignon Blanc," Carla said.

"You know, six months ago you wouldn't have known it was a Sauvignon. You've grown, you know."

"I know. Every now and then I say something to my mother and she gives me that look. You know the 'I didn't teach you that so how could you possibly understand it' look."

"Oh yes, I know it well." She sipped her second glass of the full, flavorful wine. "Carla, I have something I'd like to discuss with you."

"Sure, shoot." Carla set her glass down and her body became more alert.

"Occasionally one of my friends makes a request that I'm not sure I can fulfill." She toyed with the stem of her wine glass.

"Are you getting coy with me?" Carla asked.

"No, but this is a bit unusual and it involves you." Heat flushed Ronnie's cheeks.

"You're blushing. I don't believe it."

Ronnie laughed. "Neither do I. Anyway, I've been getting together with one friend every month or so for years. He enjoys selecting erotic stories from magazines, scenes from novels, things like that, reading them to me, then acting them out. He's very creative and I've learned a lot from him and his stories." She sipped her wine.

"You're working up your courage, Ronnie. I can tell. Just remember there's nothing you can ask or tell me that will change our friendship."

"Thanks. He read me a story about two women involved in a torrid love scene. In the story, a man first watches, then joins in their lovemaking."

"Oh," Carla said, suddenly uncomfortable.

"I realy didn't know how to broach the subject to you since we've never even mentioned that type of sex. If it turns you off, let's drop it right now."

"You obviously didn't say no to him or we wouldn't be discussing it now."

Ronnie sighed. "No, I didn't."

"Have you ever been with another woman?" Carla asked, in a small voice.

"Yes," Ronnie said. "In college. Although we were roommates, even you didn't know."

"No," Carla said, surprise showing in her voice. "Who?"

"Remember Evelyn Sage?"

"The gorgeous blond with the tremendous eyes and great skin. She had the most fantastic breasts as I recall. I always wondered whether they were hers or silicone."

Ronnie laughed. "She was fantastic looking all over, wasn't she? They were her own. Anyway, we had been in several of the same classes and we got together to study on occasion. Somewhere during our junior year she casually mentioned to me that she thought I was very attractive and she wondered whether I felt the same way about her. One thing lead to another, and another, and another. Anyway, we had been together only a few times when I met Sid."

"I remember him. You and he got pretty heavy for a while."

"We certainly did. He was into skin. Used to love to give me back-rubs with scented oils. But while we were dating, I didn't see Evelyn and by the time Sid and I broke up, she was with someone else."

"Did you enjoy it with her?" Carla asked.

"Very much," Ronnie answered. "It was new and different and very sensual. I've been with several women since then, always brief flings. I assume you've never done anything like that."

"Never," Carla said, sipping her wine. "This is hard to admit but I guess I've always been a little curious."

Ronnie looked Carla in the eye. "I'd love to show you but I don't want it to spoil our friendship."

"Would it?" Carla asked, now curious at the prospect.

"I don't know. I hope not. But if anything ever feels wrong, just tell me and I'll stop."

"Isn't that what we tell everyone before we play?"

"I guess so." Ronnie put her glass on the table, then leaned over and whispered in Carla's ear. "It will be wonderful. I've fantasized about you. In my fantasy you're here just like this."

Ronnie's breath on her ear made Carla's heartbeat speed and her breathing deepen. Her doubts dissolved and she relaxed.

"Close your eyes and just feel." Ronnie watched Carla's eyes close. "Good. Like that. Don't move. Just feel." Ronnie touched the tip of her finger to Carla's mouth and saw her lips part. "Your lips are so soft. So moist and smooth." She touched Carla's teeth and brushed her nail against Carla's tongue. "Does that tickle?"

Carla was awash in sensations. Nothing sexual had happened but her body tingled and her pussy was swollen. But she was in no hurry. She pursed her lips around Ronnie's finger and sucked lightly.

"Oh yes," Ronnie whispered in Carla's ear. "Suck my finger." She allowed Carla to draw her finger into her mouth, then pulled it slowly outward. In and out, mimicking the fucking motion that they had both experienced so often in the past. The rhythm was primitive and deeply sexual. Ronnie pressed the tip of her tongue into Carla's ear, echoing the rhythm the two women had established.

Carla had never imagined that such simple things could be so deeply sensual. She was sucking Ronnie's finger as her friend fucked her ear with her tongue. Suddenly her blouse was in her way. She wanted her breasts free.

Carla reached for her buttons but Ronnie stilled her hand. "Don't move at all. Let me be in charge of everything." With a nip at Carla's earlobe, Ronnie pulled her finger from her friend's amorous mouth and unbuttoned her blouse. "Your nipples are so swollen. Are they uncomfortable under your bra? Do they want to feel my hot mouth?"

"Oh yes," moaned Carla.

Ronnie parted the front of Carla's blouse and stroked her palm over her friend's erect nipples through the satiny fabric. "I can feel how hard they are. Do you like my hand?" When Carla moaned again, Ronnie continued, "It's real, isn't it? You want more, I know that. Your heart is pounding and you can't seem to get air into your lungs."

Ronnie leaned over and took one nipple in her teeth. Although the sensation was diminished somewhat by her bra, the nipping drove Carla wild.

"I like it that this bra fastens in the front," Ronnie said. "I can unfasten it without you moving. And I don't want you to move, even a little." With a deft flick of her fingers, Ronnie unclipped Carla's bra and separated the cups so her breasts were free. "Such beautiful breasts, baby," Ronnie whispered. "I've seen you naked many times, and each time I've imagined how your gorgeous nipples would taste."

Ronnie cupped Carla's large breast, weighing the handful. "Heavy and ripe. And hungry. Flesh can be hungry, you know, needing my touch." She drew her fingers from the outside of the breast in her hand to the pink center, pulling at the nipple. She repeated the motion over and over until Carla thought she would go mad from wanting.

"I want you," Carla said, "and need you."

"You need me to do what? Give you pleasure? I'm doing that. Need me to increase the heat? Oh baby, yes." Ronnie leaned over and licked one erect nipple with the flat of her tongue. Then she drew back and blew on the wet tip. Alternately she wet the tight bud, then cooled it with her breath. "Is that driving you wild?" she asked as Carla's hips began to move.

"You're making me crazy," Carla murmured. "My pussy is going to explode."

"No, it's not and that's the wonderful part. Your pussy will get hotter and hotter but you won't come until we're ready. And it'll be so intense I'll be able to feel it, share it with you." Ronnie quickly pulled off Carla's jeans and panties, then removed her own clothes. "I want to be naked like you are."

Carla reached out to touch Ronnie's naked skin. "Not yet," Ronnie said. "This is for you. I don't want you to do anything at all. Another time you can touch me but this time is just for you." Carla's hand dropped to the sofa. "That's a good girl. Just feel."

Ronnie licked Carla's nipple again, then drew it into her mouth. She sucked hard, causing a tightness to flow from Carla's breast to her pussy. It was as though the sucking made a path through her body and Carla could feel the pull between her legs.

"Is your pussy wet?" Ronnie asked.

"Yes," Carla murmured. "I'm so excited I don't know what to do. I can almost reach my climax, but not quite."

"I can reach it for you," Ronnie whispered. "Now spread your legs so I can see your magnificent pussy. Spread them wide. Put your feet on the edge of the table and open your knees for me."

Carla did what Ronnie's deep throaty voice told her. She opened her body as Ronnie moved so she was on her knees on the carpet between Carla's spread legs.

Ronnie watched Carla's soaked pussy twitch with excitement. How long could she keep her friend on the edge of climax without letting her over the edge? There was so much pleasure she could give. She bent her head to one side and allowed her hair to brush the inside of Carla's thigh. She allowed the strands to slide over Carla's white skin, tickling and stimulating. Ronnie blew a stream of air at the other thigh.

Carla was going crazy. She was sure she would fly apart in a million pieces and she didn't think she would even feel the explosion. "You're torturing me," she whispered, reaching for Ronnie's head to force it between her legs.

"Don't do that, baby," Ronnie said, replacing Carla's hands at her sides. "Hold still and let me show you how good this can be. Be patient."

"It's making me crazy."

"Is it bad?"

Carla hesitated. "No. It's wonderful."

"I promise I won't make you wait too long." She used one finger of each hand to part Carla's outer lips, then slowly explored her folds with her tongue. "You taste delicious," she said, continuing her exploration. Then she found Carla's clit with the tip of her tongue. "You can come soon," she said, flicking her tongue over the swollen bud. "And your climax is going to be so big I'm going to share it with you."

Ronnie took one finger and slid it into Carla's pussy, while she slid her other hand between her own legs, rubbing and circling over her clit. A second finger joined the first in Carla's pussy. As she filled her friend's cunt she flicked her tongue back and forth over her clit as she fingered herself.

"Oh God," Carla screamed. "Oh God."

"Let it come, baby," Ronnie said. "Don't say anything. Concentrate on what I'm doing to your body. Don't move. Hold perfectly still so you can enjoy my fingers and my tongue." She blew hot air over Carla's inner lips. "Yes. Share your climax with me." Her tongue licked and her fingers drove in and out.

Pressure built in Carla's belly. Waves of pleasure began to crest. "Don't stop," Carla cried. "Don't stop." Ronnie continued tonguing her friend's clit. Then she shifted her licking to her inner lips, around her fingers. She used the fingers to spread Carla open, then licked all the flesh her tongue could reach.

And then Carla came. The spasms continued, longer than Carla had thought possible. It was a different kind of orgasm than any she had ever experienced. It wasn't the hard, fast kind she had when she masturbated, nor was it the kind she had with her pussy filled with a man's hard cock. It was deep inside, and wonderfully different.

Ronnie slowed her movements until Carla's body calmed. She collapsed onto the sofa, took Carla's hand and gently guided it to her own hot cunt. "Rub gently, just the way you like to be touched." Carla moved so she could watch her fingers while they explored and massaged Ronnie's hot, wet flesh. Ronnie held Carla's hand and used it to bring her to orgasm. "Like that," she cried, "just like that." Gales of pleasure overpowered her.

The living room was quiet for a time, then Ronnie said, "Oh God. That was amazing."

"It was magic," Carla said. "Different somehow."

"I know," Ronnie said, her breathing calming. "But it doesn't detract, at least for me, from heterosexual sex. I enjoy that as much as I ever did."

"I'm glad you said that," Carla said. "I was afraid that you'd be insulted if I did. This was a treat, but I still like men."

"If the situation arises, would you be interested in doing that while someone watches and participates?"

"Yeah, I think I would. You know how I enjoy being watched. Being the passive one makes me crazy."

"And I enjoy calling the shots. We're made for each other and for this business."

"Well," Carla said, "I guess that's settled." She picked up her wine glass. "To new experiences. Especially ones that pay well."

Ronnie took a big swallow of her wine. "Salute."

Chapter 9

Over the months, Ronnie had visited Carla's house in Bronxville many times. With no family of her own, she had become Aunt Ronnie to the boys, and Carla's parents had taken her into the fold. Every time the subject of their business came up, the two women would sidestep any questions, saying only that they were in the public relations field, working for corporate clients, and doing very well.

One evening, while the boys were in their rooms, ostensibly doing their homework, Ronnie and Carla relaxed in the living room of Carla's modest house. "I envy you," Ronnie said, wistfully. "Sometimes I wish Jack and I had kids."

"Sometimes I wish I could lend them to you for a few months. Did BJ thank you for his birthday present? Ronnie, getting him his own phone was really extravagant. The bills may be exorbitant."

"He did thank me, and the bills won't go over a fixed amount that he and I have already agreed on. And I love doing it for him. By the way, don't tell Mike, but I'm getting him his own TV for his birthday next month."

"You're too much. You miss having your own children, don't you?"

"I do. But I often think that Jack and I wouldn't have made good parents anyway. We're too self-centered. We enjoy our creature comforts, like quiet and privacy."

"God knows, you get little of either with three growing boys in the house. How is Jack?"

"He's good. He's in the used-to-be Soviet Union, somewhere that ends in 'istan,' I think. I talked to him just a few days ago."

Carla saw the wistful look on Ronnie's face. "You miss him."

"Yeah, I do. I sometimes wish that he'd give up the traveling. Maybe we'd have a real life."

"Would you give up the business if he was home every evening?"

"I don't know. What about you? You and Bryce see a lot of each other. Are you two getting serious?"

"I don't know that either. He was here last weekend."

"No! With your parents and the boys?"

"Yup. We spent the day ice skating with the kids, then had a big family dinner." She laughed. "I thought my parents were going to start making wedding plans right then and there. My mother's talked to me several times since. 'He's well-off and he likes the boys' she keeps saying."

"And. . . ."

"And nothing. He's a nice man and we have great times together." She lowered her voice. "Both in and out of bed. But that's not enough to build a life on."

"Give in time," Ronnie said.

"I have lots of that. And besides, I'm having too much fun in *public relations.*"

A few weeks later Carla and Ronnie double dated for the first time. Glen Hansmann was an executive with a motion picture production company. Ronnie had entertained him several times, to their mutual delight. About a week earlier, Glen had called and left his name on her answering machine.

"Ronnie, babe," he told her when she called back. "I know I've asked you this several times, but any chance of a double date? My friend Vic O'Keefe is in from the west coast and I'd love to do dinner with you and a friend. You understand. Some dinner and entertainment."

"I do have a friend. Her name's Carla and her fee is the same as mine."

"That's super," Glen said, "and the fee's no problem. Is next Tuesday evening okay?"

"I don't know whether Carla's available," Ronnie said. "But if she's around that evening I see no reason why it wouldn't work."

"Good. Check with her and call me back. And if she's anything like you, I can't wait."

Ronnie called Carla immediately and explained the situation. "How would you feel about a double? I don't know what they'll want, but I think we're ready for anything. And it's a Tuesday."

"It sounds fine. Hang on and let me check next Tuesday." Carla flipped pages in her appointment book. "Believe it or not, next Tuesday is the only night I have free for the next month. It must be fate."

Glen Hansmann was not at all what Carla had expected. He was in his late forties, soft spoken and rather sweet, with light eyes and a dimple in his chin. His shoulder-length dark brown hair curled just above the collar of his light blue dress shirt. Carla noticed that his hands were beautiful, long slender fingers with perfectly manicured nails. Other than a functional wrist watch, he wore no jewelry.

Vic O'Keefe, on the other hand, was a Hollywood cliché. His tan was too perfect, accented by the laughter-created crinkles of lighter skin at the corners of his eyes. He wore a ruby ring on his right hand and a heavy good-and-steel Rolex watch on his left wrist. His voice was too loud, as was his tie, and he spent the first hour of the evening trying to impress the two women, dropping names and discussing all the exotic places he had been. At one point Carla caught Ronnie's eye and their expression spoke volumes about their long evening ahead.

Finally, Glen had had enough. "Vic," he said when the man paused for breath, "you're not usually like this. Remember that these girls are ours for the evening. You don't have to impress them." His fingers drummed on the tablecloth.

Vic was quiet for a moment, then looked apologetic. "I'm really sorry. I guess I'm so used to Hollywood types that I'm out of practice with real people. I know the arrangement. It's just that you two are so attractive I forgot.''

"That we're bought and paid for?'' Ronnie said, a slight edge in her voice. The evening threatened to become a disaster.

With a disarming grin, Vic said, "Open mouth, insert foot, and take a giant step. I'm really not a bad guy, you know.'' His rueful smile seemed genuine. "How about we just forget my gaucherie and start again.'' He stood up, walked around the table, and sat down again. "Hi, everyone. My name's Vic.''

Slowly a smile spread across Ronnie's face. "Hi. I'm Ronnie.''

The remaider of the sumptous meal sped by, fueled by good conversation and easy humor. As the foursome sat over coffee Vic said, "Okay, what's the difference between a tire and three hundred used condoms?''

"I give up,'' Ronnie said, "what?''

"A tire is a Goodyear. Three hundred used condoms is a great year.'' Everyone laughed. "You know, I can't remember when I've enjoyed a dinner more,'' Vic continued, looking at his watch. "And Glen and I have arranged a special surprise that we hope you'll like.''

"Absolutely,'' Glen continued. "We've gotten the private use of the spa, pool, and hot tub at Vic's hotel for the rest of the evening. It usually closes at nine o'clock, but I slipped the concierge a little cash and can pick up the key at the desk.''

"Sounds like fun,'' Ronnie said, checking her watch, "and it's already nine-thirty. We're ready if you are.''

The two couples, Ronnie with Vic and Glen with Carla, traveled to Vic's hotel. The three waited while Glen picked up the key to the spa. Together, the four slipped through an unmarked door into a back hallway. Giggling, they followed Glen through another door and found themselves in a workout room filled with exercise equipment. "Nice,'' Carla said. "This is some facility.''

"Let's try some of it out,'' Vic suggested. Quickly, the men were out of their suits and down to their shorts. "Undies only,'' Vic called so Ronnie and Carla stripped to their bras and panties.

"Have either of you ever done circuit training?" he asked, staring at the two beautiful bodies magnificently displayed in bras and panties.

"I do aerobics, when I have the time," Carla answered.

"And I'm a confirmed couch potato," Ronnie added.

"I can show you how to use this stuff. I work out a lot," Vic said.

Ronnie looked over Vic's well-developed body, his wide shoulders, heavily muscled arms, flat stomach, and tight buns and she smiled. "I'm sure you do."

Carla walked behind Glen and ran her hands over his muscular back. "I'll bet you've seen the inside of a gym too," she whispered against the back of his neck. She smiled as she felt his muscles tense and his back straighten. "From time to time," he said, sucking in his stomach.

Vic tapped the seat of an arm-exercise maching. "Let's see how you'd look on here," he said to Ronnie. She sat on the seat and Vic placed her arms on the padded upper armrests. "Now, press down," he said, "then release very slowly. It works your biceps and triceps." As she pressed, he watched her chest muscles swell, lifting her breasts. As she reached the bottom of the machine's travel, he reached out and brushed his fingers over Ronnie's nipples. Smiling, she released her pressure and allowed the machine to return to its starting position.

Glen showed Carla how to lie on her back on the platform of the leg-press machine. He positioned her feet about twelve inches apart on the footrest and showed her how to use her quadriceps to straighten her legs. Several times he adjusted the weights so it took only a moderate amount of strength to extend her legs. "Now," he said, "try to hold your legs straight." Once she had her legs straight, she locked her knees to hold the foot support as far from her body as she could. Glen slid a stool next to the machine, sat down, and rubbed his fingers against the crotch of her panties.

"Hey," Carla said, giggling, "that makes this much more difficult." With the soft warmth spreading through her body, she had to concentrate on keeping her knees locked.

"Yeah, it certainly does." He placed one hand on each of her thighs, pressing his palms lightly against her skin. "Okay. Now release and press." As Carla relaxed, then extended her legs, Glen felt the tension in her muscles under his hands. Carla's body shined with sweat as she continued to do leg extensions.

Ronnie moved from the arm machine to a device Vic called an adductor. Vic sat her down on the padded seat and, spreading her legs at a forty-five-degree angle, placed her legs in the supports. He fiddled with the weight setting. "Try to close your legs," he said.

Ronnie used all her strength to try to press her thighs together. "Not a chance," she said.

"Good," Vic said. He walked around and knelt between her widely spread legs. He yanked at the tendrils of pussy hair that escaped around the crotch of her panties and heard her gasp. Quickly, he soothed the smarting skin, then pulled her hair again. Ronnie gave up trying to force her thighs together, closed her eyes, and relished the sensations that Vic was causing. "Makes you crazy, doesn't it?"

"God, you know it." Ronnie shuddered.

Vic grinned. "I certainly do." He pressed his mouth against the crotch of her panties and nipped at the flesh and fur beneath. His hot breath warmed her lubricating pussy.

"See what Vic's doing?" Glen said to Carla. She turned and watched Vic's face buried between Ronnie's legs. "Now straighten your legs," Glen said. Carla's thigh muscles were getting tired but she pressed the footplate. Glen cupped one hand against her cunt and tweaked her nipples with the other. Carla wanted to sink into the erotic pleasure, but she had to concentrate to keep her knees locked. "Shit, Vic," Glen said, "I never imagined the uses you can put these machines to."

"Enough for now," Vic said, lifting Ronnie's legs from the adductor machine. "I'm for the hot tub."

Glen helped Carla stand and stretch and after a few minute's walking, her legs felt stronger again.

The foursome walked into the dimly lit pool and hot tub area. Glen stopped beside the steaming water and wrapped his arms around Carla. While caressing her back, he pressed his lips against hers, flattening her full breasts against his powerful chest.

Vic and Ronnie sat on a bench and Vic caressed Ronnie's face with his fingers and his lips. For long minutes, the two couples kissed, adding fuel to the building sexual fires.

Finally, Vic pulled away from Ronnie and flipped the controls for the air and water jets. "Last one in the hot tub is a rotten egg," he said. Still in their underwear, the four slowly settled into the bubbling water, hands and mouths exploring as they moved.

Glen unfastened Carla's bra and tossed the wet fabric across the tiled room. He bent his head and licked the top of Carla's half-submerged breast. "You taste of chlorine," he said.

Ronnie placed one hand on Vic's shoulder and whispered into his ear. "You do exactly what Glen does. Watch very carefully and imitate him, move for move." She felt his back tighten and then the tell-tale trembling for his shoulders.

Vic looked at Glen and saw his friend's tongue laving Carla's breast. "It feels weird to watch."

"Do it to me," Ronnie said. Vic removed Ronnie's bra and slid his tongue over her skin.

Glen lifted Carla's breast and his mouth reached for her nipple. Carla deliberately settled more deeply into the water so that, when he attempted to take a rosy crest into his mouth, he got a face full of bubbles. They giggled and wrestled until Glen had his arms wrapped around Carla's ribs and she was floating, her breasts out of the water.

Vic was kissing and nuzzling Ronnie's neck when Ronnie whispered, "Look what they're doing now, Vic. You're really not watching carefully enough." She reached down into the swirling water and squeezed his cock, hard.

"Ow," he cried, his breath caught in his throat. The pain seemed to make his cock harder.

"Then pay more attention."

Quickly, Vic repositioned Ronnie's body and suckled her breast, his breathing fast and ragged. Ronnie smiled, knowing that she had found the best way to give him pleasure.

Still supporting her upper body on one arm, Glen lifted Carla's legs onto the tiled edge of the tub. He bent her body at the hips until a jet of warm water shot directly against her swollen lips. "Oh God," she cried. "That's wonderful."

"I want you to play with the water too," Ronnie said to Vic, "but I want it to spray against your cock. Kneel here." She moved his knees onto the ledge and pressed her hand into the small of his back. His erection was now directly in the stream of another warm-water jet. "Oh shit, baby," he hissed. "I'll come if you keep doing that."

"And if you do," Ronnie said, "we'll just have to start again." She held Vic's body in the water stream until she felt him shudder. She reached around and held his cock as he came in the water, his semen feeling thick and gooey through his cotton shorts.

Carla was about to climax as well. Glen sucked on her breast and rubbed his finger against her rear as the water pulsed against her cunt. It was so quick and so intense that her orgasm took her by surprise.

"Oh baby," Glen purred. "You're hot as a pistol. I want to fuck you good, but I've got no rubbers."

"Sit up here," Carla said, patting the edge of the tub, "and let me take care of you." As he climbed up, she pulled off his shorts so that, when he was seated, his cock stuck straight up from his lap.

"Look at that hard cock," Ronnie whispered into Vic's ear, feeeling him getting hard again. "Do you know what she's going to do?"

"Yes," he murmured.

"Well, you're going to watch. Have you ever watched a woman suck cock in person? So close you can touch her?" Vic shook his head. "Good," Ronnie purred. She and Vic moved beside Carla in the water. "Now watch very carefully," Ronnie said. "Watch her mouth as she gives Glen pleasure."

Carla licked the hollow behind Glen's knee, then kissed and bit the inside of his thighs while Ronnie kept up a running commentary in Vic's ear. "She's licking his leg," Ronnie said, scratching her fingernail up his skin. "Right here."

Carla slipped her hand between Glen's thighs and tickled his heavy balls. Ronnie did the same with Vic, while saying, "I'll bet his balls feel tight and hard. See his cock? It's hard and throbbing." Ronnie pulled Vic's shorts off under the water and placed the wet garment on Glen's knee. "Hey Glen," Ronnie said. "I just want you to know that Vic is naked under the water and I'm holding his cock."

Carla wrapped her hand around Glen's cock. "Like that?" she asked Ronnie.

"Just like that."

"And if I slide my fingers right to the end?" Carla asked Ronnie.

"I'll do the same to Vic's cock under the water."

"And when I squeeze his balls?"

"Yeah," Ronnie sighed.

Glen and Vic groaned simultaneously. Carla stroked the sensitive flesh between Glen's balls and his anus. "His ass is very tight," she said.

"Vic's is too, but I think a finger will fit. The hot water makes it easy." Ronnie rubbed his tight hole, then slipped the tip of her finger inside.

"No," Glen groaned. "It will hurt."

Since she knew that Glen knew the safe word, Carla realized that he didn't really want her to stop. "Yes, it will hurt," Carla whispered, "but it will feel so good." As Carla's finger invaded Glen's ass, she said to Ronnie and Vic, "Look how hard it makes him. His cock is twitching and moving all by itself."

Glen was so excited by Carla's hands and her voice that he knew he should be ashamed at her vivid descriptions of his body's reactions but he was too far gone to care. Carla kept her finger just inside of him, not moving.

Vic felt Ronnie's finger slide depper into his rear. "Vic's able to tolerate more of this," Ronnie said, "since he came just a little while ago. I'm sliding my finger farther inside him. I can slide in and out, rubbing the sides of his channel. I'm fucking his ass and he's trembling. His cock is getting very hard again."

Carla looked at Glen's face, knowing it was difficult for him not to come. She flicked her tongue over the tip of his penis, licking the sweet drops of pre-come she found there. "Ummm, he tastes good." She pursed her lips and sucked the end of Glen's cock into her mouth.

"Look, Vic," Ronnie said, her finger still deep inside his ass, "Carla's got Glen's cock in her mouth. Touch her head as she sucks. Do it."

Barely coherent, Vic reached out and cupped the back of Carla's wet head. "Press," Ronnie said. He pressed her head and she sucked Glen's cock deeper into her mouth. "Release," Ronnie said and Vic relaxed his hand, allowing Carla's head to release Glen's cock. "Again," Ronnie said and Vic pressed Carla's head.

Glen watched as Vic pressed Carla's mouth up and down on his cock. It was the most erotic thing he'd ever seen. He held himself as tightly as he could, trying to keep himself from coming too fast but it was impossible. He filled Carla's mouth with his semen.

"Good baby," Ronnie said to Vic. "You did so well that you deserve a reward." With her finger still deep in his ass, she pressed him upward until his hard cock was sticking from the water. "Make it good for him, Carla," she said and Carla squeezed her large breasts around Vic's cock. He climaxed right then, spurting into the air above the water. "Oh fuck," he yelled.

"What about you?" Glen said to Ronnie. "You didn't come. Neither of you did. I mean you two should. . . ."

"Would you like to watch Carla and me?"

Silently, Glen and Vic stared at the two women. Ronnie climbed out of the tub and sat on the side, her feet in the water. "Come here, baby," she said to Carla.

Eagerly, Carla buried her face in her friends furry muff and licked and sucked the delicate flesh. "Is she hot?" Vic asked tentatively.

"Oh yes," Carla said. "Feel." She took Vic's finger and held it against Ronnie's pussy. "You too," she told Glen.

The two men fingered Ronnie's pussy until she was ready to come. "You know what she'll enjoy?" Carla said. "She loves having her tits sucked." With Glen's mouth on one breast and Vic's on the other, Carla flicked her tongue over Ronnie's erect clit.

"Do it good!" Ronnie yelled. "Oh yes. Do it so good!" Her entire body contracted as her orgasm roared through every part of her. "Oh yes, it's so good."

Later, the four lay silently on towels on the tile. "I think there are seismographs as far away as California that registered that." Ronnie laughed.

"I've never had a more satisfying experience," Vic whispered.

"Oh yeah," Glen added. Glen and Vic held a quick, whispered conversation. "Look, I think I can convince the folks on the west coast that Vic has to stay another week. Can we get together over the weekend? The four of us?"

Carla thought about it. She didn't usually spend weekend time away from her children, but BJ and Tommy each had a sleep-over and she was sure she could leave Mike with her parents. And she was flattered. Every time a client called her again, she felt wonderful. This was the ultimate compliment, to her and to Ronnie. These two men wanted a repeat performance.

"I think I can arrange it," Carla said.

"Me too," Ronnie agreed.

The following Saturday evening, the four gathered in Vic's room at the hotel. Glen and Vic sat on the sofa in the sitting room of the luxurious suite and Ronnie and Carla each occupied a soft chair. They were all dressed casually, the men in slacks and sport shirts, Ronnie in a soft rose wool skirt, a matching sweater, and high black patent leather boots, Carla in black slacks and a royal blue silk blouse.

"We've already ordered room service for the four of us," Vic said. "Glen and I have talked a lot about this evening and we've got a few exciting ideas."

Carla stretched her long legs in front of her and said, "Like what?"

Glen opened a bottle of champagne and poured four glasses. He handed two to Vic and kept two in his hand. "Vic and I loved the way Ronnie took control that evening. It was erotic, being told what to do, where to look. So, for the moment, we've decided to be in charge. We'll do everything, take care of you for the evening. You just relax and do as you're told." He held a glass near Carla's lips. "Have a sip," he said as he tipped it. As she drank, she saw Vic hold a glass for Ronnie.

As they finished the first glass of champagne, a white-jacketed waiter arrived and wheeled a table to the center of the sitting room, opened leaves on the sides, and arranged plates of food. "The main courses are in the warmer under the table," he said, showing Vic how to open it. "And be careful. The plates will be hot."

Vic added a large tip, signed the check, and closed the door behind the waiter. "We're going to play a game," Glen said. "We're going to make you guess what you're eating." Ronnie and Carla felt blindfolds placed over their eyes. "First course," Glen said.

Glen pressed something cold and smooth against Carla's lips. "Open," he said, "and stick out your tongue." He placed a round object on Carla's tongue and she drew it into her mouth. "A grape," she said.

From across the room she heard Ronnie say, "A piece of cheese."

"Good. Both right." Carla ate several more cold grapes, followed by some of the cheese that Ronnie had been enjoying.

Carla felt something spread on her lips and when she licked off the creamy substance she knew immediately. "Blue cheese dressing."

"Mine's italian," Ronnie said. ——

Carla chewed crunchy bits of lettuce, cold, crisp slices of cucumber, and tomato wedges, all coated with dressing. Then Glen whispered, "My finger's are all gooey. Lick them off, will you?"

As Glen placed one finger at a time against Carla's mouth, she used her rough tongue to lick off the dressing. She drew each of his fingers into her mouth to suck off the last bits, then Glen wiped her mouth with a soft napkin. "Thirsty?"

"Yes," she said. Glen held the champagne against Carla's lips and she drank.

"I hope you like oysters," he said, pressing the slippery morsel against her lips.

"Love them," Carla said, as the slippery bite entered her mouth. It was not in the least sexual, but the entire experience was sensual and being blindfolded enhanced the sensations.

"Want a drink?" Glen asked.

"Yes," she said. She felt Glen's lips, wet and cold, press against her mouth. A trickle of cool liquid flowed from his lips onto hers. Drinking from his mouth made the champagne extra bubbly and it tickled her tongue.

"More?"

"Ummm, yes," she said and they shared a few more swallows.

Vic and Glen fed the two women the main course, sole almondine, tiny roasted potatoes, and petit pois with pearl onions.

"What's for dessert?" Ronnie asked, her voice sensual and hoarse.

Vic took some chocolate mousse in his fingers and pressed it against Ronnie's mouth. Slowly she sucked each finger, and heard Carla doing the same thing.

"What about you?" Ronnie asked. "Did you get some dessert?" She pulled off her blindfold, scooped up a handful of mousse and held it for Vic. He smiled at her and ate from her palm, licking up the last of the chocolate. "That was nice," she said, "but you missed a spot." He licked the mousse from her thumb.

Glen removed Carla's blindfold and she offered him some mousse from her fingers. When the mousse was gone, the two women went into the bathroom to wash up while Glen and Vic put the table outside the door.

Carla ran a comb through her hair as Ronnie freshened her lipstick. "You know, Carla," Ronnie said, "they're waiting for something."

"I agree. You're always so quick about these things. Do you know what they want?"

"I think they want me to take over as I did last time. Is that okay with you?"

"Sure. If you don't know what turns me on by now, no one does."

"Have you ever gotten into pain as pleasure?"

"Once or twice," Carla said. "I've been slapped a few times, once until I had to tell the guy to stop."

"Bad?"

"Not really," Carla said. "As a matter of fact, until it got to be too much, it was very erotic."

"Great. Are you willing to give it a try if things go the way I think they will?"

"Sure. Are you certain that this is what they have in mind?"

"I'm not, completely, but I've developed a sixth sense over the years. I'll go slowly and read the signs. Just remember the safe word."

Carla nodded. "I'll use it if I need to."

They went back into the living room. "Carla, pour everyone another glass of champagne," Ronnie said. "You two," she said to the men, "sit down."

The two men dropped into chairs while Carla poured wine. "You've called the shots so far," Ronnie said. "Now it's my turn." When neither man answered, Ronnie knew she had been right. "Each of you close your eyes. Picture the rest of the evening. Play it in your mind like a movie—picture it exactly as you wish it would happen. Now, Glen, you first. Tell me precisely what you see.'' When Glen hesitated Ronnie said, ''Do it now.''

''This is very difficult.''

Carla walked behind Glen's chair, cradled the back of his head in the valley between her breasts, and glided her hands down the front of his shirt. ''I know it is, baby,'' she murmured. ''Tell me. Are we making love? Are we fucking good?''

''Yes, but before. . . .''

''Tell me, baby.'' She bent over his shoulder and placed her ear next to his lips. ''Whisper it to me.''

''Ronnie's making me do things to you.'' The words exploded from his mouth and his body shook.

''What things? Tell me, baby,'' Carla whispered.

When he was silent, Ronnie said, ''You must tell us, Glen. Do it.''

''Oh Carla. Ronnie's forcing me to spank you. And she's forcing Vic to watch everything.''

Ronnie knelt in front of Vic, whose eyes were still closed as he fantasized about the evening. She placed her hands on his thighs. His body would tell her even if his words didn't. ''What do you see, Vic? What are you doing?'' When he was silent, Ronnie continued. ''You must tell me.'' She had heard what Glen said. ''Am I making you watch? Are you getting hard?'' When he remained silent, she continued, ''Am I spanking you, too?''

''No,'' he whispered.

Ronnie knew there was something else, but Vic was unable to tell her what it was. ''Vic, put your mouth close to my ear. Now, whisper. Say, 'Please don't make me . . .' and end the sentence.''

She felt him shudder as he whispered. Now she knew. ''It's all right, baby,'' she said. ''I'll make it all right.''

Carla stared at her friend. She had no idea how Ronnie sensed the things she did, and got men to admit to their darkest sexual fantasies, but she felt the level of tension in the room increase moment by moment.

Ronnie stalked to the closet. She took out a wooden coat hanger and slapped it on her high boot. She pulled off her sweater and skirt and revealed a tight black satin teddy and black stockings. She settled comfortably on the couch, one ankle resting on the opposite knee. She slapped the hanger against the leather as she spoke. "Glen and Vic, shirts, shoes, and socks off. Now." The two men hurried to comply.

Ronnie's boots, Carla realized, hadn't been an accident nor had the underwear. Somehow Ronnie had known. "Vic, sit here," Ronnie said, indicating the spot on the sofa next to her, "and Glen, close your eyes and stand facing Carla. Now, touch Carla's face. Describe it to me. Tell me how it feels and smells and tastes."

Glen gazed into Carla's eyes, then closed his eyes and touched her face. "Her skin is so smooth. She smells of perfume, exotic and eastern." He licked her cheek. "Her skin tastes of salt and spice." He ran a fingertip over her lips. "Her lips are soft and warm."

"Now, Glen, open your eyes and undress Carla. Do it slowly and describe her body for us as you do. Blouse first."

Glen slowly unbuttoned Carla's blouse and slipped it from her arms. "Her skin is smooth and pale. There are no marks from the sun anywhere, just white skin." He touched his tongue to the pulse of her neck. "Her neck is slender and she tastes and feels smooth under my tongue."

"Do you want to take her bra off? Taste and feel her tits?"

"Yes," Glen whispered.

"Then do it."

Glen unfastened Carla's bra and took it off. "Her breasts are gorgeous. I saw her body last week, but I never realized how beautiful her tits were." He filled a palm with one large breast and lifted. "They're heavy and fill my hand. Her nipples are delectable," he grazed her areola with his tongue, "and so soft."

"Do they get hard if you suck them?" Ronnie asked, idly rubbing her hand over Vic's chest.

Glen drew one tight tip into his mouth and pulled. "Yes. Hard and warm."

"Use your champagne to flavor them," Ronnie said.

Glen smiled and picked up his glass. He slowly trickled cool liquid down one breast, then licked it off her erect nipple. "Vic," Ronnie said, "the other one."

Vic jumped up, dribbled champagne down Carla's other breast, and sucked it off. Carla's breath caught in her throat and her knees wobbled. Pleasure knifed through her.

"Vic," Ronnie said, tapping the sofa with the coat hanger, "over here." Again he sat beside her. "That's good," Ronnie said. "Now Glen, pull off her slacks and panties."

Glen unzipped Carla's pants and pulled both slacks and undies off in one motion. "Tell us about her body, Glen," Ronnie said.

"Her stomach is flat and her belly button is very deep." He flicked his tongue into her navel. "Tastes smoky. And I can smell the aroma of her cunt."

"Feel her pussy. Is she ready for fucking?"

Glen ran his fingers through her pubic hair. "Yes, she's steaming."

"That means we're ready for the next part." Ronnie got up and turned one of the chairs from the dinner table to face the group. "Sit there, Glen. And Carla, you know what you must do. As they say, assume the position."

Glen sat on the chair and Carla lay across his thighs. He stroked the gorgeous globes laying so invitingly across his lap, delightfully crushing his erection. "Spank her on one cheek, hard." Glen raised his hand and brought it down on Carla's bottom.

"Again." He did. "Again."

After a few minutes, Carla whispered, "Popcorn."

"Oh, poor Carla," Ronnie said. "Her poor ass is so sore. Glen, make it feel better."

Glen stroked Carla's flaming bottom, caressing each cheek softly. "Does she feel good?" Ronnie asked.

"Yes, very soft and very hot."

"Does her hot bottom make you hot as well?"

"Abslutely," he said. "I want to fuck her."

"Not yet!" She reached down and held Glen's cock. "Neither Carla nor I have climaxed yet. Lie on the floor."

When Glen was stretched out on the carpet, Carla impaled herself on his erection and Ronnie crouched over his face. As his cock serviced one woman, his mouth serviced the other. Vic squeezed Ronnie's breast in one hand and fingered Carla's clit with the other and the two women climaxed almost simultaneously, then Glen screamed and came.

"You've been so patient," Ronnie said to Vic. "Now you get your reward." She snapped her fingers and Vic stretched out on the sofa. Carla licked one side of his fully erect penis and Ronnie licked the other. The two women licked in perfect unison, until thick come spurted from Vic's member.

Vic looked at Ronnie and smiled. "Holy shit."

"Precisely," Glen said.

Later, as Ronnie and Carla were leaving, Vic and Glen stood at the door. "Next time I'm in town?" Vic said.

"Love to," Carla said.

"Just give me a call," Ronnie said. "You both know the number."

Chapter 10

"I got a catalog in the mail a few weeks ago," Bryce said to Carla as they entered the paneled room one evening in early spring. "And I did some shopping." He put a large cardboard box down on a wooden bench.

From the expectancy in his voice, Carla assumed that he wasn't talking about new shirts or remaindered books. "And . . . ?"

"And I bought us a few new toys. I know Ronnie has a bunch of stuff here, but I wanted some things of our own. Why don't you get undressed?" As Carla took off her clothes, Bryce opened the box and pulled out his first purchase, two pairs of handcuffs. "Come here." He kissed Carla firmly, cupping her firm buttocks and squeezing her cheeks. He nibbled on her neck, then fastened one cuff to each wrist. "Now let's see. . . ."

Carla had a general idea of what was to come. She and Bryce had played here often and several of their fantasies had become regular games. They had learned to easily communicate their desires. Often an evening started with one fantasy and veered off in another direction midway through. But, no matter what scene they enacted, they always ended up truly satisfied.

Bryce backed Carla against a wall and fastened the cuffs so her wide-spread arms were stretched over her head. "Nice. I love to see you like that, exposed and vulnerable." He took a sip of his wine. "Tonight, you need to learn a new sexual lesson."

"And what might that be?" Carla asked, her body already wet and hot, ready for whatever Bryce wanted to teach her.

184

"Patience," he said.

"What's that supposed to mean?"

"Tonight I'm going to see how far I can push you. It's a game that we're both going to win. As they say so dramatically in those romance novels you're so fond of, 'I'm going to make you beg for me.' "

"I'll beg right now. I want you and you know it. And you want me too."

"Of course I do, but tonight is a contest. I want to make you want me like you've never wanted anything before. I want to push your need as high as it will go, tear it down, and push it higher still."

"This isn't supposed to be an endurance contest," Carla said.

"An endurance contest might be fun." Bryce took out his wallet, counted out ten one-hundred-dollar bills and placed them on the bed. He pulled a timer from the bag and set it for fifteen minutes. "I'm putting this right here," he said as he set the timer on a bench. "If you can hold out until it goes off, the money is yours."

"This is nuts," Carla said, intrigued. "You already paid me for the evening."

"I know that, but this is a wager. I'll bet you that I can make you so hot that you'll say, 'Fuck me,' before the timer goes off. Of course, if you should climax you lose."

"Why are you doing this?" Carla asked, truly puzzled.

"I love making love with you," Bryce said, "but I've always felt that you're so busy giving me pleasure that you never reach your own limit. I want to extend you, push you to the ultimate." He grinned at the beautiful woman spread-eagled against the wall. "Is it a bet?"

"Let's get this straight. If I can keep from asking you to fuck me until that thing bings, I win a thousand dollars?"

"Yup."

"And if I fail?"

"You get the best damn fuck you've ever had."

"That sounds too good to pass up."

Bryce slid his hand up the inside of Carla's thigh, past the top of her stocking, and brushed the crotch of her panties. "You're soaked already," he said, rubbing her crotch lightly. "Want me to fuck you right now?"

"I can wait," Carla said, feeling the electricity that always jolted her body when Bryce touched her. She liked Bryce a lot and would have dated him without the money, but he always insisted on paying. He tried to explain that it made it easier for him. And whether or not she truly understood his reasons, she knew that he could afford their frequent rendezvous and Carla enjoyed watching the boys' college fund grow.

Bryce pressed his fully clothed body against Carla, entwined his hands in hers, and placed his mouth against her ear. He traced the tip of his tongue across her sensitive skin and whispered, "Remember, just say 'Fuck me' whenever you're ready." He bit the tip of her earlobe, then kissed a fiery path along her jaw and down the pulse in her neck.

"You'll have to do better than that."

"If that's a dare," he said, "I'll take you up on it." He opened the box and pulled out a jar. "This is called Slippery Stuff," he said, opening the jar and tasting a bit. "Strawberry." He rubbed some of the goo on Carla's nipples, then withdrew another package from the box. "These are nipple suction cups. I thought about getting clips, but I know you don't enjoy real pain and those things hurt. But these, well according to the package," he said, reading the cardboard, "these are supposed to 'create the erotic sensation of love-sucking.' Let's see."

"That's not fair," Carla said, heat rising through her belly.

"It's my game and I decide what's fair." He held the silver-dollar-sized suction cups where she could see them, then attached one to each already-erect nipple. "Are they right? Do they feel like my mouth?"

"Not really," Carla said, "but they're exciting just the same."

Bryce's fingers danced over her breasts as the suction cups enhanced the sensation. "They make your skin blush," he said. "Want to stop?"

Carla's hips moved of their own volition, but she said, "Not a chance."

"Good." He pulled another cardboard-and-plastic-wrapped package from the box. "Here we have a pair of 'Vibrating Ben-Wa Balls.' It says, 'Guaranteed to give maximum vaginal or anal pleasure.' You'll be happy to know that I even thought to bring batteries." Agonizingly slowly, Bryce put batteries into the control pack, then inserted the one-inch balls deep into Carla's vagina. "Now, let's see how this works." He pushed the slider so the balls hummed.

Vibrations filled her body. "Shit, Bryce," Carla said. "Oh God."

"One more thing," Bryce said, pulling another toy from the box. "An anal plug." As he unwrapped the plastic, he continued. "We've played with these before, but this is our very own, just made for your sweet little ass." He held the almost-two-inch-wide dildo in front of Carla's face. "See how big it is?" He rubbed the thick phallus through the over-sensitive valley between her breasts.

"That won't fit inside of me," Carla said, squirming. The vibrations still filled her cunt and the suction on her nipples made them almost unbearably sensitive.

"Let's see," he said. "Make it wet." He pressed the tip against Carla's lips. "Open," he snapped. Carla took the thick plastic cock into her mouth and slid her tongue over the plastic.

"Good," Bryce said. "I wonder how this will feel pressing against those vibrating balls in your pussy." It took only a little pressure to insert the dildo into Carla's rear.

"Oh God," Carla screamed. "Too much."

"Don't forget that if you come, you lose."

Carla gritted her teeth, trying to think about cold showers or trips to the dentist. It didn't help.

Suddenly, the timer sounded and Carla sighed.

"Good girl," Bryce said. "You win. Now, how about double or nothing for another fifteen minutes."

Carla's eyes were glazed and she was unsure whether she could last much longer. "Done," she said, deciding she could hold out, or at least try.

"Wonderful." He stood up and took a video tape from his jacket pocket. "This toy's a little unusual. Do you remember two men with whom you made a movie several months ago? Dean and Nicky."

"I remember," she hissed through gritted teeth. She was on fire and it took all of her concentration not to surrender to the pleasure.

"Well, when you told me about it I was curious. I called Tim who put me in touch with Dean and he made me a copy." He brandished the unmarked video cassette. "Now I want to watch it."

He turned on the TV and slipped the tape into the VCR. Familiar images appeared on the screen. For several minutes Bryce rubbed his hands over her body while, on the screen, Nicky kissed her as she lay on the couch of the hotel suite. As the scene changed to the bedroom, Bryce's hands became more demanding. Suddenly, almost angrily, Bryce removed the toys from her body, unfastened her wrists, and almost dragged her to the bed.

Bryce pulled down his jeans and briefs and forced his cock into her mouth. "Do me just the way you did him. Hold my cock with your free hand just like that."

Carla squeezed the base of Bryce's cock and his sac the way she had Nicky's, effectively keeping him from climaxing. Watching the TV screen, she sucked his erection. "Now," he cried and she released her hand so his hot semen could fill her mouth. As he came, the film ended.

Moments later, the timer sounded again. "You win," Bryce said, burying his face in her muff. "Come for me, baby." He licked her clit and fucked her cunt with his fingers until she, too, came.

Although her orgasm was wonderful, Carla was disappointed that Bryce has given up the game so easily. As he lay silently beside her she knew that something was wrong. "Tell me," she said softly, wrapping her arms around his waist and placing her head on his shoulder.

"Nothing."

"Bryce, that's not fair. If there's something you don't want to talk about, that's fine, just say so. But don't insult me by saying that nothing's wrong."

Bryce sighed and stroked her hair. A few moments later he said, "Seeing you like that bothered me in a way I didn't expect."

"I'm sorry that it upset you."

"I guess I care about you more than I thought I did. It surprises and scares me." When Carla remained silent he continued, "Would you consider giving this all up?"

"What?"

"I suddenly realize that you mean more to me than I thought and I'm suddenly very bothered by the thought of you with other men."

"But. . . ."

Bryce placed a finger across her lips. "Let me finish. I've spent a few days with your parents and your boys and I like all of them very much. If everything works out, eventually we could get married. You know that I'm very well-off, financially, and I'd make sure your boys' college was provided for. You wouldn't need to do this to earn money."

"But that's not the reason I do this," Carla said. "Sure, the money's nice, but I really enjoy giving pleasure and discovering new games in bed. And when the men that I'm with discover that their darkest fantasy isn't really so terrible, well, it makes me feel so valuable."

"We have fun together and there's nothing we couldn't do together, in or out of bed."

Carla patted Bryce's hand. "I know that, but this is what I want to do right now."

"But I love you. I want you to be part of my life forever."

"Love?"

"Of course. I guess I didn't realize it until now." He kissed her. "I love you," he whispered against her lips. "I guess it just takes a jolt like that movie to make me realize it."

"Oh Bryce," Carla said, pressing her lips against his. "I love you." But I love this too, she said to herself.

"Think about it. Please."

The following Monday morning, Carla and Ronnie sat across from each other in the living room of the brownstone. "Bryce proposed last Thursday," Carla said.

"That's great." Ronnie jumped up, wrapped her arms around her friend, and squeezed Carla. "What did you tell him? Should I break out the champagne?"

Carla sighed. "I told him that I loved him, but now I don't know. I think I said it because he did. Of course I'm very fond of him, but I don't know whether it's love. His offer is tempting: security, affection, and good sex. But although he told me he does, I don't think he loves me, at least not yet."

"What makes you think that?"

"Well, for one thing, we haven't spoken since last Thursday. You'd think that he'd have called over the weekend. I think the 'I love you' was sort of an afterthought, that his sudden decision to get serious is about me and this business. I think the thought of me with other men bothers him a lot."

"If he loves you, it would."

"Jealousy and possessiveness aren't love. Jack loves you and he understands. I think what Bryce is saying is 'I want you to love me so much that you'll give up fucking other men for money.' " Carla told Ronnie about the video that precipitated Bryce's proposal. "Bryce is a wonderful man, but the more I think about it, the more I realize that I'm not in love with him. Maybe some time in the future, but not now. And I enjoy what you and I do."

"I know."

"It's a tough decision."

"I don't think it would be a difficult choice if you really loved him."

"You may be right."

"I've got a similar problem," Ronnie said. "Jack's home."

"Great. For how long this time?"

"He's back for good. He got in late Saturday night, so excited and he wanted to surprise me. He's gotten an offer from a computer software house to develop a program about geological formations, three-dimensional modeling. He got a small advance and will get a nice royalty deal when it sells. His old boss, TJ Sorenson, has wanted him to come back here for a long time but there wasn't enough work to offer him a full-time position. Now Jack's sure that he can arrange a three-day-a-week slot with TJ, and spend the rest of his time at the computer."

"Ronnie, that's great!"

"I guess."

"What does that mean?"

"I've made a life for myself here, with our business and all. I don't know if Jack will want me to stay at home all the time and I don't know whether I want to give this up. And sometimes wonder Jack and I have enough for a full-time life. It was always easy to believe that we still had something between us when he was gone most of the time."

"You've told me often enough that your sex life wasn't very adventurous."

"Yeah. Hot and hormonal, but predictable. We fucked like bunnies all day yesterday, but I've come to enjoy the creative side of our work."

"Does he know the details of what you do? The fantasies and all? Have you ever showed him Black Satin?"

Ronnie shook her head.

"Mabye he'd be interested in meeting one of your characters."

"You think? It's silly but it's easier to share that side of me with a stranger than with my own husband."

"From all you've told me about Jack, he may be no different from some of our clients. He may have fantasies in his mind that he can't share with you. Maybe you should give him the chance."

"And maybe you should do some thinking about Bryce. I've known him for years and he's a very special person."

"You're changing the subject."

"I know but the comment's still relevant."

"I've got a date with a new guy tomorrow night. I somehow think that it will help me clarify things. And you need to have a good heart-to-heart with Jack."

Since Carla enjoyed making a bit of an entrance, she usually arrived slightly late for dinner with a client. So it surprised her when she was seated at a table in Vinnie's Waterfront Cafe, a well-reviewed yet inconspicuous seafood restaurant overlooking the Hudson River and her client wasn't there waiting for her. She placed the leather case that contained her album on the floor beside her feet and ordered a glass of club soda with a piece of lime. As she sipped, she gazed out through the wide expanse of glass at the river with the lights of the boats making patterns on the rippled surface.

Almost fifteen minutes later, Carla glanced up and saw a man weaving his way toward her. Gil, he'd said his name was. Just Gil. He had refused to tell her his last name and that was all right with her. He had been recommended by a client she'd been with many times.

As he approached, she realized that he was unusually tall and incredibly thin. He really does look like a bean pole, she thought. He's maybe six-six and he couldn't weigh more than one fifty. Carla extended her hand. "Gil," she said as she took his tentatively offered hand, "I'm Carla."

"Nice to meet you," he said. He sat down quickly and took a long swallow of the glass of water already waiting at his place. "Sorry I was late. Unavoidable."

Carla watched her newest client intently. His hands were never still. He put his glass down and fiddled with his napkin. When it was neatly in his lap, he picked up his fork and twirled it in his long slender fingers. "You sounded nice on the phone," he said, his words quick and clipped, "but I'd like to make this perfectly clear. I don't want to talk about my wife or my marriage. I won't talk about my job and I've given you a phony name so you won't be able to trace me."

Carla tried to keep her smile warm yet impersonal. If she had any desire to find out who he was, her friend Ed, who had vouched for him, would tell her anything she needed to know. But why should she? A man's personal life was his concern. "I have no intention of trying to find out who you are, Gil. I'm here because you called me."

"Yes, yes I did," he said, putting his fork down and picking up his water glass. His nails were bitten down to the quick and his cuticles were chewed and scabbed over in a few spots. He wore a casual shirt and tan slacks, an outfit that unfortunately made his almost emaciated body look even thinner. "As I told you on the phone, I have these needs that no one would understand so I decided to hire a hooker." He looked at Carla, stylishly dressed in a pair of black wool slacks and a long-sleeved, kelly green silk blouse, and his mouth tightened. "I'm sorry. You're not really a hooker."

"I am a hooker and I enjoy it. Do you know where the word hooker comes from?" When he was silent she continued. "During the Civil War a general named Hooker brought women along with his army to keep the troops happy between battles. Hooker's Women, they were called. That's what I do, after all. Keep the troops happy. And what's wrong with that? Sex is fun."

The corners of Gil's mouth turned up for a moment, then his lips returned to their original thin line. "I don't want to talk about sex either. That is, not yet."

"That's fine. Tell me what you like to do in your spare time. Do you like sports?"

"You mean do I like basketball," he snapped. "A tall guy like me has to like basketball, right?"

"Ouch," she said softly and Gil had the good grace to look chagrinned. "I thought no such thing. I'm just trying to make small talk. Wow, you've got quite a chip on your shoulder."

Gil's shoulders slumped. "I guess you're right. I'm sorry."

The waiter interrupted. "May I get you a drink?"

"Sure. What have you got on tap?"

The waiter listed several brands and Gil and Carla each ordered a Sam Adams.

"I'm sorry," Gil said as the waiter disappeared, "about my remark before. You hit a sore point and I'm very strung out."

"I wouldn't have noticed," Carla said, taking his dinner knife from Gil's hands and placing it back on the table. "Want to talk about it?" Carla had realized long before that part of her job was being a counselor, friend, and confidante. So many of her clients had problems and no one to talk to about them.

"They used to call me Zip in school."

"Zip?"

"I was already over six feet tall in junior high and I weighed under a hundred pounds. The kids used to tease, 'Stick your tongue out and you'll look like a zipper.' Thus the nickname Zip. I lifted weights but it didn't help."

"You are what you are."

The waiter arrived with their beers and they each took a long drink. "I understand you're a college graduate," Gil said.

"Unusual for a hooker. Right?" Carla winked and Gil smiled ruefully. "Touché," he said.

"I went to Michigan State and majored in English Literature. You?"

They spent the meal talking and quickly discovered that they had similar taste in movies and books. They had both vacationed in St. Martin and both lamented the commercialism of what had once been a quiet island with great French and native island food. They also shared the same taste in restaurants and each had a quiet little out-of-the-way spot to recommend. They had completely different opinions of the currrent administration and argued hotly over a recent cabinet appointment.

Over coffee, Carla decided it was time to get to the reason for the dinner. "Not that I'm not enjoying our dinner," Carla said, "but maybe it's time to get slightly more serious. What lead you to call me?"

Gil picked up a sugar packet and turned it over and over in his long fingers. "I have needs. You understand. I have things that pound on my brain, fantasies that I have when I'm with my wife. You know, in bed. It's gotten so I never really make love to her but always pretend she's someone else or that I'm someone else."

"She wouldn't be interested in playing out these fantasies with you?"

"Of course not. We've been married for twenty-four years. She's not that kind of woman."

Carla let that remark pass. "What kind of fantasies?"

He jumped up as the packet in his fingers burst open and sugar poured into Gil's lap. When he was seated again, he said, "I was talking to Ed, you know, like guys talk, and he told me about you. That you fulfill fantasies. That's what I need. Someone like you."

"I'm happy to oblige," she said, "but you'd be surprised what your wife might enjoy if you gave her the chance."

"Don't talk to me about my wife," Gil snapped. "I know her better than you do."

So many men came to her with the same story. And so many of them were wrong. Carla's sigh was inaudible. It wasn't her job to educate her clients, just to please them. "I won't say another word about your wife," Carla said.

His gaze was fixed on the corner of her leather case. "You have a book. Ed told me about it."

Carla pulled her album from its case and handed it to Gil. "Ed probably told you how this works. There's an envelope inside." When he nodded, she rose and picked up her pocketbook. "I'll freshen up and be back in a few minutes."

Gil opened the cover.

When Carla returned from the ladies' room Gil was staring at one of the pictures. She glanced over his shoulder as she took her seat. "Gil?" He was a million miles away. "Gil?" she said again. His eyes cleared and she caught his eye. "That's Sally. She's twelve and she really likes candy." She could see Gil's Adam's apple bobbing up and down.

Suddenly, Carla knew exactly what he wanted and although she'd never been Sally before, she could think of several ways to enhance the experience. She could see his fantasy playing, like a movie, behind her eyes. "I know where she lives."

Gil held the book with one hand and his fingers fiddled with the tassel of the now-filled black satin bookmark. He suddenly pulled out a credit card and dropped it onto the dinner check. The waiter whisked it away and returned with the receipt which Gil signed, his finger still in the album marking Sally's photograph.

It took the cab almost fifteen minutes to arrive at the brownstone. Carla showed Gil into the living room, then disappeared upstairs.

Ten long minutes later Gil stood in the center of the room. "Gil," Carla said as she walked down the stairs.

He turned and stared at the little girl in the pink party dress who walked toward him. Her face was freshly washed and she wore no makeup or jewelry. "Hi," the girl said, hugging a large doll under one arm. "My name's Sally. My mommy says that I should always call my elders by their last name. May I call you Mr. Smith?"

Gil could only nod, his hands still for the moment.

"Can I have that?" Sally said, taking the book from Gil's tight fingers. "Thanks," she said, her voice slightly higher pitched than usual. She placed the book on the desk at the side of the room. "Do you like my new shoes?" She stuck out one foot then polished the shiny tip by rubbing it up and down Gil's trouser leg. "My mommy lets me wear them on special occasions."

Gil cleared his throat. "They're very nice," he said, dropping onto the sofa.

"Wanna play a game Mr. Smith?" she asked. "We could play with my doll." She bent over and put the doll on the sofa beside Gil. As she bent, her short skirt allowed a clear view of her white cotton underpants.

This is a grown woman, a prostitute, Gil told himself. But oh Lord she even smells of baby soap. He rubbed his sweating palms on his trouser legs. "I'd love to play a game." He saw the candy dish on the end table next to him. "There's some candy here," he said, trying to say the right thing to make this fantasy go on and on. "Would you like some?"

"My mommy only lets me have candy on special occasions. Is this a special occasion?"

"It certainly is," Gil said, slowly slipping into the fantasy. She was a hooker, but she was a little girl and he wanted her as he'd wanted nothing else in his life. "If I give you a piece of candy will you do something that will make me happy too?"

"Okay, Mr. Smith," Sally said. Gil handed her the dish and

she selected a Hershey's Kiss. Slowly she removed the silver paper while Gil watched her very move. Reflexively he wet his lips as Sally stuck out her pink tongue and licked the surface of the chocolate.

As she watched his eyes on her hands and tongue Carla was happy that she'd taken an extra minute to remove her nail polish. He wouldn't realize how much thought had gone into creating Sally but he would get tremendous pleasure out of playing with her. "Thanks for the chocolate," she said, popping the morsel into her mouth, but deliberately leaving a chocolate stain at the corner. She slowly licked her lips, missing the stain.

"You've got some chocolate on your mouth," Gil said. "Come here." He took her arm and used his handkerchief to wipe the brown goo from her mouth. He pulled her close and placed a feather-light kiss on her lips.

"I can do a dance for you," Sally said, bouncing up from the couch. Anticipation was the best part of the game.

"That would be nice," Gil said, disappointed that she had moved away.

Sally put a tape in the player and whirled around the living room, flipping her skirt so Gil could catch glimpses of her undies. "Sometimes," she giggled, "I do this without my panties. The wind feels funny when I twirl. Wanna see?"

Gil could only nod, his fingers playing with a fold in the sofa's leather. Quickly Sally pulled off her panties and twirled. In her ten minutes upstairs, Carla had run an electric razor over her groin and now her crotch was clean as a baby's. "Wheee," she said, landing on the couch as if dizzy. "It's all tickly." Since Gil was silent, Carla continued to lead him through the fantasy. "If you give me another candy, I'll let you touch where it's tickly."

A bit dazed, Gil handed Carla the dish and she selected a carmel. She unwrapped it and popped it into her mouth. As he watched, she chewed the sticky candy slowly, moving it around her mouth with her tongue. She inserted a finger into her mouth and pulled a glob of candy free. "Now I'm all sticky," she said. "Wanna lick?" She pointed her finger at his mouth and reflexively he opened and sucked her finger inside. She pulled just hard enough to create suction, then allowed him to draw her finger back in.

He flicked his tongue around her nail, sucking at the sweetness. "Wanna touch my tickly part?" she asked as she withdrew her finger.

"Yes," he groaned. She lifted her skirt, took his hand and brushed his fingertips over her freshly shaved and lotioned flesh. "Oh Jesus," he moaned, rubbing his palm over her now-hairless mound.

"You moaned, Mr. Smith. That's too bad. You must be hurting." She patted the bulge in his pants. "When I hurt, mommy takes all my clothes off and puts me to bed. Like this." She whisked her dress off over her head and pulled off her shoes and socks. She stood before Gil dressed only in a white cotton undershirt, stretched to its limit by her large, unrestrained breasts. "You should take your clothes off if you're sick."

He stood and removed his shirt, folding it carefully and placing it on a chair. He pulled off his slacks and straightened the creases with quick, efficient motions. His shoes and socks followed, then his underwear until all his clothing was folded and stacked in a neat pile. He stood in the middle of the living room, naked, with his long, slender erection poking straight out from his body like a large thorn on a long, skinny branch. His fingers stretched across his flat abdomen, twisting and untwisting.

"Wow," Sally said, "you look different from me. You've got that thing sticking out. Can I touch it?" Without waiting for Gil to answer she cupped his prick and slid it through her hands. "It's very long and very hard," she said. She touched, examined, and stroked his cock and balls as though she'd never held one before. "What does it do, Mr. Smith?" she asked, her voice high pitched and a wide-eyed innocent expression on her face.

He pulled back, unsure of his ability to control his body for long. "I'll show you, if you want."

"Can I have candy when you're done?"

"Of course," he said, barely able to keep the quaking from his voice. He sat on the sofa and pulled the little girl so she stood between his knees. "But first I have to make you ready." The insides of her thighs were like the softest silk as his fingers tickled their way from her knee to her smooth, hairless crotch. She was already wet and his cock and balls were on fire with his need for her.

"Come here." He pulled her so that she was kneeling astride his lap, straddling his cock. "Sit down right here and you'll understand."

She opened a foil package she'd taken from the end table and unrolled the condom over Gil's cock. "A little girl is always prepared." Without any delay, she sat on his erect cock. "That way? Is this what that's for?"

Gil rubbed the sides of the cotton undershirt. Avoiding her large breasts, which would have ruined the fantasy, he bucked and arched as she bounced in his lap. "God, yes," he cried as an orgasm deeper than any he ever remembered overtook him. "Sally!"

Ten minutes later they were still in the same position and his hands had been quiet for the entire time. "Can I see you again?" he whispered.

"You have my number," Carla whispered, rising and handing Gil a wad of tissues. "Call me anytime."

He dressed quickly and, reliving the evening over and over, he left. Carla gathered her props and walked upstairs, considering. She was pleased at how deeply Gil had gotten into his fantasy. She had given him a wonderful evening and had earned five hundred dollars as well. It's amazing, she thought. I become part of almost every fantasy I play and so far I've enjoyed them all. She pulled off the white cotton undershirt and threw it and the rest of Sally's clothes into the hamper.

In the bathtub, she held the massager hose and played the spray over her freshly shaved pussy, thinking about Sally and Gil. It took only a few moments for her to climax. Bathed and relaxed, Carla climbed into bed.

Ronnie had always called her customers friends and now Carla realized why. These men were her friends, if only for one evening. She liked all the men she had been with and got tremendous pleasure out of satisfying them and, in doing that, satisfying herself.

No, she thought, a smile lighting her face. Although I like Bryce a lot and his offer is flattering, I don't want to give up the pleasures that I've found with my friends. At least not yet.

If Bryce could continue their relationship as it had been, that would be wonderful. And if he couldn't, then they would have to go their separate ways. She would miss him dreadfully, but not enough to make her give all this up.

She snuggled down, pulled the satin comforter up around her ears, and quickly fell asleep.

In Hopewell Junction, Ronnie sat in her living room with Jack, sipping a glass of diet Pepsi. She had just finished telling her husband about the lifestyle she, and now Carla, had established. "I enjoy helping my friends understand that their fantasies are not very different from the dreams that we all have at one time or another."

"I know what you were involved in, of course," Jack said, "but I had no real idea how much there was for men to experience."

"It's fun, Jack," Ronnie said, "and men pay me a great deal of money to share their fantasies with me."

"Are you going to continue in the business?"

"How do you feel about it?"

"Now that I'm going to be in New York full time," Jack said, "I guess I'd be upset if you spent time with other men. Of course, I'd love to meet Carla. You two seem to have become such good friends."

"We certainly have. But if I gave up the business, what would I do all day to keep from being bored crazy?"

"I was thinking about the amount of writing that is connected with my job. There are going to be manuals and guides and scads of documentation. I'll hate that part and you'd be so good at it."

"But what do I know about geological models?"

"Hey, babe. You've got a college degree in writing and you're very bright. I'll teach you how the model works and you can explain it on paper to the users. I know you—you'd pick up what you needed to know very quickly."

"You really think so?"

"I'd like you to give it a try."

Ronnie winked at her husband. "I think I'd like that."

"And you'd give up the business?"

"Only if I can play with you."

"Play with me?"

"Men have been paying me a lot of money to play fantasy games. Wouldn't you like that? Some different ideas to spice up our sex life."

"I guess we've never done much off-center stuff. But it's always been good just the way it is."

"I know that. But variety is wonderful. Don't you have a fantasy that you'd like to act out with me?"

"I don't know. Like what?"

Ronnie reached into a paper bag she had put beside the couch and pulled out the black satin album. She slid over next to Jack, placed the book on his lap, and opened the front cover.

"Is that you?" Jack said. He turned the page. "That *is* you. Holy shit."

Ronnie smiled and cuddled against her husband. "That's Marguerite, the stripper." He turned the page. "And that's Nita, the harem girl, and on the next page is Miss Gilbert, who enjoys disciplining naughty students. And there are many more. Wanna play?"

"Holy shit," Jack said, turning another page. "Holy shit."

Dear Reader,

I hope you've enjoyed the adventures of Carla and Ronnie. Once I created these two extraordinary women in my mind, they leaped onto my computer screen in almost no time. I'm now considering my next venture so please let me know which of the adventures you particularly liked and share any of your thoughts.

Joan Elizabeth Lloyd
POB 221
Yorktown Heights, NY 10598